If the Slipper Fits

Other Avon Contemporary Romances by
Elaine Fox

MAN AT WORK
MAYBE BABY

ELAINE FOX

If the Slipper Fits

AVON BOOKS

An Imprint of HarperCollinsPublishers

AVON BOOKS
An Imprint of HarperCollins*Publishers*
10 East 53rd Street
New York, New York 10022-5299

Copyright © 2003 by Elaine McShulskis
ISBN: 0-7394-3361-x

Prologue

Candlewick Island, Maine
January 2003

"Why not just be honest and tell him you're sorry the bastard didn't die ten years ago? I know I am." Anne Sayer's grandmother stood at the kitchen counter, clattering through the silverware drawer, behind Anne at the table. Though the old woman was tiny and frail, her voice hadn't weakened a decibel since Anne was a child.

"Well, Gramma, it's a sympathy note," Anne said. "I don't think that sounds very sympathetic."

On the sheet of notepaper in front of Anne were two words: *Dear Connor.* Written in her best script. Those two words had been staring at her for the better part of an hour.

She bit the end of her pen. It was the hardest note she'd ever had to write. And her grandmother wasn't helping.

"I thought you were fixing my lunch." Her

grandmother's walker squeaked as she wheeled it over to the pantry.

Anne glanced at the clock. "It's only ten-thirty, Gramma."

Delores Sayer made a grumpy sound.

Anne closed her eyes and pictured Connor's face. Would he be surprised to hear from her? Would he see the return address and dread opening the envelope? Was it possible he wouldn't read her letter at all?

It was all possible, she thought. He hadn't heard from her in eleven years. He would probably feel all of those things—surprise, dread, trepidation.

Anger?

And yet, she had to write to him. She *had* to. There was no better time.

She put pen to paper.

I want you to know how very sorry I am to hear about the loss of your father.

Sorry for Connor, she thought. Not Bradford Emory, Connor's father. As her grandmother'd said, the man couldn't have left this planet soon enough to please Anne.

She dipped her head with the evil thought. No use thinking like that. The man was dead, and he'd taken the past with him.

I know how much you struggled to forge a closer bond with him. I hope for your sake that you succeeded. But even if you didn't, Connor, it was obvious to all who knew him that your father loved you very much.

She paused, wondering if it was true, but she decided to let the sentence stay. It was, after all, a sympathy note. She didn't need to be scrupulously truthful.

It was also obvious how very proud of you he was, and rightly so.

Behind her, the walker squeaked back to the kitchen counter, and something heavy thudded onto the Formica. Anne hoped her grandmother could refrain from breaking something, setting something on fire, or injuring herself for the few minutes it would take Anne to finish the note.

She studied the heavy, cream-colored notepaper before her. She'd bought it just for this purpose. Because it looked classy, adult, and she wanted him to think of her that way.

She sighed. As if he would notice what sort of paper she used. She'd be lucky if he even opened her letter.

She rested her head in one hand. How much more should she say? How plainly should she speak? What in the world would he think if she just flat out said *Please come back to me*?

She dropped the pen to the paper but didn't write the words. It had been too long, of course. For all she knew he was in a serious relationship or engaged. Surely she would have heard if he'd married.

For all she knew, he'd forgotten her.

But what did she have to lose? She started writing.

Connor, I hope you will consider returning to Sea Bluff soon. It's been too long, and . . .

And what? She struggled with her thoughts. She wanted to say what she meant, but subtly. She wanted to be clear, with ambiguous undertones. Or overtones. She wanted to tell him she wanted him to come back, without actually telling him she wanted him to come back. She wanted to accomplish the impossible.

She sighed and finished, *You've been terribly missed.*

She exhaled slowly. Was it too much? Should she take out the *terribly*?

She was overthinking this. She signed the note *Love, Anne*, folded it, slid it into the gold-lined envelope, and quickly sealed it. She pulled a stamp off the roll in front of her and aligned it carefully in the upper right corner.

"Gramma, I'll be back in a minute," she said, standing.

She crossed the kitchen, went down the short hallway, and opened the front door.

Delores groused back something about missing applesauce, knowing full well she'd finished it off the night before. She'd badgered Anne at length to be sure to put it on the shopping list.

Anne closed the door behind her. She walked quickly to the corner mailbox, opened the hinged door, and slipped the note in before she could think twice about it.

Then she walked back home, wondering how

long it might be before she could reasonably expect a response from Connor.

As she closed the front door behind her and headed back down the hall toward the kitchen, reality closed in on her as tangibly as the gray walls of her grandmother's tiny house.

And she wondered if there was any chance she'd hear from Connor Emory at all.

Chapter One

Sea Bluff
Candlewick Island, Maine
Six months later

The staff had been gossiping behind her back all week. And the worst thing was, they didn't think she'd noticed.

"Mr. Franklin, be *careful!*" Anne said to the gardener more sharply than she'd intended as she rushed to grab the plant he'd nearly knocked off the pedestal in the front hall.

She was annoyed with all of them, she thought, glancing up at the bird circling the foyer's ceiling over the heads of the rest of Sea Bluff's core staff. The very staff she'd found whispering in empty rooms and darkened corners nearly every day since last Thursday. Whispering, that is, until she entered the room.

"I'm going to call Animal Control," she said, striding toward the hall phone. "The new tenants are going to be here within the hour and I don't want the entire staff in the front hall chasing after some crazed bird."

"No authorities!" the gardener cried, his flinty eyes following the bird's flight. "I got it. *Look out!*" he roared, heading toward Anne, his craggy face intent. A butterfly net—old, bent, and patched with panty hose—flew over his head like a battle flag.

Her pale blonde hair swinging into her face as she spun to follow the gardener's path, Anne jumped aside and ducked as the bird careened around the front hall of the historic mansion.

The gardener stopped abruptly in the center of the hall, his eyes alert. The net drooped above him.

Everyone stood stock-still. Anne pushed her hair out of her face and looked at the five people drawn from their jobs to the bird "crisis": the gardener, the handyman, the housekeeper-in-training, the cook, and the business manager.

Lois Marshall, who was accountant as well as business manager for Sea Bluff, had just displeased everyone by telling them to get back to work. "Work" being preparing the island's largest, most famous summer "cottage" for the arrival of this season's tenants.

Though best known for its stunning beauty—it was situated on four hundred sea-kissed acres at the northernmost point of the island—and the host of celebrities who had stayed there, Sea Bluff also had an impressive history. It had been built in the 1800s by a notorious sea captain renowned for his mercenary exploits, for a bride who would never see it. She was killed en route to the island by a roving band of pirates.

Of course, some said she was killed by her own mother, who was also in love with the sea captain, but nobody really believed that story.

In any case, the captain died alone, having never married, and he willed the estate to his nephew, Cornelius Edison Emory, whose descendents had owned it ever since.

"Back to work, she says," Prin Walter, the cook, protested. "Seems to me makin' sure the house ain't infested with wildlife *is* work."

"Yes, but it's work for only *one*," Anne said firmly. "And Mr. Franklin is capable."

A fluttering sounded to Anne's right. She whirled and pointed past the Frederic Church landscape on the wall to the Florentine marble bust of Socrates near the curve in the massive Italian walnut staircase. "It's over there."

"Lord preserve us!" the cook said, her voice issuing the statement like a command to the Almighty. One side of her gray hairdo was ruffled where the bird had glanced off her head, and flour smeared her forearms. She must have been baking bread when the commotion had ensued. "You all know what a bird in the house means, don't you?" she warned.

"Oh, I had a bad feeling this morning." Hiding behind a robust Boston fern, the young housekeeper-in-training wrung her hands in her apron. As if greenery were not the very thing a panicked bird might look for, Anne thought. A dried leaf had dropped into her baby-fine red hair. "I'm a little bit psychic, you know," the housekeeper added.

"Yes, Trudy, we know." Anne sighed.

Trudy was one of the many young people who came to the island off the coast of Maine to work summers in the mistaken belief that Candlewick Island had something to do with witchcraft. "*Wick* comes from the word *wicken*," Trudy had informed her during her interview several weeks before, "which means *to bewitch.*"

"A bird in the house means poop on the floor," Lois Marshall told the cook. "Unless we do something quickly." Her short, spiky hair and big, handmade silver earrings gave her a look in direct contrast to the old cook's gray bun and flower-print housedress.

Completely practical, Lois was frequently exasperated working in the 1800s mansion on the cliffs with its colorful crew.

"It doesn't mean anything bad, Trudy. It just means company's coming," the brash young handyman said, winking in the direction of the nervous housekeeper. "Better get your fancy dress apron on."

"If Trudy is concerned, she can just go back upstairs and finish vacuuming those drapes." Anne sent a stern glance to her young trainee.

The gardener, who'd been creeping across the

ornate foyer with the skill of a man who'd stalked many a groundhog, made a lunge for the bird with the net. He missed. The chrome handle glanced off the marble bust and Socrates teetered, then toppled to the floor as the bird took off with renewed frenzy. Anne watched in horror as parts of Socrates's face skipped across the floor to hit Prin's white Reebok sneaker and Lois's thick-soled oxford.

"Mr. Franklin, stop right now. This is not working." Anne took several steps toward him, keeping one eye on the bird's erratic flight. God only knew how valuable that bust was, and what if the next thing he took out was one of the oil paintings? Or part of the antique chandelier? "I'm calling Animal Control."

But the gardener was already reaching into the air with the net as if he might catch the bird mid-flight.

"No, it don't mean company's coming." Prin scooped up Socrates's ear as if it were a dust bunny and dropped it into her apron pocket. "That's when your nose itches. Bird in the house means you're gonna kiss a fool, that's what it means."

Lois scoffed.

Anne looked around the foyer at the staff. "Just how many fools should we be expecting, Prin?"

Lois laughed, then raised her eyebrows toward her spiky hairline and directed a pert look at Prin. "Good point. We seem rather overloaded with them at the moment."

Lois had been working with Anne for the better part of the last decade, and the two had formed a good rapport. While Anne had practically grown up working at Sea Bluff, starting out as a maid and working up to housekeeper, overseeing a staff that could balloon to twenty in the busy summer months, Lois had only arrived after graduating college in Boston. By then the Emorys, who owned the place, had stopped their yearly summer visits, and the house was leased, year after year, to whoever could afford it.

Now Anne was in the process of turning over her job as housekeeper to Trudy, so she herself could devote more time to her budding career as an events coordinator. There were so many events in the historic mansion on the cliffs each year that she'd become an expert at party planning, and was beginning to attract work outside the mansion. She'd even started a small, party-planning business on the side that she'd romantically named Glass Slipper Inc.

Still, her first love was Sea Bluff, and most of her business was there. Many tenants had passed through the mansion since the Emorys had stopped coming—the summer of 1992 being their last, Anne remembered all too well—a past list of which included corporate tycoons, foreign dignitaries and celebrities who used the place for everything from political benefits to charity balls.

Even Mara Hubert, decorating and lifestyle doyenne of the new millennium, had used the house. Not only had she filmed several Christmas specials there but she'd also looked into buying the place. The Emorys, however, had not been interested in selling.

"Bird in the house means," the gardener said, turning ominously toward them, gray eyes fierce in his rocky face, "death."

Even though the gardener was macabre on a daily basis, Anne felt a chill.

"Death?" Trudy breathed. "Oooh, I knew bad luck was coming . . ."

"Maybe it just means bad luck, like losing your keys or spraining your ankle," the handyman told her, drawing himself up and putting a hand manfully on the hammer holster at his hip. He smiled reassuringly at Trudy. "Yeah, I think it's just plain bad luck."

"A bird in the house is bad luck for Socrates, anyway." Lois bent and picked up the bust's nose.

Anne laughed. Lois glanced her way and smiled cynically, which was the only way Lois knew how to smile.

"I don't know what you're giggling about, Miss Sayer." Prin turned on Anne with a warning look. "You're the one most likely to be kissing the fool, when he comes."

"*Missus Walter!*" Lois admonished, sending the woman a scorching glance.

Anne looked at her in surprise. Prin loved nothing better than to warn people about their behavior, so why was Lois upset with her this time? Something had been making Lois tense all day.

Anne stepped into the center of the foyer. "As I said earlier, it's time for everyone but Mr. Franklin to return to their duties. I'm sure our able groundskeeper will have no trouble keeping track of the bird until Animal Con—"

At that moment the ancient grandfather clock on the north wall decided to chime. Everyone in the room jumped.

Adrenaline shot through Anne's veins, and she wished for the thousandth time she could get rid of the damn clock. It kept terrible time, chimed only when it felt like it—which was usually every six or seven days, but sometimes three times in one day—and had a gong so loud that it could peel the skin right off your body if you were standing too close.

Startled, the bird dive-bombed her head. Anne ducked as it careened toward the front door, which, she noted in her astonishment, opened just as the creature reached it.

"Whoa!" The man in the doorway dipped back, limbo-like, as the bird grazed his forehead. Just before falling over, he twisted to watch it fly past him into the wild blue yonder.

The clock struck eight, despite the fact that it was noon, and stopped.

Sean Crawford straightened, one hand on the small of his back and the other pulling a garishly

Elaine Fox

orange tie off his shoulder. He smoothed the tie down his expansive chest in a practiced motion.

"What the hell was that?" he demanded.

"Here's your fool now," Prin sniffed, with a last glare at Anne before turning to head back to the kitchen.

"Well, there you go," Lois said, relief in her voice. "Problem solved. How you doing, Sean?"

Anne shook her head. Sean wasn't *her* fool, she thought firmly, though she knew—as everyone in town did—that he might be if she ever indicated she was interested. To her he was just the realtor who handled the leasing of the house, and she tried to limit her contact with him to whatever that required.

"Hey, Lois." Sean entered with an obvious effort to regain some dignity. "What's all the commotion? I thought you people *worked* here. Or is there some party element to your jobs I was unaware of?"

Anne noticed a bird dropping on the floor a few paces in front of her and moved to clean it up before he could step in it. She pulled a paper towel from her apron pocket and stooped to the floor. "Only a minor crisis, which you just helped usher out the door."

Lois turned back to the others. "All right, everyone. We've got a lot to do. Sean's here to talk to Anne about the new tenants—" Lois stopped abruptly and shot a worried glance at Anne.

Anne thought she even detected a blush on her normally unflappable friend's face before Lois continued.

"The new tenants," Lois continued, shooing everyone down the hallway in front of her, "who we will all meet for the first time in a few short hours."

"But I thought—" Prin began.

"You can tell me what you thought in the kitchen." Lois's words drowned out Prin's as they disappeared from the foyer.

Anne rubbed at the bird dropping on the floor.

"That's enough of that," Sean said, heels clicking on the marble as he moved toward her. "Off your knees, Cinderella. I've got something to tell you."

Anne wiped the spot clean and stood, pretending not to notice the hand he held out to help her. Last time she'd taken his hand, to let him help her out of a car, he'd moved his own suggestively up her arm and she'd had to scrape him off on a parking meter.

"Would this have anything to do with the new tenants?" she asked.

Sean gestured to the door of the morning room and looked at her in surprise. "Yeah, actually, it does. Let's talk in here."

Anne gave him a long look. It wasn't like Sean to ask for privacy. On the contrary, he usually sought out an audience.

Fast work, she thought. *That bird was only in the house fifteen minutes and bad luck's apparently already here.*

She walked into the morning room, acutely aware of Sean's eyes on her back. She reached the couch and sat. "So what's up, Sean?"

He sat across from her on the other couch and smiled in a way that was probably meant to put her at ease.

"How're you doing, Anne?" His tone was one a doctor might use to say *He's stable at the moment.*

Anne felt a curl of dread in her chest.

"I'm fine." She narrowed her eyes at him. "What's this all about? You're making me nervous."

He looked offended, in that manner he had of looking whatever way might get him what he wanted. "I ask how you are and that makes you nervous?"

Anne directed a raised brow toward him. "Forgive me, Sean, but you usually get right to the point. Are you about to tell me something awful?"

She stopped, her stomach jumping with fear.

"It's not my grandmother, is it?" she asked.

Perhaps Sean had heard something in town. Just a week ago Anne had moved her grandmother into the Candlewick nursing home, and ever since she'd been waiting for disaster to strike. It would be just like her grandmother to succumb to death so soon after being taken to the home, if only to prove that Anne had well and truly broken her heart this time.

He waved a hand dismissively before him. "No, no, it's nothing like that. It's the new summer tenants, Anne. They're not . . . ah . . . well they're not exactly *tenants*, is what I'm trying to say."

Anne exhaled with half a laugh. "Well, what are they? Freeloaders?" Then her face fell. "They're not—the Emorys aren't—"

Sean started to nod, and Anne's stomach lurched.

"They're *selling*?" she breathed, eyes wide, her hand at her heart.

Shock made her nerves ripple.

They couldn't, she thought. Well of course they *could*, but surely they *wouldn't* sell this place, would they? It had been in their family for almost two centuries. Besides, this house was more home to Anne than the one she'd grown up in, the one in which she still lived, now minus her grandmother.

Not that the Emorys would keep it just for *her*. On the contrary. If they did anything because of her, they'd be more likely to sell it just to spite her.

"Selling!" Sean's face cleared, and Anne expelled her pent-up breath. "Don't be ridiculous. Why would anyone sell a moneymaker like this?"

"Oh, thank God." Anne decided not to point

out that the Emorys had to worry about money like polar bears had to worry about ice.

Sean sat back and fingered the hideous tie. "The fact is, Anne, they're coming back. Or rather, *he's* coming back. With some guests."

Anne looked at him. " 'He'? You told me the new tenants were an Italian man and his family."

Sean looked at her as if she might do something unpredictable, like break into song or spontaneously combust. "I'm not talking about the Italian man."

"Then who are you talking about? God? Santa Claus?"

Sean looked at her in exasperation. "Jesus, Anne, it's *Connor*. I'm talking about Connor Emory. *God*. I was trying to be delicate."

Ordinarily Anne might have shot back something about Sean's delicacy being so rare that it was understandably imperceptible, but not this time.

He was coming, she repeated to herself. *He*, Connor Emory, her first love.

If she were honest, her only love.

Every summer from the time she was nine years old and he was eleven, to the year when she was nineteen and he was twenty-one, he came with his family to spend the magical Maine summer at Sea Bluff. And every summer Anne and Connor's relationship had grown. Until the summer the family left and didn't return. The summer of 1992.

She hadn't heard from Connor since September

1st of that year, she reflected, a day on which they'd had one conversation. One that she'd re-lived a thousand times since.

Of course, he'd only heard from her once in the intervening years. She winced inwardly thinking about the note she'd written to him after his father's death. The note he'd ignored.

She leaned back in her chair and studied Sean. In addition to his duties as local realtor, Sean wrote for the small island paper. Specifically, he wrote the gossip column, though he refused to call it that and gave whoever did a lambasting. The *Anonymous Observer* was merely a chronicle of island life, he'd said on many, many occasions. Occasions on which he hadn't convinced anyone.

It wouldn't do, she knew, to show any reaction to Connor's return, since Sean was the one person on the island who could put it in print.

"Why were you trying to be delicate?" she asked.

He rolled his eyes. "Correct me if I'm wrong, Annie, but I was under the impression that mention of the prodigal son in your presence was to be done only when absolutely necessary."

She folded her hands in her lap. Her fingers had gone cold. *This* must be what everyone had been talking about behind her back. Connor Emory was coming back. And they all wondered what the still-single, still-Emory-employed, still-on-Candlewick-Island Anne Sayer was going to do about it.

"Why should I care what's said about Connor, or any of the Emorys, for that matter?" she asked coolly.

"Well . . ." Sean seemed to search for words.

Anne waited. "Okay, you think about it. In the meantime, let's get down to what I need to know. How long is he coming for? Is he staying the whole summer with Mr., ah, Tucci, is it? Will they require any more staff? And will they be entertaining?"

Sean frowned. "Weren't you two . . . *involved*, once upon a time?"

"Involved?" Anne crossed her arms over her chest and tilted her head.

"Yeah, you and Connor."

"In what way? Oh, I do remember painting the boathouse with him one summer, if that's what you mean."

The words were barely out of her mouth before she remembered that while supposedly painting the inside of that boathouse she and Connor had shared some pretty steamy moments on a pile of old canvas sails.

Anne kept her expression neutral.

Sean sighed. "All right, don't tell me. But you know I'll find out eventually. There aren't any secrets around here, and the moment Connor sets foot on this island the gossip'll be flowing like wine. Little Helga will know everything before he's even unpacked."

Anne grimaced. Little Helga worked in the post office with her mother, Big Helga. Between the two of them they processed—with malicious glee—more information than the *Bangor Daily News*.

"Fine, I'll leave you to her, then," Anne said.

Sean sighed. "He's coming for the rest of the summer. About two months."

"Okay." She nodded. "Anything else I need to know?"

"Yeah." Sean leaned back and put one arm along the back of the sofa. "He's coming with three others. The Italian man and his two daughters."

Anne's mind raced over the contents of the attic. "There are some beach toys and rafts in the attic, I believe. Buckets, shovels, and some pretty sophisticated sand-castle-making equipment, in fact. We could—"

"Hold on, Mary Poppins, the girls're grown. In their twenties, I believe."

"Oh, well." An unbidden image of youthful Sophia Loren–type beauties frolicking on the beach in front of an appreciative Connor Emory sprang to her mind.

"Is something wrong?" Sean asked, leaning forward.

"Of course not." She frowned. *Fine time for him to get perceptive.* "We'll just make up another room for Connor. Or rather, for Mr. Tucci, since Connor will probably take the Galleon Suite." She paused. "I take it each of the daughters will need a room?"

"Of course! What, you think one of them's gonna sleep on the floor?" He scoffed elaborately, obliviously, while Anne took a deeply relieved breath.

"All right, then, other than that, we're ready."

Sean looked around. "Yeah, I can tell. I can't believe it, but the house looks great. You sure put it together fast after that Fourth of July bash last week."

Anne brushed aside the compliment. "Do they need anything special for when they arrive?"

Sean's hands turned palm up, casually uncurious. "He didn't say. Though he did say he wanted first-class treatment for these guests."

"All of our guests get first-class treatment. He should know that." Despite herself, Anne asked, "So . . . you spoke to him?"

He gave a one-shouldered shrug. "Sure. I talk to him every time the place gets rented these days."

"*Every* time?" she blurted.

Sean's eyes narrowed. "Of course every time. Why? What difference does it make?"

"I just thought you'd speak to his stepmother or someone. Not Connor."

"No, I've been dealing directly with Connor since his father died," he said with a self-important air. "His stepmother retired to that Mediterranean island, you know. Whatsit called? I can't remember. Anyway, Connor must have inherited the house."

"Aren't his sisters involved at all?" She leaned back in her chair and casually crossed her legs.

"Not from what I've heard. They never liked it here anyway, and besides, I understand they're both married now too. Snagged successful men with their own high-class vacation properties."

"A cottage or two in Newport?" Anne chuckled.

Connor's sisters were as pretentious as his step-mother. But while they were merely snooty, Connor's stepmother was downright evil. Anne had been profoundly grateful when they'd given over leasing of the property to Sean's realty company a few years back. Not having to talk to Mrs. Emory about each prospective tenant had made Anne's job infinitely more enjoyable.

"I wouldn't be surprised," Sean said. "They were definitely a couple of snobs. But then, the whole family was, really. The sisters were the worst, though."

"And looking for husbands even then," Anne recalled.

Then Sean's words hit her anew. *They're both married now too,* she thought. *Too?*

"Is Connor . . . well, he's . . ." She assumed an offhand expression. Surely she would have heard, she thought. She didn't actually have to voice this question, did she? And certainly not to Sean Crawford, of all people.

But she had to know.

Sean grinned slyly while she searched for appropriately casual words.

"Is Connor's wife coming?" she asked finally.

"Connor's wife?" Sean smirked. "No. No, Connor's *wife* isn't coming."

Anne gave him an exasperated look. Neither of

them was fooling anybody. "You know what I'm asking, Sean. Does Connor *have* a wife?"

Sean laughed. "No. You can put the hanky away, Cinderella, Prince Charming's not married."

She resisted it, but a light breath of relief blew through her anyway. "That's a shame." She folded her hands in her lap and smiled benignly at Sean. "I mean for him. He deserves to find a good woman. Maybe he's . . . you know, lonely."

Sean gave her a significant look. "Yes. *I* know. I know just how it is to be lonely." He leaned forward, suddenly intent. "Don't you, Anne?"

Anne was silent a moment. She certainly did know how it felt to be lonely, but she wasn't about to give him that opening. "Not really, Sean."

He looked at her skeptically. "Oh, please. How can you not be lonely? You're a beautiful woman on a tiny island with nothing but old men and summer people. Why don't you let the only eligible bachelor in town take you out Friday? I know you've said before you weren't interested, but there's no need to play hard to get. You and I both know we're going to end up together. We're the best-looking people in our age group on the island."

Anne laughed. "Oh, well, if you put it that way." She couldn't help indulging in some helpless sniggering. "Sean, you get more romantic by the day."

Sean's eyes narrowed. "All right, so you want to be wooed. I get the message. But think about this, Miss Anne Too-Good-For-The-Island Sayer, do you really want to be without even *a boyfriend* when Connor Emory comes back to town? With two gorgeous Italian women, no less?"

Chapter Two

Somewhere over the coast of Maine
July

Connor Emory felt the throb of the helicopter's engine throughout his entire body. As the chopper's blades sliced the air with a steady *whomp, whomp, whomp* he tried vainly to unclench the muscles from his neck to his shoulder blades.

He was tense. He'd been tense for days. Months. Maybe years, if he was honest.

Connor stared out the window at the rugged Maine coastline scrolling below—the thread of jagged rocks, the deep green trees, and the sea, lace-trimmed where waves crashed against the shore.

Beside him, Connor's uncle, Marcello Tucci, had twisted in his seat to talk to his daughters, Gabriella and Nicola, about God knew what in Italian. Ordinarily Connor would have enjoyed hearing their conversation, although he didn't understand a word. Marcello had always amused him with his big voice, his broad gestures, and his ready laugh.

But today Connor longed for quiet. In fact, he wanted it all week. All summer, if he could get it. If he could find some peace, some solitude and contemplation, maybe then he'd know what the hell he was doing with his life.

Which was just one reason he was returning to Sea Bluff.

"Connor, my brooding boy," Marcello boomed over the roar of the chopper. "You look as if you are heading in the direction of the hangman. We are on holiday, are we not?"

Connor rubbed the back of his neck with one hand. "I'm just tired."

"Tell me you are not thinking of that Nancy, are you?" Marcello's face was skeptical. "She was nothing, nothing for a man like you to pine over."

Connor grimaced. "No, I'm not thinking about Nancy."

In fact after she'd severed their relationship two weeks ago, he'd barely given Nancy another thought. Except maybe to be grateful that she'd done it. Ordinarily it was Connor who ended relationships. Having one end without his effort was a relief.

Of course, it had helped that he'd wanted out too.

"I hope you are not." Marcello shook his head. "Because that one was not worth the time it took to say good-bye. Some women, yes. Some women, you must mourn them. They have become a part of your soul. But not that one." He brushed something off the leg of his pants with the back of his hand, a gesture that seemed to be brushing Nancy away too.

Connor shot him a look. "She was important to me," he said, perhaps wishing to justify the last year of his social life. "She had some very good points. She split up with me, didn't she?"

"What? Why do you say this? Any woman is a fool to lose you, *il mio ragazzo.*" *My boy.* Marcello loved endearments and used them liberally, though usually in Italian so nobody knew exactly what he was calling them.

"Nancy was in it for love. And she didn't love me. So she ended it." It was refreshing, really, Connor thought, wondering if that made him strange, figuring it did.

"Nor did you love her, I am convinced of this."

Connor tilted his head in acquiescence. "No, I didn't love her. But I haven't loved others either, and they've stayed. For the money, maybe."

"For love, maybe," Marcello suggested.

Connor laughed doubtfully. "Maybe."

"So when will we be there, eh?" Marcello laid a broad hand on Connor's shoulder. "I have a great hunger for something smothered in gravy. Food of the soul, *capire*? Did the driver get that case of Amarone I bought? I don't want to have to settle for some cheap island Chianti."

Connor turned from watching the ocean pass beneath them and smiled at his uncle's warmth. "It'll be another ten minutes or so. And the case of Amarone is right behind you. You must know by now I would never serve you substandard wine."

Marcello laughed. "Of course not, *il mio ragazzo*. I know you are the soul of generosity and good taste. But then you are usually in Italia, where there is no substandard wine. It is these island people who are the problem. I remember how . . . ah . . . provincial they can be. Drinking wine out of boxes and eating Parmesan from the grocery shelf." He made a helpless gesture. "Eh! What can you do? They do not know any better."

"I imagine things have changed a bit since you were here last, Marcello. The island has much more to offer now than it did twenty years ago, you'll see. It'll be perfect for you."

Connor glanced back at Gabriella, who stared moodily out the window. *It won't have enough to satisfy her, though*, he thought. They had just been in California, where Connor was planning to move, and she had hated it there, too.

"I don't know how you would know," Marcello said. "When was the last time you were here, eh? Not so very short a time, I think."

Connor shifted his gaze to Nicola, who had re-donned the headphones to her Discman and rocked silently in her seat. Nineteen-year-old Nicola seemed happy wherever she went. The perfect counterpart to her discontented sister.

"It's been a while," Connor admitted. "But it was still more recently than you've been here."

Marcello had been married to Connor's aunt Corinne twenty-three years ago for about five minutes. After they'd split, Corinne had married seven more times, but Marcello had returned to Italy and remarried only once, to the mother of Gabriella and Nicola. That woman had died several years ago.

For some reason, Connor and Marcello had formed a bond in the short time Marcello had been a part of the family, and the two had kept in touch over the years. Now Marcello had come back to the United States to expand his business, and Connor was helping him.

"How long, eh? One year? Two? When did you last go on holiday? I think a long time. I see it in your face."

"Hey, I take holidays. I was in the Bahamas three months ago."

"With that Nancy."

Connor looked at him. "Yes. So?"

"And how long since you have been here? To this place you used to love so much? I remember once you told me it nourished your soul, something like that. Do you remember?"

Connor frowned and gazed out the window. "No. I don't remember."

"How long, *il mio ragazzo*, eh?"

He shrugged. "Ten years or so."

"Ten years," Marcello pronounced. "It has been a decade since you were in a place that nourished your soul. Ah . . . and now I think I remember it. You left because of a woman, is it not so?"

"I left because it was the end of the summer," Connor said mildly. "I always left at the end of the summer."

Marcello scoffed and threw out his hands. "You Americans. Always trying to pretend that love is not important."

Connor sighed, faintly amused. "Love? How about two teenagers with raging hormones."

"You know," Marcello said as if he hadn't spoken, "I think you should have married that girl, whoever she was. If you had, perhaps you would never have left this little island and then you might not have spent ten years of your life unhappy in your family's grand empire. And you would not now be lost and looking for meaning in your life."

"I'm not lost. I've got plenty of meaning in my life. I've just had enough of Emory Enterprises. I want to do something different."

Marcello grinned at Connor's scowl. "Sure, sure. Something new. Something on your own, away from the family business. Something to define yourself. I understand. A man must be a man. But, I wonder. Is she still there, this raging teenage girl?"

"*She* wasn't raging," Connor corrected, the mistake prompting a smile. "Her hormones were. And I don't know if she's still there or not."

Marcello's brows shot up.

"All right, yes, I think she is."

Marcello sat back. "Ah ha."

"She works as a maid there. She's *always* worked as a maid there. Her *mother* worked as a maid there. The Sayers have been a part of Sea Bluff for as long as anyone can remember."

Connor could explain the whole thing. How Anne's mother had been the housekeeper at Sea Bluff until she'd died when Anne was fifteen. How Anne had worked at the house every summer until she'd graduated high school, when she'd become the full-time housekeeper. How nearly every summer she and Connor had done everything together. Sailing, clamming, swimming, hiking, exploring, even fixing up the boathouse together one July.

How in the last two summers he'd spent there, their relationship had become something more than friendship. And then, everything they did together had included so much more than those simple childhood pursuits . . .

"I see." Marcello watched him, bushy brows raised over heavy-lidded eyes.

Connor laughed. "I'm sure you see something, Marcello, but God knows what it is. The fact of the matter is, I'm not even sure I could pick Anne Sayer out of a lineup at this point."

"*Sí, sí*, I understand." Marcello nodded.

Connor looked at him. "You want to make something out of this, but there's nothing to make."

Marcello gave an elaborate shrug. "Whatever you say, Connor. I simply find the whole thing interesting, *quello è tutto.*"

"Right."

There was a momentary silence that Connor had no illusion would last.

"Yes," Marcello said, and Connor sighed. "I find it interesting that you had a relationship with this girl. Your parents must have been so proud. Their only son diddling with the maid."

"That's a pretty coarse way of putting it." Connor shifted in his seat to face him.

"And now," Marcello continued, "after not seeing her for many years' time, you will see her again. I am merely interested in how you think that will be." He smiled again at Connor.

Connor studied him. "You're trouble," he said, "which is something I've always liked about you. But in this case you're barking up the wrong tree. I'll be fine seeing Anne again. And I'm sure she'll be fine seeing me." He thought briefly about her note after his father died. He wondered, still, if it had meant more than it had said.

Not that he would consider—*ever*—being burned by that match again.

"But I would appreciate your not trying to stir anything up," Connor continued. "The last thing I need right now is—" He broke off and gave Marcello a suspicious glance. "I just don't need you putting ideas into anyone's head. She's a nice girl but we don't need any misunderstandings."

Marcello grinned and slapped Connor jovially on the leg. "Ah *ha!* Now I *do* see. You think this Anne might still have some affection for you, is that it?"

Connor shook his head, picturing Anne's quiet prettiness. At nineteen she had glowed with youth, her shy eyes shining with intelligence. She'd been beautiful but fragile, like an early bloom destined to be crushed by the last frost.

A frost that had come and hit hard, according to the realtor who leased the place for him. Sean Crawford had spoken of Anne just recently, in fact, and the woman he'd described had borne little resemblance to the Anne Sayer he remembered. Apparently she'd grown pale and faded, that gentle radiance extinguished by the world and her own insecurities.

"I have no idea if she ever thinks of me at all." An image of her popped into Connor's head. She was standing on the beach, bent with laughter, her bright blonde hair whipping around her face in the ocean breeze. "Probably not. But I don't want her or anyone else getting ideas from some bored Italian businessman looking for a way to complicate my summer."

"Connor, you wound me." Marcello frowned, one hand at his heart. "You accuse me of something so ugly. I do not toy with the lives of other people. Least of all yours, *il mio nipote favorito.*"

That one Connor knew: *my favorite nephew.* He also knew he was Marcello's *only* nephew.

Connor laughed slightly and looked away, knowing he was being teased but feeling chagrined nonetheless.

After a moment, Marcello added, in a far less injured tone of voice, "But I am confused. Why would you worry I could stir something up? If this thing happened so long ago as you say, what could I do?"

"I don't think you *can* stir anything up. I just think you'll try."

"No really, I want to know. You think this girl might have some feeling for you still?"

Connor looked at him. Marcello's hand stroked his own chin contemplatively.

"If she has feelings for me," Connor said, "I'm sure they're not warm ones. I just don't want anything bringing up the past."

"Why not?"

Connor sighed. "It's a long story."

Marcello raised one shoulder. "Make it ten minutes."

He shook his head. "I can't."

Connor let his gaze drift to the window. He remembered the ugly scene his parents had pitched when they'd found out he'd been "diddling with the maid," which was about as romantically as they had put it too. They were convinced she'd get pregnant to trap him.

"You'll like Anne," Connor predicted impulsively. "She always said she'd never in a million years fit in with my family."

"*Pah!* What normal person would?" Marcello's expression was indignant.

Connor shot him an amused glance. Marcello hadn't fit in with the family, either, but then no one would ever accuse him of being normal.

"But she's a quiet girl," Connor added. "Painfully shy. Bright, but a wallflower. Can you imagine someone like that involved in my life? All that travel, and entertaining business associates. She'd have hated it, and I would have resented her for holding me back."

"Because you love that travel and entertaining and socializing with business associates so much," Marcello said with mock solemnity. "That is why you have so recently quit this dream job, no?"

Connor shrugged. "Hey, it got me where I am, and that's what's important. I didn't love the job, but I'm glad I put my time in."

"So now you and this girl from your past will be just friends, yes? In that curiously bland American way. Or perhaps not. You are her employer, I believe, yes? That will be comfortable for you both." Marcello crossed his arms over his chest and looked at him smugly.

Connor frowned. "It'll be fine. It'll be the way it's always been."

Marcello grinned. "Really?"

Connor shot him a look. "Minus the raging hormones."

Marcello laughed.

Connor hoped to God it was true, that Anne

didn't harbor any romantic thoughts about him. It was not something he would have feared, ordinarily, since it had been such a long time and things had ended so badly between them. But after receiving her note, then having that last conversation with Sean, Connor had gotten the impression that Anne was desperate for someone to sweep her off her feet and away from the island where she had lived her entire life.

Well, except for that stint in college. About a year after he'd left Sea Bluff for the last time, he'd overheard his father talking on the phone, arranging for a new housekeeper at Sea Bluff. Connor hadn't been able to resist asking what had happened to Anne.

"She's going to college," his father had said, and there'd been a note of satisfaction in his voice. Glad, Connor had thought, to be rid of the girl who'd tempted his son to "forget where he came from."

But she hadn't left forever, he'd found out later. She'd come back on holidays and had returned for good after finishing school in three years.

He'd wanted to ask her about that, he remembered now. Why she'd decided to go to school. Or, more precisely, how she'd been *able* to. When he knew her she hadn't been anywhere close to being able to afford college. And even if she'd been able to get a scholarship or financial aid, she'd never have been able to afford the time off to go. She was taking care of her elderly grandmother even back then.

Somehow, she'd figured it all out. So why, after getting such a golden opportunity for change, had she returned to her old job, her old home, her old life?

Even now her belligerent grandmother was still alive, Sean had explained. Anne was in the same job she'd had since high school, and she was a single woman on an island with little to no social life outside the short summer season. She'd taken up with several summer executives over the years, according to Sean, only to be heartbroken when they'd left the island without her.

No wonder she'd gone after Sean Crawford with so little dignity, as Sean had confided in that last conversation. *Sad*, he'd told Connor, and Connor was inclined to agree.

The worst part, however, was not that he wouldn't be saving her from the island. Quite the contrary. He was coming to drop a bomb on her that he knew she didn't see coming.

He was coming to fire her.

Chapter Three

"He's a Southerner." Prin Walter threw the lump of dough onto the counter, causing a cloud of flour to billow into the air.

"Well, sure, he *lives* in Atlanta," Anne began.

"And has lived there all his life," Prin added.

"But his family has owned this house for generations," Anne continued. "Aren't there mostly Emorys in the cemetery by the chapel? Didn't Captain Leland Emory build this house? How can you say that just because he doesn't live here year-round Connor Emory doesn't belong at Sea Bluff?"

"Because he doesn't live here year-round." Lois donned her reading glasses and began flipping through a batch of stapled spreadsheets she held in her hands.

"And never has." Prin punctuated this statement with two wags of a floury finger.

Anne frowned. "Well, I disagree."

As far as she was concerned Connor belonged here more than anyplace else on earth. Certainly more than he belonged in Atlanta. He used to say so himself, even.

Then again, that was before he became an adult and began living a whole life in Georgia she knew nothing about.

"Well, you would," Prin said in the exact same tone. She sprinkled flour on a rolling pin and pushed into the ball of dough, flattening it with a simultaneous roll of her shoulders.

"Besides," Anne said, "he's coming back now. Maybe that means the family will start using the place again."

"That or they'll decide to sell it," Prin said. "Now that Mr. Emory's gone."

"Now, Prin," Anne said, "Connor's in charge now and he's always loved this place. Nothing's going to change just because Mr. Emory died."

Prin snickered. "Except now we won't have to be afraid of being caught alone in a room with him anymore."

Anne felt herself flush.

"What?" Lois asked.

Anne shook her head. "Nothing. Mr. Emory was just a little . . . flirtatious."

Prin snorted. "More'n flirtatious, I'd say. Let his fingers do the walking, that one did. Mosta the girls employed here during those old summers learned pretty quick to avoid him or get their bums pinched. Or more."

Anne rubbed suddenly damp palms on the sides of her skirt. "Do we have to talk about this now? The poor man's dead, after all."

"Fine. I'm just bein' grateful for small favors,"

Prin said. "We can talk about whatever you want. Like why Connor Emory's coming back this summer, maybe?"

Anne's heartbeat accelerated. The question hadn't left her mind since Sean had told her Connor was coming. Why *was* he coming now? Could it possibly have anything to do with the note she'd sent six months ago? Could this visit be the answer she'd never received?

She tried not to think about it, but her stomach fluttered nonetheless. She would know as soon as she saw him. When he looked in her eyes she'd know if he'd come back for her, she thought.

And he'd be looking in her eyes in a matter of minutes. Excitement bounced in her stomach and made her skin flush.

"Maybe he never came back before because he couldn't. His parents always had the place rented out," Anne considered out loud.

"He's rented the place out too," Prin said. "Ain't he coming with some group a Italians?"

"Speaking of which," Lois interjected, looking over her glasses at Anne, "did you get me that itemized list of expenses from the Fourth of July event? If the big boss is coming I'd like to be able to show him I'm earning my keep."

Anne brushed smatterings of flour into a pile on the counter in front of her. "It's on your desk."

"Great, thanks. So tell me about this Connor," Lois said. "He's handsome, I guess?"

Prin snorted. "Like asking the roof if it likes the

sun. Sun just shines all over everything. Warms up some things more'n others, though."

Lois looked at Anne, who stuck her tongue out at the side of Prin's face.

"Guess he warmed you up pretty good, then," Lois said.

"We had a teenage fling," Anne said. "He was handsome, and fun. All the girls on the island were a little in love with him." She paused, remembering how stunned she was to discover his interest in her. Awkward, misunderstood Anne Sayer, whose domineering grandmother raised her to be invisible. "But it was just a fling, nothing serious. We were from two different worlds. *Are* from two different worlds."

She said the words, but she didn't believe them. Sure, eleven years ago the shape his life was destined to take had scared her to death. But not now.

What scared her to death now was having the chance to get things right and blowing it.

"You don't feel strange about him coming back, then?" Lois asked.

"Of course not." Anne's voice was too high and quick to be believable. She took a deep breath and continued more slowly. "I don't know why everyone's being so careful around me about this. Goodness, it was *eleven years* ago. I can barely remember what *I* was like then, let alone him."

"Hmph." Prin scooped up a lump of butter and

rubbed it vigorously along the sides and bottom of a pie plate.

Overhead, the sound of a helicopter thudded into range. Lois and Anne looked up, as if they might be able to see it through the ceiling and the three floors above them.

"There must be the young lord of the manor now." Prin did not raise her head.

"Why are you so disdainful of him, Prin?" Anne asked. "I thought you liked Connor."

"How do I know if I like him or not? I hain't see him in years."

"But you *did* like him," Anne insisted. "I remember. You used to make picnics for us, and one time you even included a half bottle of wine the Emorys hadn't finished the night before. Boy, were we shocked to see that." Anne chuckled, remembering their illicit joy.

"Maybe it was you I liked." Prin pulled at the edges of the now-flattened dough and dragged the sheet of it toward the pie plate.

Anne turned to Lois. "It was Connor. Everyone liked Connor. His parents were awful, but he wasn't. He could charm a smile out of anyone, Mrs. Walter here included."

Lois looked impressed. "That's quite a skill."

"He was a boy." Prin pushed the dough into the pie plate. "That don't mean the man will be the same. You mark my words, Anne Sayer."

"Oh, Prin, it's not as if I'm expecting to take up

where we left off." Anne was touched by the old woman's concern. "In fact, the only thing I'm expecting is to continue on about my business just like I do with any other summer tenant."

She stood up, straightening her skirt. The sound of the helicopter drew closer, and the tone changed. Landing, she knew from experience. Many of Sea Bluff's tenants arrived by helicopter, despite the bridge that linked them with the mainland. Not all of them produced the same accelerated beat of her heart, however.

"I'd better go meet him." Anne headed for the door.

"Give him a kiss from me," Prin called, with a cackle of glee.

"I'm coming with you." Lois rose and laid her papers on the little desk Anne used in the corner of the kitchen.

They stepped out the back door, footsteps quiet on the moss-covered walk, and headed up the short hill into the back garden. They wound their way through the landscaping, past walls of boxwoods and beds of dahlias and daffodils, tulips and daylilies. Carefully constructed paths passed through rose-covered trellises and wandered by thoughtfully placed wrought-iron benches in secluded garden coves.

"That Mr. Franklin, for all his oddness, is one helluva gardener," Lois said as they walked.

"Did I ever tell you about how he started here?" Anne asked, remembering the tale she hadn't thought of for years. Strangely, she felt as if Connor's return was bringing back a whole host of memories she'd forgotten.

"No. But if I had to guess I'd say someone turned over a rock one day and there he was."

Anne smiled. The sound of the helicopter blades was much slower now. It must be on the ground. She gripped her hands together and kept talking. It seemed the only way to keep her heart out of her throat.

"Well, maybe." Anne pushed a pine branch out of the way and held it for Lois. "He arrived way before I or even my mother did."

"Jesus, that means he's been here, what—?"

"About forty years. And rumor has it he came here with no gardening experience at all, just a shovel and some story about how he knew everything there was to know about plants. Connor's grandfather hired him, and Franklin set about digging holes all over the property. Not planting anything, mind you, just digging holes. When he was asked, he said he was preparing the soil. But it finally came out that he'd heard Leland Emory, the sea captain who built the house, had buried some sort of treasure here."

"Treasure!" Lois burst with a spike of laughter. "You mean like gold coins or something?"

"Something like that. And Mr. Franklin was dead set on finding it. Old Mr. Emory apparently didn't care, just told him to for God's sake at least put some trees in the holes, and Franklin's been here ever since." Anne glanced at a hardy thicket of roses climbing up the side of a well-hidden potting shed. "Apparently he's learned a lot about gardening along the way."

"Goodness. Who knew the old guy was such an optimist?" Lois laughed. "Believing in buried treasure . . ."

"Well, I think he's given up by now."

They passed under a huge oak tree overspreading the lawn in front of the summer house. This spot had always been one of Anne's favorites because it was private and silent when someone was not arriving by helicopter. She often came here to relax or figure out some problem or other.

But now, with the advent of Connor Emory and many of her long-buried memories, Anne remembered a night when she'd crept out of her grandmother's house and met Connor in the deserted place. It had been cobwebbed and musty, but he had cleared a spot in one corner and lit a bunch of his mother's best dinner candles in cut crystal candlesticks. She could still see his face in the warm glow of light, flames reflected in each of his light gray eyes, and that smile, the tender one that was just for her, was on his lips.

Huh, she thought, *the sun may shine on everything during the day, Prin, but at night it's more particular.* She felt again the remembered glow of pleasure that had suffused her so many years ago. The amazement that handsome, charismatic Connor

Emory had chosen her, out of all the young girls on the island . . .

But that was a long time ago.

They passed through a thick stand of conifers and arrived at the edge of the woods near the helipad—the broad, flat field on the cliff overlooking the north shore.

One helicopter door was open, and two young women stooped next to it, grabbing fitfully at their flying hair while reaching for suitcases being handed out by a stout, balding man.

"How much older than you did you say he was?" Lois leaned close and spoke loudly over the drone of the helicopter's engine.

Anne looked back at her. "That's not him." She waved a hand negatively.

"Holy God, are those the daughters?" Lois called, leaning close again.

"Must be," Anne called back, looking dispiritedly at the pretty girls being helped by their father.

"Jeez, look at them," Lois said as one of them turned, running away from the swinging blades.

After a second, the other followed. It was obvious to Anne what Lois meant. They looked like movie stars running from the paparazzi, graceful and curvaceous at the same time. Thick dark hair wild in the wind but still curling with old-Hollywood perfection.

Anne squinted toward the group, clutching her sweater around her as the breeze from the ocean combined with the copter's swirl. She shivered. She should have worn something other than this dull skirt and knit shirt. She should have pitched the sandals and worn stockings to make her legs look better. Higher heels. Shorter skirt. She wished her hair wasn't so straight.

She should move forward and greet these foreign beauties, but she didn't want to move. Not before she caught sight of Connor. For some reason—probably the girls—the nervousness that had eluded her before sprang up now like a wall she could not walk through.

How could she not have known how awkward it would be to see Connor again after so much time?

"Maybe he didn't come," Lois said, voicing a fear Anne hadn't even thought of.

But a second later he appeared. Unfolding himself from the cockpit with a box under one arm, Connor reached to take a small carry-on suitcase from the Italian man. The rest of their luggage would be arriving from the airport by car, Anne knew. Then the two of them ducked out from beneath the helicopter's reach, straightened, and walked toward them.

Anne caught her breath. She could barely focus on his face at this distance, but the way he moved was instantly familiar. Lithe, coordinated, like an athlete in the middle of a game. All warmed up and comfortable in his skin.

His hair blew as the copter rose behind them,

tousling it with the Hollywood perfection the Italian daughters shared, and Anne knew at that moment that she was in trouble.

Yes, she had changed. She was no longer the bashful, awkward girl she'd been so long ago.

But he hadn't. No, Connor Emory had not changed nearly enough.

Connor strode away from the helicopter's blades, breathing in the brisk salt air, and he knew immediately that returning to Sea Bluff for the summer was the right thing to do. He'd forgotten how invigorating it was. The ocean breeze, the scent of pine, the sense of freedom and wildness.

For a moment he considered telling Marcello he'd meet them at the house. Then he could turn back to the cliff and descend the rocky path to the beach. He even looked back, as the helicopter rose and swept away into the postcard-blue sky, to see if the brushy opening to the beach path was still apparent, but it wasn't. It didn't matter anyway; the beach would have to wait.

Connor turned back to see two women standing against the deep green backdrop of pine and spruce. He froze.

One of them was Anne—he knew it the moment he set eyes on her. So much for not being able to pick her out of a lineup.

Two steps later, Marcello glanced back at him, and Connor resumed his pace.

She stood there, her blonde hair bright as a new

penny in the sun and her slight figure as straight
and graceful as ever, clutching her sweater around
her middle in a gesture that seemed at once familiar and strangely comforting.

She hadn't faded, he could tell as he approached.
She wasn't the pale, retiring figure Sean had led
him to expect. She had hardly changed at all, in
fact, except her hair was shorter. Cut chin length in
a straight shiny style that suited her perfectly.

Damn, he thought, then banished the thought.
It didn't matter to him how she looked. In fact, he
was glad she looked good. Glad for her. Happy
that she hadn't become someone pitiable. And he
was glad for himself, that he didn't have to feel
melancholy for all the changes that had taken
place.

His legs carried him closer. Before he could put
together an appropriate expression to greet her
with, she approached him.

A smile on her lips, she held out a slim hand.
"Connor, it's so good to see you again."

Her voice was the same, soft and northern, but it
lacked what he used to perceive as hesitancy. Her
eyes were the same brilliant blue, but they were
more direct than he remembered. Had he remembered incorrectly, or had she changed after all?

For just a second, he wondered what she saw
when she looked at him.

He set the suitcase down and took her hand,
half expecting some kind of historical jolt, but it
was simply warm and firm.

On impulse, he bent and kissed her cheek.

Big mistake.

A whiff of fragrance catapulted him back a hundred years, and his hand automatically tightened on hers. Hers responded. He experienced an intense momentary flashback to the time when he would have scooped her up in his arms and kissed that sensual mouth of hers.

Getting off the helicopter and seeing her was always the first moment of summer.

He drew slowly back, and their eyes met.

Her gaze seemed to glow from her sun-touched face. Her smile grew rich with warmth and intimacy.

He realized he'd stopped breathing.

He inhaled sharply, dropped her hand, and took a step back.

Chapter Four

"Anne Sayer." He forced a smile onto his face, the broad, automatic one he used with business associates. "Good to see you too. I'm glad you're here."

"Me too," she said, a bit breathily. "That is, I'm glad you're here. Well, I'm glad I'm here too, but I'm always here." She laughed, her eyes dropping shyly away from him.

Connor barely noticed her discomfort, it paled so beside his own. What in the world was he doing? Hadn't he just made it clear to Marcello he didn't want any misunderstandings? Hadn't he just told himself the last thing he needed was Anne Sayer thinking he wanted to revisit the past?

He hadn't needed to kiss her hello. That was just plain stupid. The woman worked for him, after all. Was he supposed to kiss the cook too?

"I'd begun to think Maine had seen the last of you," she said.

Me too, Connor thought.

As the group shifted and headed for the path toward the house, Connor introduced Gabriella and Nicola, who nodded perfunctorily at Anne.

Anne introduced him to Lois Marshall, who then led the girls through the trees and out of sight.

"Dill should be along in a moment to get the luggage," Anne said. "Can I help carry anything now?"

He shook his head. He needed to get a hold of himself. "No, no. I'll take these. Who's Dill?"

"Oh!" She laughed again. Her fingers pushed one side of her hair behind her ear, and she glanced up at him. "Dill's the handyman. You'll have to remind me if there's anyone else you don't know. I keep forgetting how long it's been since you were here."

"Eleven years," he said, then regretted it. It wasn't as if he'd been counting the days.

A moment of awkward silence passed before Connor realized Anne was looking expectantly beyond him.

Connor turned, something like a cold sweat breaking out on his forehead. He saw Marcello standing behind them. He'd forgotten all about the man.

"I'm sorry," he said. "You two haven't been introduced, have you? Anne Sayer, this is Marcello Tucci."

Marcello moved toward her, casting a sidelong glance at Connor as he passed. He grinned at Anne. "No, we have not had the pleasure."

He took one of Anne's hands and held it, looking deeply into her eyes. Connor had seen this performance many times before. While it wasn't insincere, it was still Marcello's foolproof way of winning people over. Connor stood back, his right arm suddenly aching from carrying the case of wine.

"You are even more beautiful than I imagined," Marcello said.

Connor closed his eyes. Now she'd know they'd been talking about her. How had this gotten off to such a disastrous start?

But Anne simply laughed, the sound somehow more carefree than he'd remembered it. Certainly more carefree than he was feeling.

"No one told me that the gentleman accompanying Connor would be so charming," she said in return.

Which is when Connor realized he didn't know her at all anymore.

Anne made sure the guests were settled in the appropriate rooms, oversaw the preparation and serving of dinner, then got resolutely into her car and drove home. Though she caught some flak from Prin for staying so much later than usual, she'd stayed only to make sure everything was in order for the owner of the house. She wasn't hanging around to see Connor. She'd have done the same—perhaps even more—if it had been his parents.

As it happened, she didn't see much of Connor anyway. He'd taken off for the beach shortly after changing his clothes.

No matter, she told herself. There would be time. The whole summer, in fact. Once he was settled she'd seek him out so they could talk the way they used to. Surely it hadn't been so long that they couldn't make their way back to where they'd been. Not if they both really wanted to.

She thought again about the hello kiss he'd given her. It had meant something, hadn't it? It had to have. Why else would he have kissed her?

But it was just a kiss on the cheek, she reminded herself.

Well, what was he supposed to do? she argued. Sweep her up in his arms? She admonished herself to be reasonable. A lot of time had passed. She knew what her feelings were, but his had to be different. After all, he'd lived the last eleven years believing a lie.

At the nursing home, where she'd arrived just minutes before the end of visiting hours, Anne found her grandmother wide awake and full of questions. Her grandmother knew—as she knew all things that happened on the island—that Connor was back.

"What did he say to you?" Delores demanded the moment Anne walked into her room.

It was not going to be a pleasant conversation, Anne knew, but at least it would be a change from the daily tongue-lashing she'd been receiving about putting her grandmother in the nursing home.

"Did he imply anything about your past?" Delores insisted.

"Who are you talking about?" Anne drew the drapes and turned out a couple of the many lamps her grandmother kept on. Delores insisted on keeping the room lit like a stadium on game night.

"Connor Emory, of course. Don't play coy with me, Anne Sayer. Everyone knows he came back today. Him and two young women."

"*And* the young women's father."

"Well? Did he say anything to you? Did he mention anything about what happened between you to anyone?"

"That's ancient history, Gramma. And it wasn't that interesting to begin with."

But her grandmother was on a roll, choosing this moment to employ her selective deafness. "Because it doesn't do to have new people learn about that childish romance you had with him. People talk, you know. Like mother, like daughter. People will speculate, and speculation only breeds gossip. You should tell people nothing happened, that it was all groundless rumor."

"If I bring anything up out of the blue as groundless rumor they're rather more likely to think there's something to it, don't you think?" Anne asked, tucking the industrial-grade sheets in tight around her grandmother's spindly legs the way she liked them. "Besides, Connor is not the type to gossip."

"Don't matter. If he says anything about you and him people will start up all over again. 'Remember what her mother did? Those Sayer girls never could resist a summer boy,'" her grandmother mimicked. "Those Helgas down to the post office will have a field day."

"Gramma, stop it." Anne straightened from tucking in the sheet at the bottom of the bed. "What Mother did and what I did are two completely different things."

At least, she could say that now. Eleven years ago it was not so clear. Not to her grandmother, not to the Helgas, not to Anne herself.

Not for the first time Anne wondered how much influence her mother's history had had on her own actions.

"You can think that if you want, but I still don't see why he has to come back now and risk stirring up a new scandal."

"There was never an old scandal," Anne said. "Not of mine, anyway."

"There might have been." Her grandmother poked a finger in the air at her.

Anne gave her a hard look. "Gramma," she warned.

Their gazes held fast for a long moment.

Then her grandmother continued with a wave of one frail hand. "There was your reputation. You've decided not to remember, but your carrying on with that boy all those years ago didn't do anything for your reputation around here, Miss Anne Martha Sayer."

Anne sighed. "Nonsense," she objected perfunctorily. She took her grandmother's robe from the foot of the bed and hung it up in the closet. "I didn't have any reputation around here."

"Yes you did. You were a nice, quiet girl who didn't take anything from anybody, 'til you tried to take up with that Emory boy. Carrying on with a rich boy made you look like a social climber. Yes it did. Why do you think none of the other boys ever asked you out during the school year, hm? They knew you'd been sporting around with that rich Emory boy all summer long, that's why."

"They didn't ask me out because I was shy and awkward and nobody wanted to go out with me."

Anne knew this argument by heart, though they hadn't had it in a long time. While her grandmother didn't usually bring up her mother, Anne always knew she was thinking of her. Remembering the last "summer boy" who had ruined a Sayer girl's reputation.

But she was not her mother.

"Don't be silly." Delores's nightcap quivered with her indignation. Her gnarled hands kneaded the covers at her waist. "You were a beautiful girl. They all would have asked you out. But they thought you had airs. It's not good to put on airs, you know, and that's what that Emory boy did to you. Gave you airs."

"He didn't give me airs, Gramma. He might have given me confidence." She stacked some magazines and tossed some tissues in the wastebasket.

"You didn't need confidence. You were a beautiful girl and nobody needed to think you knew it. They all thought you were waiting for Connor Emory to marry you, that's why they didn't ask you out."

"Well, I didn't marry him, now, did I? He never even asked." Anne stopped and gave her grandmother a severe look. Then, with a wry twist of her lips she added, "Besides, even if he had we all know that would've been getting too far above myself."

"That's right! He'd always have thought of you as the maid, Anne. Him and his whole family. You know it's true now just as you knew it then. How did he treat you today? Like the maid, I'll bet."

"He treated me like an old friend." She thought of the kiss, then shoved the thought from her mind as if her grandmother might read it. She rolled the cart that held Delores's dinner dishes from the foot of the bed toward the door.

"An old friend, eh? He ask about your old grandmother then? He ask if you're married yet? Have children? Family of your own?"

"No. Nor did I ask him."

"It's thanks to him you don't have a family, you know. Why do you think no one asks you out even now? People don't forget these things. Little Helga's been going on about you two all day long. People don't forget. Those Helgas especially, the old cows. They don't forget anything."

Elaine Fox

Anne squelched a smile. "Don't be mean, Gramma."

"Think *he's* forgotten, do you?"

"Gramma, I work for him. I talked to him about my job, about the house—"

"Huh! See? He didn't forget you were the maid. That you didn't go to some fancy college. He'd never have forgotten you were the maid. You should be glad you haven't seen him in so long."

"I'm *not* the maid." Anne stood up straight. "Not anymore. And I *did* go to college."

She wanted to say more, but, as she often did, Anne held her tongue. Her grandmother was an old, opinionated woman, and Anne had learned years ago that she should feel sorry for her, not angry. She was, Anne knew now, just trying to protect her only grandchild from suffering the same fate as her only child.

Besides, she didn't have power over Anne the way she used to. These days it was best just to let her carry on until she grew tired and that was usually that.

"Doesn't matter. It was a small college, and you came back to be a maid for the Emorys again anyway." Her grandmother shook her head, working her lips around her bare gums, eyes bitter and resolute. "And he'll always think of you that way. That's the problem with him. Him and his ilk."

Anne exhaled slowly.

"You knew it. You knew it all along."

Anne nodded and picked up her purse. "That's right, Gramma."

She *had* known it. That had been half the problem. She'd swallowed her grandmother's fears hook, line and sinker.

Which had made things *so* much easier for Connor's parents, who'd been the other half of the problem.

"Listen, I have to go," Anne said. "But I'll be back tomorrow night. Do you need anything?"

"That Sean Crawford, now," her grandmother continued. "*He* doesn't think you're a maid. He thinks you're a strong woman. A woman who'd make a good partner for him and his business."

Anne stopped at the door and turned, scoffing. "His business. Do you even know what his business is, Gramma?"

Delores looked offended. "He's the realty man. He sold Pat Newland's house last spring to that nice Hoskins couple. Got them a nice price too, as I understand it. And the Hoskins, they're hoping to bring back those apple trees, I heard. Sell cider and applesauce like they used to out there."

"Sean Crawful—Crawford," Anne corrected herself, snickering at the unexpected elementary school nickname, "is an egotistical blowhard, and if he didn't spend so much time blinding you with his flattery you'd see right through him yourself."

"I'm not blinded by anyone!" Delores brought a bony fist down on the bedclothes. "I know he's full of himself. But he makes a good living and he knows everyone in town. I knew his folks and his grandfolks. Russell Crawford used to court me, did you know that?"

"Yes, I knew that."

"He's an island boy who'd understand an island woman. He wouldn't hold your airs against you."

Anne sighed. "I don't have any airs, Gramma. I'll see you tomorrow."

"He'd know you had to work as a maid the way your mother did just to keep food on the table!" her grandmother said, pointing a finger at her as if that would freeze her where she stood. "But you didn't get weak like your mother. You stood up for yourself. Somebody like Connor Emory'd never see that in a million years. No siree. If you weren't out there being a millionaire like all his other friends you'd just be the maid. The maid who owed him everything."

"But I *didn't*, Gramma. That's the point. Now I've got to go. I have a lot to do tomorrow." Anne started to turn.

"You just remember one thing."

Anne turned back to her with a sigh.

"I know you're thinking things can maybe be different now that you're both grown-up people. But remember this," her grandmother said darkly, "the apple doesn't fall far from the tree."

"Gramma . . ." Anne warned in a throaty voice. Heat traveled up her neck to bathe her face.

"I know, we were never going to bring that up again. And I haven't, you know I haven't. And I won't, after this. But you remember now, Annie." Delores's eyes were fierce in her fragile face. "*You* remember. The apple doesn't fall far from the tree."

Anne opened the closet door in the tiny, rarely used guest room of her grandmother's house. The house she now—suddenly, it seemed—lived in alone. The door hinge creaked, and the smell of must wafted out from a row of her grandmother's old coats hanging within, several of which hadn't been used in forty years, she would bet. Next to those was a waxy zippered clothing bag containing Anne's christening gown, a velvet Christmas outfit from when she was twelve, and her prom dress, which she'd never worn.

Though the house was now essentially hers, Anne still had done nothing to change the ancient décor or even clean out any of the junk her grandmother had collected over the years. The fact was, all of Anne's homemaking abilities went into Sea Bluff—so much so that she often felt like a visitor in her own house. She was only at home while at the mansion on the cliffs.

Sure, the worn floral sofa and armchair in her grandmother's living room were as familiar to her as her own hands, but how much more comfortable was she sitting at her little desk in the kitchen at Sea Bluff? And while she kept her grandmother's house neat and clean, it was the furniture at Sea Bluff that she polished with tender care, the pillows on the Queen Anne sofa that she fluffed daily, and the sunroom in the east wing that was stocked with fresh flowers whether there were tenants in residence or not.

That was why she'd come back to work for the Emorys again, she thought. Because she loved the place. And because she'd had to come back anyway to take care of her grandmother.

Anne sighed.

On the floor of the guest room closet were stacked several sagging cardboard boxes, the old Bell & Howell film projector, some squashed and battered shoes, and three faded hatboxes from various now-defunct department stores.

Anne leaned down and pulled the bottom hatbox from the stack, leaning one shoulder against the coats to keep them out of the way and holding the top two boxes against the wall so they wouldn't overturn. The top one, she knew, contained several of her grandmother's pillbox hats—one with the eye of a peacock feather on one side, which had fascinated her as a child. The other held some of Anne's old school papers, most of which carried As but one of which was a scathing D. Her grandmother had kept that one, perhaps believing it would remind Anne that she wasn't perfect.

Rubbing the dust from her nose with the back of one hand, Anne backed out of the closet with the bottom hatbox. The rounded blue-gray cardboard was rich with familiarity, yet at the same time she felt shocked at how old it looked. She hadn't sought it out in years—eleven years, to be exact—and in that time it seemed to have aged far more than she had.

She brushed a hand along the dust-blurred top, then, drawing the string handle out of the way, she pulled off the lid. There, lying right on top, was a gull's feather, long, gray and white, with a clear quill tip. She picked it up, dismayed at its frayed condition.

She remembered this feather when it had first been found, on Cinder Beach, by a reckless, smiling youth who on a whim had made her pledge to keep it forever. She'd thought it perfect, had brushed its softness against her own cheek, then his. How had it aged so much when she hadn't opened this box in eleven years?

She set the feather aside and pulled out the stack of photographs, now slightly curled with age. A brown-haired boy with a free and feisty grin teased her from the top one.

He looked so *young*, she thought with awe. Yet they had felt so grown up.

And they had made such grown-up decisions.

She set the pictures aside and examined the collection of oddities rattling around a stack of letters in the bottom of the box. Several chipped shells, a couple of pebbles she'd once thought pretty, a piece of string with a Catholic saint's medallion attached to it, a bottle top, some rubber bands, one clip-on earring strewn with fake rubies, and a cheap metal ring, partly corroded, with a gap on one side so it could be sized according to whichever childish finger wore it.

She took out the ring and slid it onto her left-hand ring finger. The glass stone shone slightly against her tanned skin. She closed her hand into a fist, felt the metal ring expand on her finger, and held it briefly to her heart.

She remembered the night she'd gotten this. She remembered every detail. They'd attended the carnival, and Connor had won it by throwing a dart into the bull's-eye of the target, and the center of the items.

Until the real thing comes along, he'd said in a voice that had sent a delicious array of shivers up her spine. Then he'd slid the ring onto her left hand.

Their fingers had clutched each other's then, Anne's holding on for dear life.

She took the ring off and put it back in the box with the rest of the items.

It looked like a collection of treasures from some child in the 1920s, so much older than her memories. The magic they'd once held seemed to have aged, too. Become as cobwebbed as an old ghost story.

Finally she pulled out the stack of letters, tied

with a pink ribbon she remembered had come on a box of chocolates her grandmother had received one Easter. She sat with them a moment on her lap and looked at the contents of the box strewn around her. Every item was attached to a memory each and every second of which she recalled. Or did she? Now she wondered how much she had changed them, romanticized them in her youthful mind, and adapted their import to the circumstances of optimism, then defeat.

She had planned to read these letters, to remember what he had been like, to remember what *she* had been like with him. But now, looking at the stack of yellowed envelopes and the boyish script upon them, she found herself unwilling even to untie the ribbon. At one point, years ago, she'd had most of them memorized, but at this moment it suddenly didn't matter to her what they said. Nor did it matter how much pain these items had contained for so long.

It didn't matter, she realized, because he'd come back.

Connor Emory had come back.

And all that mattered was what was said *now*, she thought with a private smile. What *happened* now. Their history, apart from having gotten them to this point, was immaterial.

She took a deep breath and packed the contents back into the box. Then she put the box back in the closet, beneath the other two.

Her grandmother's warnings were understandable, but they were wrong. As wrong as they could be. Things *were* different now. For one thing, she was no longer the shy, intimidated young girl she used to be.

And for another, Connor's father was dead.

Chapter Five

Connor had forgotten the peace the sea could give. How the expanse of it, the unbreakable mass and power of it, could comfort a man used to conquering less inspiring things.

He walked along the beach under the Widow's Bluff. Cinder Beach it used to be called, because of the blackness of the cobbles that made up the shore. It was a shallow cove, with rocky, pine-dotted points jutting out on either side, and he used to put the Sunfish in at this site, since it was easy to push the small sailboat out over the shallow waves.

He took a deep breath and held it, feeling the salt air clean his lungs of city smog, clear his muscles of stress and his throat of insincere words. This was just the break he needed. The honesty of this place. The memory of the idealistic boy he'd been when he was here. *What had happened to that boy?* he wondered briefly, then laughed at himself. That boy had grown up and grown smart. He'd also grown rich on his own political adroitness.

Connor skipped a few rocks, kicked some down the beach, and walked close enough to the water to feel its icy tendrils when a shallow wave lapped over his cross-trainers.

He should buy another place like this, he thought. In California. Big Sur. He could change his life completely and buy a vineyard. That would be enjoyable.

A shift in the wind caught his attention, and he turned to look at the shore. He wasn't surprised to see Anne Sayer making her way down the path from the bluff. He knew it was her from the way her bright hair flapped and shone in the breeze, the way her head bent and her slender body made its surefooted way down the slope.

He liked looking at her from this vantage point. It was like watching a home movie of someone you loved once in a far-off time. It warmed him, from this distance.

She was coming to him, he assumed, because he had summoned her. He'd told the cook to let Anne know when she came in that he wanted to talk to her. He hadn't expected her to track him to the beach, of course. He'd thought they could talk at the house, but this was better. More private.

For a second, he remembered how things had been eleven years ago. How she would have run to him and he would have gathered her up in his arms, breathing in the scent of her, his face buried in her neck and hair. Each of them sure they were the only two people on earth who mattered.

This, however, was now. She walked toward him soberly, picking her way over the cobble beach easily even though she wore heeled shoes with her skirt. With her slim build and light blonde hair she would blend in in California, like every other all-American girl on the beach. But here, in this moody gray landscape, she stood out like a ray of sunlight. This was where she belonged, he thought. And she knew it, too. Had known it all her life.

Where did he belong, he wondered. Nowhere? Everywhere. Anywhere he chose. But that wasn't the same thing. No, not the same thing at all.

She glanced up and waved at him, still too far to speak, and he abandoned the uncomfortable train of thought.

"I thought I'd find you here," she said once she was close.

His memories vanished in the face of this Anne. She looked the same as she had when he'd known her all those years ago, but she was so much more self-assured that she seemed like a different person. A confident and savvy twin.

Connor lifted a brow. "Did you, now?"

She nodded. "The landward breeze. It tends to draw people to the beach. As you know," she added, clearly an afterthought.

"I'm a long way from knowing anything about this place anymore, Anne." He regarded her a moment, assessing her mood in light of what he had to say to her. "You didn't have to come all the way down here, you know. I was just about to go back up to the office."

He hadn't had any intention of returning yet, but he didn't want her to think he'd summoned her to the beach. Old habits died hard, he guessed. He was still trying to prove he didn't think of her as a servant.

Her direct gaze slid off him then, went out to sea for a moment. "It's no problem, Connor. You know it's never a hardship to come to the beach."

Against his will, Connor noted the glow of her skin, the way it seemed subtly lit from within. He took a moment answering.

She looked back at him and smiled. "Besides, I was hoping we'd get a chance to talk. It's so strange, seeing you after so much time, and having to make conversation in front of everyone else. Remember how we used to run off as soon as we possibly could when you arrived?"

He noted the shallow dimple in her right cheek. A dimple that had no left-side mate, he remembered suddenly.

The wind whipped up a moment, ruffling his own hair and sending hers into disarray. She smoothed one side behind an ear with her fingers.

"I needed to talk to you about the house," he said brusquely.

Her smile faded. "Is something wrong? Were the rooms not right?" She looked suddenly sure. "You don't like the ship's wheel at the window in your suite. I told Lois it was too kitschy."

He shook his head. "No, no, it's nothing like that. The place looks great."

Her gaze warmed.

He looked down. "But, as you know, it's a commercial property and has been for years. Deborah and Astrid don't want anything more to do with it, and when my father died he left it for me to manage."

"Yes, I know." She appeared confused by his tone. "I sent you a note. After your father died?"

"I got it." He nodded.

The note had been short, somewhat remote, the way first communications after ten or eleven years tended to be, but kind. He hadn't debated whether or not to answer it—not any of the five or ten times he'd read it—he simply hadn't answered.

But he'd kept it.

"I just ask because . . ." She waved a hand dismissively, but her expression belied the airy gesture. "Not that I expected an answer or anything, I just wanted to make sure you got it. Not that it was important . . . I just wanted you to know . . . I was sorry you lost your father, Connor."

He nodded again. She *was* sorry he'd lost his father, but she *had* wanted an answer. She'd wanted absolution.

"I know," he said. "Thank you."

He paused, wondering how to proceed. *Just say it, Emory*, he told himself. *It shouldn't be that hard.*

She laid a hand on his forearm. "And I'm glad you've come back to the house, Connor. I really am. The place, well, this'll sound strange"—she laughed lightly and removed her hand—"but it seems the place has missed you. It feels right with you in it again."

Connor felt the weight of the years descend upon him. *I can't do this,* he thought with a moment of desperate surprise. He couldn't pretend that what had happened between them was nothing and now everything was fine. He couldn't get chummy and nostalgic with her just because some years had passed.

She may have been right—hell, she *had* been right. The courses their lives had taken had been the right ones. But the fact was, he couldn't forgive her. And he could never tell her why.

"It's funny," she continued. "When I heard you were coming back I suddenly started remembering all these things, things I hadn't thought about in ages. Like how Mr. Franklin got his job, and how the staircase was made from your grandfather's ship's mast and how strange those paving stones in the—"

"Anne, I'm selling the house."

She stopped so abruptly that her mouth stayed briefly in the shape of her next word.

"I'm selling the house," he repeated more forcefully, as if she'd asked what he meant. "And I need you to help me with the staff."

The blood rushed through Connor's veins. She hadn't moved a muscle, but he found himself bracing to catch her just the same.

"Not immediately," he continued. "I don't want word getting out right away. But in the coming weeks we're going to have to figure out how to get everyone jobs and what everyone's severance ought to be, issues like that." He watched her face turn ashen as he continued in his best CEO tone. "You're the one who'll know best what needs to be done for these people, so I want you to start thinking about it now. Make me up a list of employees, length of service, current salary, benefits, et cetera. Nobody's going to be turned out on their ear, of course, but they'll have to be gone by the new year.

"Most of them can probably find jobs at one of the other summer places on the island. I know for example the Chasens are looking to staff year-round starting next year, and the Holloways are always looking for a decent cook. I'm sure we can work everything out, and we'll cover any transitional lapses or costs, of course."

He paused. She was frozen, her eyes on him, unreadable. She looked as if she'd been captured on film, paused in the moment he gave her the news, and any minute now the film was going to burn up in the projection light and she'd be gone.

"But," he added, not wanting to stop until it was all out, "no one's to be let go before the end of the summer. Labor Day weekend we're having a party to introduce Marcello to island society and it's going to be picked up and filmed by the Style Network. Everything needs to be perfect for that. Once that's over the transition can begin."

He exhaled. That was it. He'd done it. He'd

taken her world and turned it upside down.

He kept his gaze on her face, his expression kind yet firm, his nervous system as agitated as if he'd just proposed a multi-million-dollar deal to a cynical board.

She was just a woman losing her job, he told himself; but not without a more-than-generous severance package. Besides, from what he'd been told, she had quite a bit of business outside the house these days. She'd be fine, he told himself. *Fine*.

After a moment she closed her mouth, and he saw her swallow. Her eyes were on his chest, her back straight and her hands in delicate fists at her sides.

"You'll be fine, Anne," he said impulsively. "It's not as if I'm going to turn you, of all people, out on the street without help."

The look she gave him could have chilled ice, and he wished he could take the words back. So much for not making her feel like a servant.

"Not that you wouldn't do fine on the street," he added. Hearing his own words, he suffered the unfamiliarity of a blush. "I don't mean *on the street*, of course. I mean, you've got other business, other sources of income, as I understand it."

Her look turned to surprise.

"Not that I expect to leave you to sink or swim on your own, with just your sideline." He took a deep breath. "What I'm trying to say is I'll take care of you."

"You'll *take care* of me?" She looked incredulous.

He coughed, frowning, his mind spinning. "Well, no. Not *me*, per se. I mean . . . well, I *don't* mean 'I'll take care of you' in the way that it sounds. What I'm saying is there'll be an extremely generous severance package for you. We—and by 'we' I mean *all* the Emorys—we recognize the service you've given over the years, and we want to reward you for it."

She dropped her head, looked at him from the tops of her eyes. "The service I've been giving?" She glanced down at the beach, folded her arms across her stomach. "You've been paying me for that *service*, you know."

"Of course, and paying you well, I hope. What you deserve, that is." What a goddamn mess he was making of this, he thought as the words continued to blunder out of him. "We just—I want you to know we intend to be fair, in light of the contributions you've made, and those your mother made. The contributions everyone's made, of course, but especially you."

He stopped, knowing he had gone way too far and said way too much of exactly the wrong things.

Slowly, she inclined her head, her eyes on the beach beyond him. "Thank you," she said. Then she turned that direct gaze he was so unfamiliar with upon him again. "Mr. Tucci is the one who's buying it?"

Her voice was low. She looked dangerously composed.

"Yes. Dad left it to Patsy and me, and we agreed it was time to let it go. Patsy, especially, wants to get rid of it. I do too, of course, no reason to keep it. But she has some . . . plan for the money."

Anne nodded—stiffly, he thought.

"Marcello intends to turn it into a European-style guest house, whatever that means, and staff it with nothing but Swiss people. Gabriella claims they're the only ones who know how to run a guest house." He shrugged, attempted a laugh.

She looked at the ground.

"Anne, I'm sorry." He took a step toward her, suddenly wanting to talk to the real Anne, the Anne of old, not the one he was currently treating as an employee. "I know this must be a shock. I want you to know that I wish there was another way. A way that didn't impact your life so much."

She raised her chin. "Don't be silly. I'm fine."

He straightened. "Of course. I know you're fine. It just must be surprising."

She looked at him evenly, but he could see her pulse beating in a vein in her neck. "It isn't as if I thought everything would stay the same forever. I knew this day might come. Things change. I've always known that."

"Yes." He nodded, gazing at her. "Yes, things do change, don't they?"

She attempted a smile then, a wry one, but

didn't quite achieve it. "And it seems they're always changing right here on this beach."

He glanced around. At the sand, the surf, the immutable cliffs. It might have been eleven years ago, he thought, when she had ripped his life from under him just as he was ripping hers from under her right now.

"Anne," he said gently, "I want you to know that I'm not harboring any ill will toward you because of . . . well, because of what happened in our past. This decision was made independent of any of that."

And it was, he told himself. It was.

Her lips parted, but she paused. Then, finally, she said, "Connor, I would never have thought that of you. You know that."

He didn't know that. In fact, he'd been sure ever since making this decision months ago that that was exactly what she'd think. That he was exacting some sort of revenge.

"Good." He inhaled deeply. "In fact, I want you to know that I see now that you were right, all those years ago." He wanted to step toward her, take her shoulders in his hands, feel some connection to her other than the words. But he didn't move. "I wanted to thank you for that. For being so much wiser than your years."

"I was right?" she repeated. The blue of her eyes seemed to have darkened with the heavy clouds scudding across the sky.

"Yes. To call things off at the end of that summer. You were smart. It would never have worked. *We* would never have worked."

Her cheeks flushed. "You've seen me for one day and decided that?"

Connor shook his head. "No, that's not what I mean. I've known for a long time, for years. I've thought time and again over the last decade how right you were. I just wanted you to know that."

She swallowed. "So . . ." She paused and cleared her throat. "So what you're saying is that for over ten years now you've been wanting to thank me for not being with you? You've thought this 'time and again'?"

"What? No. That's not what I said—"

"That's just what you said, Connor." She pinned him with a look. "Look, this whole conversation is awkward, I know that. We haven't seen each other for a long time and you've had to give me some difficult news. But let's at least be honest here. You're saying you've been happy to be without me. Fine. I understand."

"That's not what I meant. I meant that—" He sighed.

Why wouldn't anything he was saying come out the way he meant it?

"For example," he started over, "last year I went to four charity balls, half a dozen corporate banquets, and a slew of events as a very visible sponsor. I gave speeches. My dates were interviewed on television. You'd have *hated* my life."

God knew *he'd* hated it.

"So . . . your public persona . . . your rich and famous lifestyle . . . *That's* the reason you were glad to be without me?" She looked at him carefully. "I mean, the main reason?"

"Come on, Anne. You know what I'm saying. You'd have hated the lifestyle, which is just exactly what you said. You knew it even a decade ago."

"You know what, Connor?" She turned to the ocean, her cheeks pink. "There really isn't any need to get into this. All of that was a long time ago." He saw her jaw clench. Then she added with a sidelong glance, "Besides, what I would have hated a decade ago has very little to do with who I am now."

He crossed his arms over his chest and sighed. "Okay. I just want you to know that what you gave up is nothing you'd want even now."

She turned back to him slowly, brows drawn. "Do I seem as if I want something from you now?"

"No. Don't misunderstand what I'm saying. I just meant that—"

"Connor, listen. Decisions were made a long time ago based on a very different set of circumstances." She looked at him squarely and spoke deliberately. "I don't think we need to get into all the reasons now. It's been a long time, and those reasons are gone. Forgotten, mostly. So let's not get into what a great decision it was, okay?"

Despite himself, Connor felt his skin prickle. Eleven years ago, out of the blue, she had dropped him like a bad apple. Did she regret it now?

His heart hardened. So she'd had some time to think about it. Had had time to realize she was stuck on this tiny island with no one but Sean Crawford for company. Had had time to think that maybe the ostentatious lifestyle she'd turned her nose up at back then might not have been so bad.

Well, tough luck, he thought, steeling himself against her. She'd betrayed him eleven years ago, and he had no desire to be lured back into trusting her again now just because she'd changed her mind.

"I agree," he said, his eyes steady on hers. "What's past is past. That's all I'm trying to say, Anne. Things worked out for the best."

For a moment they stared at each other.

Connor had had that speech in his head for nearly eleven years, in one variation or another, though never as badly botched as it had been today. He had even dreamed of this moment, both asleep and awake, in various incarnations and intensities, believing telling her all of this would bring him peace.

It hadn't, though.

"Then I suggest," Anne said finally, "that we don't indulge in any intimacies left over from our past."

"Of course not." He paused. She was looking at him significantly. "What do you mean?"

"I mean, that kiss by the helipad, for example."

He drew himself up. "I meant nothing by that. It was just a hello."

Her breathing was quick now. Peripherally, he noted her sweater rising and falling with it.

"Just a hello," she repeated, skeptical.

"That's right."

She scoffed, and he felt his spine go rigid.

"Listen," he said heatedly, "if that sort of friendliness disturbs you, then I'll refrain from here on out."

"Oh, it's nothing to me," she said briskly. "I just want to make sure we don't get our signals crossed."

"I'm not sending any signals."

"Good," she said.

"Yes, good," he shot back. "Glad we got that straightened out."

They stood looking at each other a long moment. A couple of gulls screeched from high up the cliffs.

Connor knew he should leave, he should walk away, but he couldn't. Did he want to prolong the conversation? Did he hope she'd admit that she *had* regretted her decision after all? He had no idea. All he knew was that he was angry, and he wasn't sure why.

The breeze kicked up and blew a strand of hair across her cheek. He thought of the time he might have reached up and moved the lock with a finger, grazing the petal soft skin of her cheek.

The distance between that time and this one stood between them like a wall.

Her blue eyes, crystalline in the sunshine unveiled by a passing cloud, seemed to read his mind.

"So, can we be all business now?" he asked finally. He held his hand out to hers, to shake.

She hesitated a moment, then took it.

"All business." Her voice was steady. Her nod decisive.

But she did not relinquish his hand, and his grew warm in hers.

He tightened his grip and shook her hand once more. "Good."

He loosened his fingers to let go, but she didn't. They stood a pace apart, hands clasped across the distance, eyes studying each other as if seeing someone new. The moment stretched into one too long to be casual. And still she didn't take her hand from his.

Slowly, she closed the gap between them.

The breeze blew another lock of hair across her cheek. Connor watched her, immobile with uncertainty.

She got close, reached up, and touched his lips with hers. Despite himself, his mouth moved in response.

He could have backed away, asked her what the hell she thought she was doing. But he didn't.

If he moved, he risked not finding out.

She stepped closer and put her other hand on his chest.

Desire surged within him as her body touched his. Her fingers tightened around his hand and her lips touched his again, opening beneath them.

Connor swept one arm behind her, pulling her close as their tongues met and twined in a dance they once knew quite well together. His heart pounded in his ears, thrusting blood through his veins to every limb, electrifying him.

She was familiar yet strange. They were in synch because they'd kissed a thousand times, and yet she was exotic in a way that he had given up hope of ever finding again.

How had he forgotten this desire?

He longed to run his lips down her neck, to feel her skin beneath his fingers, to make her tremble with the power of their connection.

He imagined laying her down on the beach and stretching his body the length of hers, to feel every inch of her against him. To take her as if she were his. As if they were eleven years younger and knew nothing of what the future would bring.

But she stopped, then shifted so that her mouth was close to his ear.

"Just business," she said quietly, then straightened and turned away, walking off down the beach away from him.

Chapter Six

Anne walked back into the house through the front door—unusual for her—telling herself that if Connor was going to let Marcello Tucci fire them all and turn Sea Bluff into a guest house, then she was damn well going to act like a guest.

She was unprepared, however, to find the estimable Mr. Tucci standing in the front hall, arms outstretched, bellowing out "O Sole Mio" in a dramatic, yet decent, tenor to the enormous antique chandelier.

His voice met her at the door like an otherworldly presence and shivered the crystal droplets on the chandelier frame.

She stopped. Her heart, already shaken by her own audacity, vibrated with Marcello's comically melancholy voice.

As his back was to her, her first impulse was to leave, and retreat to the kitchen entrance, near where she parked her car every morning. But she was so flustered by her encounter with Connor that standing in the doorway listening to Marcello's voice felt soothing.

He was so absorbed in song that he hadn't

heard her open the door. Nor had he appear to notice the freshening breeze that stirred the hall, rustling the mail on the table and waving a sensitive frond of the Boston fern.

She wondered how on earth one became so assured, so receptive to the transports of one's own mood, to have the nerve to stand in the front hall of a house populated by dozens and sing as if one were utterly alone.

As if, she thought wryly, one owned the place.

And yet, what had she just done? Where had *she* found the nerve? She'd taken a situation spiraling out of her grasp and jerked it back into her control like a foot on an escaped dog's leash.

She shook her head in wonder at herself, not sure what she'd been thinking. She'd gone down there with the highest hopes, only to hit the depths of despair moments after he'd begun talking.

When he'd told her about selling the house, her first thought had been that in the last eleven years he'd discovered something, that he now knew what she'd gone to such lengths to keep from him.

But then it had become obvious that no, he'd simply come to the conclusion on his own that he'd been better off without her.

So she, in a completely uncharacteristic moment, had taken an incendiary situation and dumped gasoline all over it. She had no idea what had made her do it. Had no idea where she'd found the nerve to step in and kiss him like that.

All she knew was that one moment she was upset that Connor was so obviously over her, and the next moment she was sure he was lying.

And she'd set out to prove it.

Now she found herself wanting to laugh at her own insanity, but she was too appalled at herself to pull it off. Was this hysteria?

Well, she had proven one thing, she told herself with a deep breath. Connor may no longer feel love for her, but he certainly felt passion. The question was, how far apart were the two?

Anne had no idea if Marcello finished the song, or if he simply ran out of lyrics that he knew, but he turned and saw her standing there. She immediately wished she'd left before he'd noticed her. The last thing she was in the mood to do was play hostess to this man who was buying away the thing she'd built her entire life upon.

She mustered a smile, however, and clapped her hands several times in appreciation.

Marcello's face lit up, and he stretched his arms out toward her.

"Signorina Sayer!" He approached her, and she had the uneasy feeling he meant to pull her into a bear hug. But he brought his hands together as he neared and held them, prayer-like, under his chin. "What a delight to see you on this beautiful day."

Anne's brows drew together, but she couldn't help smiling. "Beautiful? Why do you say that? It's getting cloudy and looks like it might rain. And you were singing such a sad song."

"It's beautiful because it *is* cloudy, because it is not California perfect."

She liked the way he said California: Calee-fornee-ah. Somehow, despite all she'd just learned, he made it impossible to hate, or even begrudge, him.

"And I sing a sad song," he continued, "because they are so powerful, just like this place. Like this house. Like the weather. It is all so much bigger than we are." He smiled broadly and extended one arm toward the front parlor. "Come. Have a drink with me."

She looked at him in surprise. "A drink! But it's only nine-thirty in the morning."

"So we will have orange juice. Coffee. Whatever you Americans deem proper at *only nine-thirty in the morning.*"

His grin was devilish as he ushered her toward the parlor. There was no graceful way she could refuse, and frankly, after what she'd just done, maybe a drink wasn't such an absurd idea after all.

Squaring her shoulders, she preceded him into the room and made for the bellpull in the corner by the fireplace. She gave it a tug and, putting on her best hostess smile, said, "What shall we have? Prin makes a wonderful pot of tea, and I'm sure she's got some pastries left over from breakfast. Or maybe you'd prefer a Bloody Mary?"

"Perfect," he exclaimed. "You see what a perfect day it is?"

Anne let go of the rope, took a deep breath, and

moved toward the sofa. "Yes, perfect." The words echoed surreally all the way into her soul.

"Beautiful signorina," Marcello said, his voice low. He leaned forward in his chair. "What is the meaning of this look upon your face, eh?"

Anne whipped a smile into place. Had she been looking as resentful as she felt?

"Oh!" She forced a laugh. "Am I looking like thunder again? I'm told I always look angry when I'm tired. I didn't get much sleep last night."

Which was true. She'd been thinking about Connor. About all the possibilities of his return. About all the possibilities of the future.

She had not been thinking that less than twelve hours later her life would be utter chaos.

"*Per favore*, Signorina Anne," he said, his face reflecting disappointment. "I know I am a meddlesome old man, but I hope that I am not so apparently stupid."

"Mr. Tucci, I never meant to imply that you were stupid." She was aghast that her expression might have conveyed such a thing, then annoyed with herself for fearing his opinion at all when she had just learned he was largely responsible for upsetting her entire life.

He leaned back in his chair and regarded her as a teacher might a student who perplexed him.

He smiled slightly. "I believe, *sí*, it is clear that you have spoken with Connor. No?"

She met his eyes, suddenly tired of trying to conceal her thoughts. "Yes."

Words filled her head, comments both scathing and subdued, hardened and heartfelt, to convey to this man what he and Connor were doing to her—to all of their lives—but she only pressed her lips together and looked at him. They had a right to do whatever they wanted.

Trudy bustled into the room, wringing her hands in her apron. "Did someone ring the bell?"

Anne looked up. Apparently Trudy's psychic skills did not extend to perceiving when someone actually took the effort to summon her.

"Yes, Trudy. Have Prin prepare two Bloody Marys and a pot of tea for Mr. Tucci and me. Ask her to include some of the morning's pastries too. Oh, and Trudy? Close the door behind you, please."

"Bloody Marys?" Trudy repeated.

Anne nodded and gave her a stern look. The staff was not to question what the guests wanted, ever. "That's right. Thank you, Trudy."

But Trudy didn't leave. She stood for a moment with a distracted look on her face and murmured, "I had a dream about someone named Mary last night . . . or was it Patty?"

Anne smiled apologetically at Marcello, then returned a dark look to the new housekeeper. "That will be all, Trudy."

Trudy's eyes refocused on Anne. "Oh, yes,

sorry. Coming right up." She backed out the door, knob in one hand.

Anne looked back at Marcello, who watched her quietly. They sat for a moment in silence.

"I want to say," he began then, "first of all, that I believe you are the mistress of this house, absolutely. That you are deserving of all of the loyalty the Emorys have bestowed upon you and more."

Anne inclined her head. Words backed up in her throat.

"But I'm sure you understand," he continued, "that I, too, have people to whom I must be loyal. People with whom I have worked and lived over the course of many years."

She began to nod, then stopped. "I'm sure that makes you a man of great integrity in Italy, or Switzerland, or wherever it is these people currently work for you. But it will do you no favors in a community this small, Mr. Tucci."

Marcello sat back and steepled his fingers. "I understand you are sorry to lose your position here—"

"I don't say that because I'm bitter." He looked surprised to have been interrupted, but she barreled on anyway. "I say it because it's true, because it's something you should probably know if you're going to do business here. Island people are very protective of their own."

"Are you saying there might be . . . repercussions, Miss Sayer?" His formidable brows rose.

She shook her head. "No. Not in any overt way, at any rate. I only mean that you might find yourself starting out on the wrong foot with the islanders, if the first thing you do as Sea Bluff's new owner is turn out a local staff who has been loyal to the place for decades." She raised her brows back at him. "The plight of out-of-work locals is not taken casually by the general population. We're a community of fishermen and shopkeepers, a few small farmers. But mostly we rely on tourists and the few wealthy families who make their second homes here. If you take one of the largest estates on the island and staff it with people from away, the locals will have little to thank you for, and less desire to help you." She swallowed and looked at her hands in her lap.

"I'm not speaking for myself, of course, I have other job options, and I do understand your predicament. But the other employees—some of whom have been here even longer than I have— they may have a difficult time adjusting."

"Of course. You are quite selfless, I understand," he said mildly.

Anne's blood pressure rose. "Not really. I'm upset about my own situation too, of course, because I love this place. But I'm not afraid for my future. People like Prin Walter, however, or Edward Franklin, the gardener, they don't have backup plans. Sea Bluff has been their life. And they anticipated it being their life until they retired."

"There are other estates, signorina. Some lovely inns—how are they called? Bed and breakfasts, yes, as well."

She sighed. "Of course there are."

"And a guest house this size would bring even more tourists to the island than a house only rented to a family or two each summer."

Anne closed her eyes against the vision of careless multitudes traipsing through the gardens, leaving trash on the beaches, or hanging their Bermuda shorts from the upstairs balconies.

"I have no desire to argue with you, Mr. Tucci," she said finally. "I'm only thinking of what's best for Sea Bluff and its people."

Marcello was silent a long moment, studying her. Anne had the impression that he hoped to make her uncomfortable, but instead her heart fluttered with indignation.

"Permit me, signorina," he said finally, "but I think perhaps you are not upset so much about the house, or even the staff. The staff we will take care of. I think you know that." He said it easily, offhandedly, as if she were a fool to think twice about it. "Connor told you we expect to find jobs for all of them, did he not? But you . . . no, you are upset for yourself, Signorina Sayer, and not about this house."

Anne nearly choked on her scoff. "I beg your pardon?"

"I mean, that I think this house only . . . how do

I say . . . represents what you think you are losing. It is *simbolico* . . . symbolic, *sí*, that is the word, of what you might perceive as the greater loss." He watched her like a police interrogator toying with a suspect.

Anne sat up straight. "And what, exactly, is that?"

He shrugged, arms outstretched, in that classically European way that made everything seem so self-evident. "Connor."

Anne sat still for exactly four beats of her heart. Then she leaned forward and marshaled all of her defenses.

"Mr. Tucci," she said firmly, "I don't know what you know, or what you think you understand about me or my life. Clearly, you know something of the past circumstances between Connor and myself."

She hesitated, wondering how far to go, wondering too if she should keep her mouth shut until she'd had time to digest all that had happened today.

But his presumption irked her, and she found she couldn't stop herself.

"If you'll forgive my bluntness," she continued, not really caring if he didn't, "Connor and I lost each other a long time ago. What I am losing now is a job and a place I have loved nearly all my life. I am, in effect, losing my home. I'll also be losing coworkers who are like family to me and a connection to this island that can never be duplicated." She raised her chin. "That's life, Mr. Tucci, not symbolism. That's life when you live on someone else's good graces, and I accept it. I'll move on, because life goes on."

She stood up abruptly, suddenly embarrassed at having revealed her thoughts in such a way. It wasn't even his business! How *dare* he preach to her! How dare he tell her what she was feeling! As if even *she* knew what she was feeling right now.

"Maybe I should check on that tea." She headed for the door, not wanting to expose any more of her ire.

"You will accept it, Miss Sayer?" Marcello said placidly from his chair. His tone stopped her from opening the door.

She turned and fixed him with a hard look. "Of course I will."

"You'll accept losing all this that you love?" His expression, the look in his eyes, told her he was talking not about the house, nor the job, nor the coworkers.

"I don't know what other choice you think I have," she said, throwing up her hands. "I accept what I can't change. I have to."

Why was she trying to explain any of this to him? Who was he to ask what she thought or felt about the situation?

The look he gave her felt like an accusation.

"Mr. Tucci," she snapped, "what are you getting at? *You* are not giving me choices, are you? *Connor* is not giving me choices. I suppose you would say I have set myself up to *have* no choices."

The moment the words were out, she regretted saying them. They sounded weak and self-pitying, the last thing she wanted to be in front of this man.

She turned and opened the door. At the same moment, the blasted grandfather clock in the hall chimed, sending one cacophonous chime into the room and her blood pressure skyrocketing.

Anne took a deep breath and turned back. She couldn't just walk out on the man. "Mr. Tucci, I'm sorry. I guess this is just too difficult for me to talk about right now."

Marcello smiled, which might have upset her further except that his expressive eyes showed nothing but kindness. "I understand, signorina. But remember, there are always choices, *cara mia*. For example"—he held up a hand to stop her protest—"you have the choice to fight for these things that you love, no?"

She laughed incredulously. "Are you inviting me to fight you for this house?" Her gaze flew to the ceiling, then back to him. "I'm sorry, but I don't know where I'd get the four or five million dollars it would take to be a contender."

He shrugged again. "I merely point out that you can choose to fight for what you love. That is the only way to get it in this life. Or you can choose to give up. *Accept*." He enunciated each letter of the word, then stood. "I think perhaps we should have tea in the dining room, if that is all right with you. Perhaps others will join us."

She stared at him, stumped by both his words and his attitude, and watched him walk toward her.

"*Cara mia*," he said again, when they were opposite each other at the door, "you have so much more power than you believe." With a sly smile, he added, "Perhaps you should sing in the foyer, *bella*. It awakens the sleeping soul."

Fight for what you love, fight for what you love. A week later the words still echoed in her head like a march as Anne walked from her grandmother's little clapboard house behind the grocery store toward the docks.

You have so much more power than you believe. If that were true, she thought, Connor would have melted at her feet when she'd initiated that kiss on the beach. If she was honest with herself— and she tried not to be when it came to Connor—she would admit that she'd hoped the moment he laid eyes on her again he'd realize that he'd never stopped loving her.

Well, that hadn't happened. And it hadn't happened again when she'd kissed him. So what was she supposed to do now?

Fight for what you love . . .

Her sneakered feet trod lightly on York Street, past the tiny police station, the laundromat, the Salvation Army store, and the barbershop. It was her day off and she was supposed to be shopping for the Marshalls' dinner party Glass Slipper was handling later that week, but she was still thinking about Sea Bluff, as she always did. What the place needed, what errands she could run, what the tenants would likely want to do the next day. It was rare that she had a true day off, when she went somewhere and thought about something else entirely. She couldn't even imagine what she'd do once Marcello Tucci took over and Sea Bluff was no long hers to think about.

She'd been avoiding Connor for a week—not hard to do, as he was apparently avoiding her too—because she wasn't sure how to act around him after their last encounter. But that couldn't go on forever. She didn't even want it to. She just wanted to figure out how to get back to at least being friends with him. Then they could see what happened from there.

Turning onto Water Street, she could see the lobster boats tied up at the harbor. It was four o'clock, so they'd probably just arrived. She'd get lobsters fresh from the sea to drop off at Sea Bluff for tonight's dinner. She couldn't be coy with herself and say this was something she always did on her day off. No, she wanted the running of the place to be impressive for Connor. Even if he was selling out and moving on.

The breeze kicked up, blowing her hair in her face as she turned onto the pier. Clement's Seafood Shack was about midway down the pier on the right. Boats unloaded their bounty at his back door, and patrons picked it up just inside the front. Freshness was guaranteed.

She pulled her hair back from her face in one hand, and her eyes lit on someone coming down the pier from the other end. She squinted against the sun-bright sea behind him, but the way he walked was as distinctive to her as her own reflection.

Connor.

Her heart did a little leap, and she marveled again that he was back. For a second the years melted away and she pictured his boyish face, the one she knew so much better than the man's.

They approached each other. Anne tried to gauge the moment Connor saw her, but his body language gave nothing away. He just kept moving forward until they were across from each other and his sharp gray eyes were upon her.

Anne could not contain her smile, though she tried, and she could think of nothing to say other than, "Hi."

He smiled back, a small, reluctant one. "Hi."

It was obvious to Anne that they were both thinking about the kiss.

"Out touring the town?" she asked brightly. God, she sounded like a hostess; she really needed to start taking more time off.

"Yeah, sort of. It hasn't changed much." He glanced around, his eyes taking in the weathered sign over Clement's Seafood Shack, the lobster pots piled in front, and the slick of oil on the asphalt from some once-parked car.

She looked at Clement's too. "Well, we work at it. You know how islanders are. We don't like change much."

He shot her a look.

"Not that I don't, personally," she added. "Like change, that is. Change is good, in fact. I've changed, I think." *God. Just yank off your foot and shove it in your mouth, why don't you?* "You've changed too. You look older, you know."

His brows rose. "Thanks."

"I mean, in a good way. You look more mature. More . . ." *Manly,* was all she could think, but she wasn't about to say that.

She glanced up at his face. His expression was slightly amused, and the smile playing about his lips made him look more familiar.

"More . . . ?" he prompted.

"Well, less boyish, I guess is what I mean." She swallowed, wondering how to breach the chasm that had opened between them. Far from drawing him closer, the kiss she'd given him on the beach had, it seemed, broadened the distance between them.

His eyes studied her a moment, moving from her face to her hair and back. "You don't look any different at all."

"Oh! Well." She laughed and tucked one side of

her hair behind her ear. "I guess that's good."

His lips were definitely closer to smiling now. "Except your hair's shorter."

She put a hand to her hair again. "Yes. I got tired of it being so long."

They smiled at each other a second, but she couldn't sustain the eye contact. Was he wary because he was afraid she'd throw herself at him again? Fat chance. She felt like a fool for having done it once already.

She looked past him, down the pier, hoping for some conversational inspiration there.

"So how does it feel," she asked, "being back in the old house?"

He started to nod. "It feels . . ." He gave her a sidelong glance, stopped nodding, and tilted his head to one side. "Strange, to be perfectly honest. It's been a long time. As you know."

She nodded encouragingly. "But . . . you're glad you came back?"

His lips curved again, diffidently. "Yes, I suppose. Yes." He watched a young couple leave Clement's. "I'm glad to be able to bring Marcello with me."

She kept her expression open, though the mention of Marcello brought back the reality that everything was now temporary.

"I think he's having a good time," Connor said, then raised his brows at her questioningly. "Don't you?"

She nodded too. "Yes. Yes, I think so. I found him singing in the front hall last week."

Connor chuckled. Anne's blood warmed with the sound.

"He sings wherever he goes," Connor said with a smile. "Including business meetings."

Anne laughed with him, wishing the moment would last forever. "His voice isn't bad."

"No, it's not. But it's loud."

She nodded some more, and they sank back into an awkward silence. Her fingers twisted together as she racked her brain for something else to say. She was so afraid he'd leave and this moment of friendship, however slight, would be over.

"Well, if you're going to do it, go all the way, I guess," she added, but her rejoinder was too late.

He looked puzzled. "Do what?"

"Sing."

"Of course." He nodded.

She hated this. She couldn't think of a thing to say. They stood there in the bright sunlight talking like strangers. Like people involved in an accident, waiting for the police to arrive.

Yet this was a person whose body and mind she'd at one time known as well as her own. A person on whom her own well-being had depended almost entirely.

Until she'd let him go. *Forced* him to go. For reasons that now seemed so distant.

"Connor—"

"Anne, listen—"

She stopped short. "Yes?"

"No, go ahead."

"No, you go ahead." There was no way she was going to miss whatever he had planned to say.

He smiled again, briefly. "You really haven't changed."

She blushed. What did he mean? How had she been, and what was he seeing now? The questions seemed too silly and self-centered to actually ask, though, so she waited for him to continue.

"I just wanted to say, about the other day . . ." He paused, not looking at her.

Dread pooled in her stomach. He was going to say it shouldn't happen again. He was going to put her off, put her away. She could tell by the look on his face. The polite, detached look on his face.

". . . I just don't think—"

"Hey, why don't we step in there for some coffee?" She spoke a little too loudly and blushed again. She gestured toward the Black Fly Café, a tiny hole-in-the-wall diner on the pier across from Clement's.

Connor looked startled and glanced behind him to where she'd gestured. She looked at his hair, drinking in the sight of him so close while he was not looking at her. It was darker than it had been, a burnished auburn instead of sun-kissed brown.

He turned back to her. The man, not the boy.

"Just a cup," she insisted. "I'm sorry, I didn't

mean to interrupt, but we can talk in there. You can finish what you were going to say."

He looked at his watch, then up at the sky, as if it might be about to rain. There wasn't a cloud in the sky.

The shadows were lengthening for the afternoon, however, so she smiled and said, "Don't worry. They won't start dinner without you, if that's what you're thinking. I'm the one picking it up at Clement's for Prin, so nothing'll happen until I get there."

He smiled and looked down, a motion she remembered well. She used to think it was like he took his smile and kept it to himself, as if savoring whatever it was that amused him.

"I don't know, Anne. I don't want to be responsible for delaying dinner. If Prin finds out you're late because of me, my name will be mud."

She laughed. "I'll keep your name out of it. Promise."

His eyes grazed her face again consideringly.

She took a step toward him and started to put her hand on his forearm. She wanted so badly to get back to their old friendship, their old easy camaraderie. They'd never had trouble talking, never been stuck in a conversation as stilted as this one.

But he started slightly as she moved and looked at her hand as if she were about to lay a scorpion on his arm.

She let her hand drop. "It's been a long time, Connor."

He nodded. "Yes. It has."

"Let's just talk for a minute. Can't we? Like the old friends we used to be?"

His eyes met hers. "We were never *friends*, Anne." His voice was low, and even though the words were contradictory, they sent a thrill up her spine.

The wind blew her hair into her face and she tucked it behind her ear again. "Yes we were. That was what made it so great."

He shook his head, his expression shuttering. The warmth she thought had been developing was suddenly gone. "If it was so great—"

He stopped, shook his head again, and looked down. Keeping the scowl to himself.

"Connor, it *was*—"

"No." He spoke abruptly and brought a hand up. "I don't want to do this."

She started to move toward him again. "Do what?"

"Rehash the past. I told myself before I came here that I wasn't going to get involved in any kind of—reminiscing. I don't want to go over what happened and try to figure it all out in the light of a new day. I don't want us trying to act like the last eleven years haven't made a difference. They *have* made a difference."

"I know, but Connor—"

"No. What happened, happened, Anne. And I'm glad it did, frankly. That's what I was trying to say on the beach the other day. Life has worked out the way it should have. So let's not do this. Let's not pretend to be something now that we weren't then. We can't be *old friends*. If nothing else, that's the point of what happened on the beach the other day."

Anne felt panic sweep into her chest. She wanted to grab him and shake him. Couldn't he see her, really *see* her, the way he used to? And even if that was asking too much, why couldn't he see that now, as adults, they could be so much more to each other?

"The kiss, you mean? You think the point of that kiss is that we were never friends?" Her voice was suddenly high.

Connor glanced past her and nodded to someone.

Anne spun her head, saw a man enter Clement's, and knew she had to calm down. The very fact that Connor had shifted his attention from her felt to Anne like a reprimand for being too emotional.

"The point of the kiss is that we can't be friends *now*," he said in a lower, more controlled voice. "You know that as well as I do."

"So what can we be?" she asked. She didn't want to sound unreasonable, but he was trying to brush her off like an old problem, one better off ignored, and she would not be brushed off.

"I . . ." He shook his head, put his hands out in a helpless gesture. A used car salesman saying *I just can't take any more off the price.*

"Employer and employee?" She couldn't help the cynical tone that emerged.

His eyes darkened, and his mouth went firm. "A professional relationship is not a bad thing, Anne."

"A *professional* relationship." God, he was impossible.

"Yes. I don't see why not. In fact, I don't see any other option." His gaze was flinty.

She swallowed. She should have known he would treat her this way. She should have known he would keep his distance. Why wouldn't he? *She* broke up with *him* all those years ago.

He leaned toward her and, as if reading her mind, asked heatedly, "Anne, what did you *expect*?"

"I expected to be treated with a little more—I don't know. Warmth!" She shifted her weight to one hip and crossed her arms over her chest. Glancing to the side, she saw a couple of tourists enter Clement's. Clearly, she needed to rethink her approach.

"Warmth," he repeated and laughed mirthlessly. "Most people don't expect 'warmth' from someone they've dumped."

"But there are things you don't understand about that, Connor. There were circumstances you didn't know about. Things had happened—"

"No." He shook his head, his expression

adamant. "Don't make excuses for what happened. Don't try to rewrite history by telling me all the reasons you did what you did. And for God's sake, don't tell me things are different now. *I don't want to hear it.*"

Anne flushed crimson. Her face was so hot that she felt perspiration prickle along her scalp.

She certainly *wasn't* going to tell him all the reasons she did what she did. Some of those reasons were dead and buried, and she would make sure they stayed that way. What she wanted, though, was to get through to him *now*, relate to him now as the new people they both were. But he obviously didn't want to let her do that.

"And what makes you think that's what I'd say?" she said. "Are you so sure of yourself that you think anyone who had let you go before *must* be regretting their decision now?"

"Of course not." He looked down the pier.

She stepped closer to him, the better to be adamant without making a scene. "Well, that's what it sounded like, Connor. It sounded like you were all ready for me to—to have designs on you."

"That's not true." His gaze flashed back to her.

"Well, you know what, Connor? I think the breakup was for the best, too. Neither one of us was ready to make a commitment, and what else did we have? Summers? Not even that, really. Not after you took that job your father offered. And were we really going to sit around and *wait* for the few days a year we could see each other? No, I don't regret anything."

"Right. Glad we agree."

"You say that like you don't believe me."

He expelled a sharp breath and looked skyward. "You see? This is why we shouldn't talk about this. This is why we should keep our distance and maintain a purely professional relationship."

"*Fine*," she said, flipping her hands up. "You know what? That's sounding pretty good to me too right about now."

"Good." He shoved his hands in his pockets.

"Yes, good." She glared at him. Then, feeling as if she'd just argued herself into a place she had no desire to be, she turned and stalked away.

Halfway down the pier she remembered the lobsters. *Dammit.* Well, she wasn't going back now. She turned the corner onto Water Street, out of his sight.

"Fight for what you want, my ass," she muttered to herself. "Not so easy when what you want fights back."

Chapter Seven

Candlewick Island Herald Press
July 19 edition
The Anonymous Observer

The Anonymous Observer has it on good authority that a most distinguished member of our exclusive little community has returned to the fold, as it were, bringing with him a bevy of beautiful Italian women and their prominent father. The party in discussion—whose last name begins with the most Excellent letter "E"—was seen in town a day after his arrival, at the Cork & Curd, stocking up on that shop's fine assortment of classic wines and cheeses.

Speculation ran rampant when word reached us that Mr. "E" was returning, as he has not been on the island since the summer of 1992. At that time, speculation was he had a relationship with a certain female member of our community who shall remain, as all AO subjects do, nameless (though her initials, as you no doubt remember, are AS).

The AO's insider knowledge is well aware that Things Change, however, and Mr. "E' "s sights have apparently been set elsewhere for this return Engagement on the island. (Does the AO use the term "Engagement" lightly? We think not. In fact, we believe the Italian family is here not for a simple vacation. But the party is party to a party that could otherwise be termed—dare we say it?—a celebration!)

With the AO's certainty on this subject comes the news that the "E"-family matriarch will soon be joining the assemblage, lending support to any and all marital suppositions . . .

"*What* an idiot!" Anne exclaimed, tossing the weekly newspaper down on the kitchen counter and scowling at Prin. "The man can't even write a coherent sentence, let alone try to nuance it into something resembling discretion." She picked the paper up again and read, " 'The AO's insider knowledge is well aware . . . ' " She threw the paper down again. "*Knowledge* can't be *aware*. My God, it's a wonder Sean ever graduated from high school."

Prin harumphed and continued stirring the bowl of muffin batter she had resting on one hip.

"And a 'bevy' of Italian women? Since when are *two* considered a 'bevy'?" Anne glared at the offending paper, tempted to pick it back up and read it again. Between the mention of her former relationship with Connor and Sean's hint at Connor's engagement to someone else, she was a mass of uncalculated emotions.

But it was the threat of Connor's stepmother showing up that really unnerved her.

"Where does this information come from, anyway?" she continued. "Does he just make it up? Because it sure seems like it. And if he doesn't, is it true? *Is*, for example, Patsy Emory coming?" she demanded of Prin. "Because if she is, you'd think he'd let us know about it. *We're* the ones who have to get this place spic and span for her royal highness. Does he think the shock value of his column is more important than the readiness of the staff here?"

"Don't take that long to make a bed," Prin said.

Anne glared at her as the back door opened and Dill sauntered in.

"Hey all, what's up?"

"It's a lot more than making a bed, Prin, and you know it," Anne said.

A *lot* more. If Patsy were to come she'd need to prepare to be robbed of her dignity, threatened, lied about, and generally treated like dirt.

Add to that the fact that Patsy Emory was the last surviving custodian of Anne's deepest, darkest secret, and the danger of her arrival was palpable.

Dill stopped and gave Anne a look. "What's wrong with you? Coon get your trash?"

Prin chuckled. "Anne's upset 'cause Sean

Crawford says Connor Emory's getting married."
Prin gestured toward the counter behind her
with an elbow. "Coffee's nearly done. Give it two
minutes."

"I'm *not* upset that he's getting married," Anne
protested. "For one thing, he's *not*, I'd be willing
to bet. Sean's just trying to stir something up. I'm
upset because Sean Crawford's a moron."

"No relief in sight for you, then." Dill grinned
and walked to the coffeemaker. He leaned over to
watch the water dripping into the coffeepot.

Prin laughed. "You read today's *Herald*?"

"Yeah, I read it." He straightened and leaned
one hip against the counter. "Which one you think
it'll be, eh? I vote for Nicola, myself. Just seems a
little nicer."

"Ayup. He'd have his hands full with that older
one, that's a fact," Prin agreed. "Whatser name?
Gabinella?"

"Gabriella," Dill said. "Think she's called Gabby?
By her friends, I mean?"

"Think she's got friends?" Prin quipped.

"What I'm upset about," Anne insisted, trying
to speak calmly, "is that Sean obviously knows
Mrs. Emory is coming but he hasn't told *us* yet.
He'd rather wait and let it slip in this stupid column that he thinks everyone hangs on, when in
truth nobody could care less what the blasted
Anonymous Observer erroneously observes."

Dill chuckled. "Yeah, you seem pretty unfazed
by it."

"Doesn't he remember how exacting Mrs. Emory can be?" Anne railed, glaring first at Dill, then Prin. "If she's really coming, we'd better know about it so Trudy can repolish the silver for the umpteenth time and *you*, Dill, can retrim those hedges at the bottom of the drive so that they're actually even. For all we know she'll want to serve dinner for twelve on them the first night."

The joke made both Prin and Dill laugh. Prin knew firsthand, and Dill had heard, of the infamous dinner parties Mrs. Emory had thrown. One year she'd had all her guests perched on horseback, each saddle fitted with a small table complete with linen tablecloths, crystal goblets, silver cutlery, and fine china dishes. Even the horses had had gold-trimmed feed bags full of oats.

She'd had Mr. Emory—who was always bulldozed by Patsy into participating in bizarre ways—attempt to play Taps on a bugle. But that had only lasted a few seconds, as the sound had been so awful that not only couldn't the guests stand it but the horses had threatened to stampede.

What Patsy hadn't counted on was her feisty Arabian Midnight Snow's antipathy for her neighbor's aptly named gelding, Put 'Em Up.

Another time, when she'd been hosting a fellow millionaire friend who'd attempted to circumnavigate the globe in a hot air balloon (and failed), she'd set up the table, chairs, and serving dishes on a platform on pulleys, eventually raising the seated group to a point ten feet from the twenty-five-foot ceiling in the Great Room.

Aside from being set into nauseating motion every time someone moved, the arrangement had proved quite the challenge when any of the guests had needed to use the rest room.

"And why would *I* have to trim the hedges again?" Dill asked. "That's Franklin's job."

"Because you made such a mess of them the last time," Anne replied. "And furthermore, doesn't Sean realize he could be jeopardizing his own job by speculating about Connor and one of the Tucci girls?"

"Connor wouldn't fire him for that," Prin said, pouring batter into a large muffin tin.

No, Anne thought grimly, *but Marcello might*. Fathers could get awfully touchy about what showed up in the paper about their daughters. Particularly, she could guess, when it concerned their love lives.

Anne hated the fact that she had to keep Connor's secret about the sale of the house. She was so used to talking to Prin and Dill and Lois—pretty much everyone at the house—that she was scared to death she was going to let it slip.

Though frankly, she wasn't sure it would do all that much harm if she did. It wasn't as if there was a wealth of opportunities on the island. If word got out that the employees were to be laid off by the end of the year, the likelihood of all, or *any*, of them bailing out of Sea Bluff for new jobs before the all-important party at the end of the summer was slight.

She'd made a list of all the employees and what she thought they were owed, but she hadn't been able to bring herself to speculate on replacement jobs for them. It was simply inconceivable to her to imagine, for example, Prin making blueberry muffins in Sylvia Holloway's kitchen, or Mr. Franklin pruning Edna Mallock's rosebushes.

Still, she didn't want to be the one to leak the information. She'd already made a fool of herself in front of Connor by kissing him, then arguing with him. She didn't need him thinking she was a gossip, too.

"You sure you ain't just mad 'cause the crown prince himself didn't tell you?" Prin asked, sliding the muffin tin into the oven and turning to her. "Seems to me he'd be the one to let you know if his stepmother's coming, seeing as how he's here and all. Not Sean."

"That's not how it works." Anne slumped onto a stool and stared at the floor.

The coffeemaker burped and gurgled, spitting the last drops of water into the carafe.

"We don't know how it works, really." Dill poured himself a cup of coffee. " 'S long as I been here none of the family's ever come to stay. Maybe Sean thinks everything works different with them here."

"Then he should tell us that," Anne said. She shook her head. "God, I just hope he's wrong about Mrs. Emory. I can't stand that woman."

"Oh, she ain't so bad," Prin said.

"What are you talking about? She's a *terror*." Anne nearly shuddered with her last memory of the woman. "She's practically psychotic, if you ask me. Don't you remember, Prin?"

"Maybe she's improved in her old age."

The double doors to the kitchen swung open from the hallway beyond, and Connor walked in.

Anne caught her breath. He looked startled to see her, too.

"Morning, Mr. Emory," Prin said as easily as if it had been Lois who'd entered. She wiped the counter and put the batter bowl in the sink, filling it with water.

"Morning, Prin." Connor turned, nodded to Dill, then glanced at Anne. "Anne."

"Good morning," she said, blushing to the roots of her hair. She looked away. Had he heard her say she couldn't stand his stepmother? Was he aware of Sean's piece in the paper that morning, and was he hoping Anne had seen it?

Anne shot a desperate glance at Prin, who sighed and turned to Connor. "What can we do for you?"

Connor took a couple of strides into the room, effectively cutting Anne and Dill out of the conversation as he directed his comments to Prin.

"I'm having Mrs. Carmichael and Mrs. Mallock

for lunch today," he said, with such a lord-of-the-manor air that Anne knew she'd hear about it later from Prin. "Mr. Tucci will also be joining us. I was hoping you could make something cold—lobster salad, something like that. Maybe some rolls. And some iced tea."

"Dill got some lobsters just last night." Prin nodded toward Dill. "Good 'n fresh."

Connor looked over at him. "Great. Dill. Okay, good. Anything else you need to know?"

"What time?" Prin set her hands on her hips and looked at him as if she were his mother asking what time he'd be home from the party.

Connor appeared not to notice. "They're coming at twelve-thirty," he said, looking at his watch, "so let's say we eat at one."

"You want it laid out like a buffet or served?"

"Served." He nodded once with the word, then glanced again at Anne.

She raised her brows. "Did you invite them, or did they invite themselves?" she couldn't help asking with a smirk.

Shirley Carmichael and Edna Mallock were both notorious social climbers, and Anne was just put off enough by Connor's imperious tone—not to mention yesterday's discussion—to want to tweak him.

"I invited them," he said. His expression was lazy, his eyes hooded. "It there a problem?"

She smiled. "Oh no. Just, well, good luck with that. They'll talk your head off, if you let them."

She felt Dill's incredulous gaze upon her. Perhaps he didn't know her history with Connor. He certainly didn't know they were all being let go at the end of the summer. Why on earth should she care what Connor, as her boss, thought of her? But all Dill knew was that she was talking not just casually but impudently to the man who was their employer.

"Thanks for the warning. I won't let them." Connor turned for the door.

Anne watched his back, willing herself to maintain distaste for his arrogance despite noting how his polo shirt clung to his muscular shoulders and draped from there to his trim waist. For a second she was seized with the memory of her fingers tracing the indentation of his spine between the hard-toned planes of his back.

He turned at the door, and her eyes flicked innocently up to his face.

"By the way, Prin, I'd like lunch in the sunroom. Have Franklin cut some flowers or something. These ladies are head of the garden club, aren't they?"

"I believe they are, at that," Prin said.

"Anne, you might want to clear out for the afternoon, since you don't like my guests." In his eyes was a challenge. To what, she wasn't sure. "Prin can serve. Or whoever you want."

"Oh no," Anne said airily, "I'd be happy to. Except that it's Trudy's job."

At least for now, she thought, giving him a significant look.

His gaze told her he knew exactly what she was thinking.

They looked at each other a long moment before he shifted his eyes to Prin. "Fine. That's it, then. Thank you," he said and strode from the room.

Anne turned to see Dill gaping and Prin frowning at her.

She looked defiantly back at them and then intoned, in her best Yul Brynner voice, "So it is written, so it shall be done."

Dill snickered.

Prin shook her head.

Anne felt something inside herself come unglued. She had to work to keep from laughing in a way what would surely be perceived as insane.

She was without a job come the end of the summer; Connor had as much as told her he'd spent the last eleven years being glad he was without her; and Marcello Tucci was turning the place she loved most in the world into a "European-style guest house."

Would it really be better for Candlewick if Sea Bluff were converted to a hotel? Was it all just about more people, more wallets, coming to the island?

What about the history, the solitude, the peace and beauty Sea Bluff offered? What about the fact that they regularly offered beach access to children's scout groups and classroom field trips? What about the fact that marine biologists were frequently welcomed to study the delicate ecosystem of the western marshes and the shoals in the east bay?

Wouldn't a guest house also prevent the locals from hiking the pine and spruce forests, or clamming down on Leland's beach?

No, she thought, it shouldn't just be about money. There was more to be protected here than income. And she, being about to lose her job anyway, was the one to protect it.

What else did she have to lose?

Nothing, she thought, an idea clicking into place in her mind like the tumblers in a safe. Nothing at all . . .

"Prin, Dill . . ." She paused, wondering if she had indeed lost her mind. Then she leaned forward. Her mind spun excitedly. Her conscience told her she was being rash, but she clapped a mental hand over its mouth and said, "I need to tell you something. But it has to be kept in the strictest confidence. You can't even tell Lois." She leaned her elbows on the counter between herself and Prin.

"What have you got up your sleeve?" Prin frowned, but she leaned toward Anne just the same.

"Something that might just save us," Anne said.

Dill narrowed his eyes. "I don't think I need saving."

Anne shifted her gaze to him and said solemnly, "Yes you do, Dill. Trust me."

He swallowed. "Why do I have such a bad feeling about this?"

"Come closer." Anne gestured him toward her and turned to Prin. "I don't want anyone overhearing what I've got to say."

"Oooh, a party!" Shirley Carmichael crowed.

Anne knew she was tickled pink to be let in on the plan. She probably even fancied herself the *first* one to be let in on the plan, Anne thought sourly as she leaned against the wall outside the downstairs sunroom where lunch was being served.

"A big one?" Edna asked. "Like those wonderful soirees your stepmother used to throw?"

"Something like that," Connor said. "Only maybe not so . . . unusual as some of the ones she did."

"No circus horses performing on the lawn," Marcello chimed with a deep chuckle. "And no carousel with live animals."

The ladies tittered appreciatively. "Oh Mr. Tucci, you are so clever," Shirley said.

"It is not cleverness, trust me, signora. These are actual things she has done." He laughed again as the ladies gasped. "I remember hearing she once ordered a plane to fly her favorite calypso band up from St. Thomas. There is no need for anything like that at this party, I assure you."

"Well, we'll be looking forward to it, nonetheless," Shirley said.

"We were hoping," Connor said, "that since we are without my stepmother's party, uh, influence, you might be able to help us."

Aha! Anne thought. *So Patsy Emory isn't coming! Thank God.*

"Why certainly!" Edna gushed.

"Whatever you need!" Shirley seconded. "What can we do for you?"

"I understand from Helga, down at the post office," Connor said, making Anne wonder when he'd talked to her and what gossip *that* conversation had produced, "that you two have thrown some of the most elegant parties on the island. I was hoping to get your input on what sort of planning we should do, maybe some ideas on themes we might incorporate. Maybe you know, too, who on the island can be trusted to provide such things as food, flowers, decorations, all the essentials."

There was a silence during which Anne had to grip the wall behind her to keep from flouncing into the room and demanding he tell her what the hell he thought *her* job was.

Then it struck her: He *did* think she was just the maid.

Her grandmother was right.

"What is it?" Connor's voice came again, confused. "Did I say something wrong? I didn't mean to imply that either of *you* do the work . . ."

"Goodness, no," Edna said, sounding relieved all the same. "We didn't for a second think you meant that. It's just that . . ."

"Well," Shirley said, "we just naturally would have assumed you would use Glass Slipper."

Thank you! Anne thought, glad that someone in the room remembered her own fledgling party planning company. Though Connor should have known that her job description at Sea Bluff included doing just this sort of thing herself.

She slumped against the wall.

"But maybe he heard about that sumo wrestler?" Edna said in a worried tone.

Anne straightened.

"No, dear, that wasn't Glass Slipper," Shirley replied, nanoseconds before Anne actually would have burst into the room.

"What's Glass Slipper?" Connor asked.

"Sumo wrestler?" Marcello repeated.

Another moment of silence passed in which Anne hoped Shirley and Edna were giving Connor looks of amazement at his ignorance.

"Glass Slipper is Anne's business," Shirley said finally. "She's planned all of my parties the last two years and done a beautiful job. Edna's too."

"Anne?" Connor repeated.

Was his tone disbelieving? Anne wanted to smack him.

"Anne Sayer," Shirley clarified. "You know . . . your . . . ah . . ."

Anne felt herself blush. His *what*?

"Tell us about the sumo wrestler," Marcello said again.

Edna tittered. "It was supposed to be Pan or someone, wasn't it, Shirl?" Anne could picture her cocking her head, birdlike, at Shirley. "Some Greek god, I think."

"Cupid, dear." Anne imagined Shirley patting her hand.

"Oh yes of course."

"Made of ice," Shirley explained. "For the punch."

"This was for Paloma Peterson's wedding."

"A nice, chubby, winged Cupid," Shirley said reasonably.

"But when it showed up," Edna said urgently, "it was a huge fat Oriental man—"

"*Asian*, dear."

"Wearing a diaper!"

"Obviously a sumo wrestler," Shirley said knowledgeably. "In ice, of course."

"Well, that was a disaster," Edna said. "People talked about it for weeks. Nobody even noticed what the bride wore."

"But that was a Theresa Wilks party," Shirley said. "She planned it. Not Glass Slipper."

"Of course not. I don't know what I was thinking. Glass Slipper is first rate," Edna said.

"First rate," Shirley concurred.

Yes! Anne rejoiced, then slipped down the hallway as Trudy approached with the blueberry cobbler for dessert.

Several hours later Anne and Trudy stood in the solarium. Trudy held a squeegee.

"I don't see why we don't wait for a sunny day," Trudy said. "You can see the streaks better."

"That's because you *get* streaks on a sunny day," Anne said. "The sun dries the solution too quickly, and you see a residue. Cloudy days are best, remember that. It'll save you a lot of time."

Trudy nodded soberly. "Okay."

"Then, once you've done that," Anne said, "you use this." She bent over a canvas bag and pulled out a blackboard eraser.

"An eraser?" Trudy asked.

"This gives the glass a little extra shine. You don't need to do all the windows with this, just the ones facing the ocean. Or wherever you see a need for it."

Distant footsteps sounded at the top of the stairs down the hall.

"Oooh, someone's coming," Trudy said. "I can feel it."

Anne shot her a look to see if she was joking, but her eyes were closed.

Anne guessed it was Lois. Nobody clomped on these old wood floors like Lois in her thick-soled oxfords.

"I believe it's Lois," Trudy said. "I'm getting a darkish aura, a mood . . . you know how Lois is." She opened her pale green eyes and gave Anne an astral look.

Anne debated several responses.

"Anne," Lois's voice called into the room.

Trudy smiled serenely. "Ah."

Lois swung around the doorjamb, one hand on the molding. "There you are. The prince is looking for you."

Trudy gasped. "Is Mr. Tucci a *prince*?"

"She means Mr. Emory," Anne said. "Lois, you and Prin are going to have to stop calling him that. It's going to get back to him."

Lois sighed and stepped into the room. "You're probably right. But he's been such a royal pain in the ass today it felt like he deserved the title. He's been storming around all morning and now he's out on the patio, looking like he expects you to come scurrying the moment you get his message."

"He's been storming around? What for?" A mixture of dread and elation spun through Anne's chest. After the surprise of the kiss and the disruption of their argument at the harbor, he was probably annoyed that he needed to ask for her help with his precious party.

It seemed egotistical to even think it, but Anne was sure he did not know what to do with her. There was no doubt in her mind that he'd responded to her kiss, no matter what he'd said afterward, over and over again, about wanting to forget about the past. And now here she was in the same house with him. He was caught between a rock and a hard place, she thought. Or the past and the future.

On the other hand, she countered, willing herself back to reality, Shirley or Edna could have said something to bother him. Or maybe he'd seen Sean's column. . . .

In any case, it wasn't like Lois to talk this way about the boss. For all her tell-it-like-it-is, no-nonsense attitude, Lois was about the most loyal, straightlaced employee Anne had ever met.

Lois shook her head. "I don't know, but he's got Dill jumpy as a pig at Easter, and Franklin was just ordered out of the garden because His Highness wanted to sit outside. *Alone.*" She drew the last word out, Greta Garbo-esque.

"Did his meeting with Shirley and Edna not go well?" Anne asked.

Lois rolled her eyes. "Who knows? They seemed happy enough when they left, but he's been a bear all day. I'd get down there PDQ if I were you."

"All right." Anne paused. "Wait a minute. Did you tell him where I was?"

"No. I didn't know where you were. I told him I'd find you. I was half afraid he'd fire me if I didn't." She headed back toward the door but turned when she reached it. "I can see now why things didn't work out between you two. Definitely temperamentally incompatible."

Anne felt Trudy's curious eyes snap to her face. She could have kicked Lois for bringing up her past in front of the housekeeper.

Lois looked from Anne to Trudy and obviously realized her mistake. "Oh, damn. Sorry, Anne. I don't know where my head is today."

Anne shook her head. "Lois, do me a favor and tell Connor I'm in the summerhouse."

"The summerhouse! What on earth for?"

"I've, uh . . ." She thought rapidly. "I've got, there are some candlesticks there I thought would look nice on the table for dinner. Something different. I want to get them."

"Can't you see His Highness first?" Lois looked seriously put out. "If I have to go tell him to find you . . . well, he strikes me as the type to behead the messenger, if you know what I mean."

"He won't behead the messenger." Anne laughed as she untied her apron and tossed it toward the squeegee bag. "Trust me."

"I don't know . . ." Lois's shoulders slumped as she left the room.

Anne turned to Trudy. "I'll be back before you're finished with the windows."

Trudy put a light hand on her forearm. "What did Lois mean, that you and Mr. Emory were incompatible?"

Anne slid out of her grasp and headed for the door. "I don't know. Maybe she meant he should have fired me years ago."

Trudy looked scandalized. "Fired you! Nobody would ever fire *you*."

So much for clairvoyance, Anne thought. *Don't quit your day job, Trudy.*

Chapter Eight

Anne trotted down the back stairs and out the side door, then wound through the tangled rosebushes and made it to the main garden path. She walked swiftly past benches and trellises, through a small copse of trees, until she reached the old summerhouse.

She had to push hard to get the door open—the summerhouse was never used anymore—and then she had to wipe spiderwebs from her face as she passed through the jamb. While she loved this place, she hadn't actually been inside it for years. She would come sit on the front steps or lean against the giant oak that shaded the structure when she wanted a break, but the inside was too full of memories she had not wanted to relive.

Today, however, she wanted to be inside.

The place smelled musty as she entered. It had been so long since anyone had been here that cobwebs softened every corner and a thin layer of dust coated every flat surface. The air was stale too, but the long mahogany sideboard managed a slight gleam in the muted light from the windows.

It was inexcusable, really, for the place to be in such a state. Just because Anne hadn't wanted to come in here was no reason for it to have been so neglected. She was sorry now she'd arranged for Connor to come here, and she made a mental note to have the place aired and cleaned.

She walked silently into the room. The house was small, more like a large gazebo for hosting semi-outdoor dinner and cocktail parties, with tarp-covered couches and chairs, the sideboard and a long dining table. But the window and door moldings were ornately carved, and a stained-glass window on the sunny southwest side dabbled colored light onto the floor.

Some problem with the roof was the reason it hadn't been used in so long, but Anne had never gotten the go-ahead to get it repaired. So the place had sat, unused, for years. Maybe Connor would give her that go-ahead once he saw the place again.

The last time they had been here together, that last summer he was at Sea Bluff, was the night they'd discovered their passion was unstoppable. Anne had met him here late one night. She'd come through the door in bare feet, long after everyone at Sea Bluff was asleep, ready to give herself to him in a way she could never give herself to anyone again. At that moment she'd been ready to pledge herself to him forever.

She remembered vividly the look on his face as

he'd watched her approach, as if he was drawing her to him with the intensity of his love. And when she'd reached him, he had taken her in his arms and—

The door to the summerhouse slammed back against the inside wall and Anne jumped, spinning around.

A much older Connor stood in the doorway, looking as surprised by the noise as she was, and a great deal more annoyed.

"Sorry," he said brusquely. "It was jammed."

"It's all right," Anne murmured. She swallowed, suddenly nervous.

In contrast to that night eleven years ago, when she'd approached a Connor who knew her, loved her, and wanted her absolutely, today she faced a stranger. And after yesterday, a contentious stranger.

This was not the pal she had wrestled with, the buddy she had swum with, and, later, the love-struck boy she had physically explored with all the wonder of first love. This was a full-grown, determined, potent man, whom she had angered yesterday and now brought to this place intentionally, as if she knew what the hell she was doing.

He wore pressed khaki pants and a white polo shirt. His leather belt matched his expensive shoes. His watch was heavy and thick—a Rolex. His hair was cut perfectly, unmussed, and his face was chiseled in a way the boy's had never been. His chest was broad, his arms well muscled, his body solid and toned; a far cry from the whip-lean, slightly gangly body of the boy's.

But it was his eyes that bothered her most. When they looked at her, they were guarded, impersonal, cool.

Yes, this was a man. A man she didn't know.

"What are you doing here?" she asked, finally remembering she wasn't supposed to know he was looking for her.

"Lois said you were here. I wanted to talk to you." As he spoke he looked around the musty room, his face unreadable but his eyes jumping from one spot to another as if looking for something he'd lost.

Anne continued slowly toward the sideboard, knowing the candlesticks were inside. She recalled vividly that on the night she'd met Connor here he had lit every candle he could find in the place. She still remembered the way his skin had glowed gold in the candlelight . . .

Connor cleared his throat.

Anne stopped beside the sideboard and turned to look at him.

"I understand you do some moonlighting planning parties." He was all business, but in the cozy cavern of the room his voice sent an illicit thrill along her nerves.

Anne gazed at him a second. "You knew that. You mentioned my side business the other day, when we talked about you firing me."

That shook him a little and added some life to

his expression, even if it did move closest to a scowl. "I am not *firing* you."

She raised her brows. "No? Just relieving me of my job at the end of the summer?"

He crossed his arms, stood just inside the door with his feet braced apart. "No. I'm selling the house. If anything, Marcello's firing you."

She smiled and ran her hand along the top of the mahogany piece. Her fingers left a streak in the dust. "Passing the buck, Connor. That's not like you."

He lifted a brow. "It might be now."

Her eyes flicked back to his. His expression was firm. Hard, even.

"I don't think so," she said. "I read about what you did at Emory Enterprises. About cutting your compensation in half and increasing the stock in retirees' portfolios when the market dropped. That's not the action of a man passing the buck."

He had the grace to look embarrassed by her praise.

After a moment he asked, "Have I got it right? Do you plan parties?"

"Yes, Connor," she said in a similarly businesslike tone. "What did you think I did? In fact, what do you think I do here, at Sea Bluff?"

"You're the housekeeper. I thought maybe you had a . . . well, a housekeeping business on the side."

She wanted to laugh and cry at the same time. Instead she swallowed and took her time answering. "You thought I was the maid."

She looked down at the rug, noting in true housekeeper style that it needed to be vacuumed. She hated it when her grandmother was right.

He said nothing for so long that she looked back up at him. He was watching her.

"Did you think I was the maid?" she pressed. "Still?"

His eyes narrowed. "Anne, I'm not involved in the day-to-day operation of this place. I knew you still worked here, I knew there was a staff, I knew Sean leased the place and you took care of it. I didn't know and frankly I didn't care what was in everyone's job description."

She raised her chin. "But you care now."

He sighed. "All I want to know is if you know how to plan a damn party or if I need to hire someone."

He was angry all right, she thought. He was trying to tell her, again, that he didn't give a damn about her. Because the one thing that was obvious when they were together—obvious because of both the kiss and the argument—was that their passion hadn't died.

No doubt that was why he was still standing ten feet away, barely inside the door.

"Yes, I plan parties," she said. Then she squatted down and opened one of the cabinet doors to rummage around for the candlesticks. If she made enough noise he'd have to come closer for her to hear him.

She poked around for as long as she realistically could, then rose with two silver candlesticks in her hands. They were tarnished nearly beyond recognition, but she remembered them well. She hoped he would too.

Standing again, she saw that Connor hadn't moved. He still stood just in front of the door with his arms crossed over his chest.

She wondered what it would feel like to have those strong, adult arms around her body. Not like it was on the beach, but like it was years ago. Would he feel like a different person? If she touched him the way she once had, would those well-defined pectorals and those powerful thighs make him feel like someone new?

"Good," he said. "I need a party planned. Why don't you come to the study in the morning and I'll let you know just what we want."

Anne moved forward and set the candlesticks on the end of the long dusty sideboard. She didn't look at him. Instead she tried to wipe some of the grime off the base of one candlestick.

"Do you remember that night when you lit all the candles in here?"

At least she was a little closer now. She could reach him in four, maybe five, strides if she wanted to. Or vice versa. She glanced up.

He looked at her stonily. "Why?"

She let her hand drop from the candlestick. "Why?" she repeated. "Why what?"

"Why do you want to know if I remember?"

Belligerent, she thought. She opened her mouth to respond, but he spoke again.

"Because of course I remember." His voice was impatient. "I remember lots of things about that summer, most of which I wish I didn't. As I keep saying, I didn't come back here to walk down memory lane with you, Anne. I came back here to sell the damn house and get out. There's nothing I want to relive from that time, understand? So let's just let it lie."

Anne's cheeks heated and her heartbeat accelerated. She looked again at the sideboard. He was so bitter that she wondered again if it was just the breakup or if he was upset about something more.

"I know why you came back, Connor," she said finally. "And I'm sorry for bringing up things you'd rather not think about. I know it must be hard . . . I mean, it's hard for me too."

She looked up at him. He watched her suspiciously.

"I don't know why that would be," he said evenly. "Since you got what you wanted."

"Did I?" Her eyes searched his face.

He shrugged. "You got rid of me. That was obviously one thing you wanted."

"But Connor—"

"*Anne.*" He sighed heavily. "How many ways do I have to tell you, I don't want to talk about it."

"Why not? Is it still so painful for you?"

He laughed and looked at the ground. After a moment his eyes rose back to hers, though he didn't raise his head. It was a look she suddenly remembered well.

"It's not *painful* for me, Anne. My God, it's been over a decade. How pathetic do you think I am?" He raised his head and looked at her consideringly. "I just don't think it would be—productive to get into who hurt who and why. Do you?"

She exhaled. He didn't know. He couldn't.

"No. I don't."

"Good. So let's just—get on with life."

"Fine." She pushed herself away from the sideboard and moved toward him. "Let's forget everything we once were to each other. Let's act like we're nothing to each other. Like we're old acquaintances. Employer," she drew the word out, "and employee."

She reached him and stepped as close as she dared, not touching him but not out of reach either. She tilted her head to look up at him, her heart in her throat.

"The trouble is," she said softly, her brow furrowing, "we don't have any precedent for how to act around each other. Not as business associates. We were always"—her eyes dropped to his lips—"together."

In a flash, he grabbed her by the shoulders and pushed her back away from him.

"I don't know what you're trying to do, Anne." His voice was low and severe. "But I suggest you stop trying."

Her eyes jerked back to his face, shocked by his extreme reaction. His hands gripped her shoulders with bruising force. To her they felt good, however, and she wondered how sick that made her, to be gratified by even this kind of contact.

She put her hands on his forearms, holding them tightly.

"All I want . . ." she began, but her mouth went dry, and she could not complete the sentence.

He was breathing rapidly, but the expression on his face was changing. Anger was slowly being replaced by something else, something . . . calculating. His lips curved so slightly that she might have imagined it.

"*What* do you want?"

She swallowed and saw his gaze descend to her throat. Her hands tightened on his arms.

His grip loosened, became almost a caress, as his eyes moved back to hers. She remembered this look, too. This sleepy, hooded look that was so seductive.

"You called me an egotist yesterday," he said, "for implying that you might regret having dumped me. So what are you doing now? I thought you said you didn't regret it."

"I don't," she said, thinking there was a great deal of difference between not regretting a decision and having the time and space to change your mind about it. "I just—you're just not as detached as you want me to think."

"Ahh." He tipped his head back. "So that's it. You want to prove something to me, Anne? That I still want you? Is that it? That you can kiss me and still get my blood going?"

Heat rose to her cheeks. She glanced away, then forced her eyes back. "Maybe."

His lips curved further, into a smile that felt dangerous and titillating at the same time.

"Well that's a two-way street, Miss Anne," he drawled, his smile lazy, mocking.

She dropped her gaze to his lips. It certainly was.

"Connor . . ."

"No, Anne," he said softly.

Just as she was sure he planned to let her go and leave, his mouth swooped down onto hers. His arms enveloped her, arching her neck and raising her onto her toes.

Anne wound her arms around his back. Her lips fervently kept up with his.

And her heart spiked with a desire so strong that even she hadn't anticipated it.

Her fingers found that indentation of spine and grasped the flexed muscles of his back. This was nothing like the kiss on the beach. This was a kiss

Anne was powerless to stop, powerless even to *want* to stop it.

His tongue plundered her mouth, pushing her head back. His hands were hot on her waist and her back, his arms could have crushed her. The strength of him, the force of him controlled her absolutely, and yet she felt as if passion imbued her with a power every bit as strong.

Heart careening wildly in her chest, Anne realized that yes, he was a different person. And while the stranger made her blood run hot, the familiar part that was still Connor made her feel as if she'd finally come home.

One of his hands dove into her hair, gripping the back of her head so he could deepen the kiss even further.

His other hand slid around her rib cage. She arched into him, gasping with the sensation as his lips left hers to travel down her neck.

Roughly, he pulled her shirt from the waistband of her skirt, letting his hand slide up the bare skin of her side to her breast. He grasped it, lightly pinching the nipple between two fingers.

She inhaled sharply, and he immediately let go. But she said, "No," and moved his hand back to her breast.

With an utterance that might have been a curse, he turned them both so that her back was against the closed door. He leaned into her, kissing her and pressing his hips into hers. He was hard, she could feel through both sets of clothing, and one of his hands gripped her hip and pulled her into that hardness.

She moved her hands to his buttocks, then slid one around to the front of his pants.

He jerked as she touched him, exhaling with the sensation, and grabbed the hem of her skirt, pulling upward, until his hands touched the bare skin of her thigh.

The touch sizzled through her body. She fumbled toward the buckle of his belt, blind with a passion that was as dominant as it was unexpected. She wanted him *now*.

At that moment he pulled back.

The hem of her skirt dropped to her thigh and he gripped her hand with one of his. Her fingers stopped on the buckle.

They stood there a moment as he lowered her hand to her side. His eyes were shrewd upon her face.

"Is that what you wanted?" he asked. His voice was breathlessly gentle.

"I—" She hesitated, breathing hard.

Yes, part of her screamed, *yes it's what I want, and for God's sake don't stop now.*

But she hadn't gotten what she wanted. No, she was getting what she deserved, she could see it in his face. This was retaliation. It was exactly what she'd done to him on the beach.

Well, not exactly . . .

Still, he'd made his point. Where making each

other crazy was concerned it *was* a two-way street.

The difference was that she wanted all that they'd just done and more.

She wanted him back.

He stepped away from her, looking down and straightening his clothes.

She thought about telling him she was sorry, that she hadn't really dumped him all those years ago. Or rather, she had but she hadn't wanted to, not the way he thought she had. She wondered what would happen if she told him everything, came completely clean. But she couldn't do it. For one thing, she couldn't sully the memory of his father—no matter how much Mr. Emory deserved it—a bare six months after his death.

Besides, things were different now. She was a different person. She was ready, she was capable, she could handle things she could not have handled before. Maybe that was enough.

Connor was different too, though, and she was scared to death he would tell her he was different in a way that would prevent him from ever loving her again.

He started to leave.

She stepped sideways as he reached for the door handle behind her. Before opening it, he stopped.

"Don't play the game," he said with a half smile she found ridiculously attractive, "if you're afraid to lose."

He pulled open the door and stepped into the

dappled evening sunlight of the summer yard.

Anne watched him go until he'd passed into the copse of trees and was no longer visible.

Out loud, to no one, she said, "But I'm not going to lose. Not this time."

Chapter Nine

Connor pushed through the kitchen door and nearly ran over Trudy. She spun out of the way, sending a basket full of dinner rolls spiraling across the room to land like a bunch of dead tennis balls near the refrigerator.

"*Damn*. Sorry." Connor scowled at the rolls.

"Lord, what's the commotion?" Prin said, turning from the stove.

"Ooh, Mr. Emory! Your aura is *black*." Trudy stepped back from him, green eyes as wide as saucers.

Connor stopped short and glared at her. "Women," he muttered, shaking his head.

He pushed through the double doors from the kitchen and ran smack into Marcello.

"*In nome del dio!*" Marcello exclaimed. "*Che cosa è errato con tu?*"

"You're in America now, Marcello," Connor growled.

Both Marcello and his booming laugh followed him down the hall. When he reached the foyer, Connor grabbed the finial with one hand and rounded the banister onto the stairs.

Marcello put a hand on his arm to stop him. "Not so fast, *figlio*. Come with me. I think you need some conversation."

Connor felt as if his head were going to explode. He didn't need conversation, he needed exorcism. "Marcello, I really don't think you want to talk to me right now."

"And I think I do. Who should we believe, eh?" Marcello tilted his head in the direction of the parlor. "Come with me."

Unable to think of another reason not to, Connor followed him.

Marcello closed the doors behind him, then moved toward the grand salon and closed those doors too.

"Now," he said, turning back to Connor, "what will you be drinking?"

"Hemlock."

Marcello laughed. "I think perhaps wine."

Connor slumped into a chair. "At least make it whisky."

"Whatever you say."

Connor ran both hands through his hair, bringing them back to rest on his eye sockets. If he pressed hard enough, maybe he could destroy whatever part of his brain turned him into an idiot around Anne Sayer.

Marcello cleared his throat.

Connor uncovered his eyes and took the drink Marcello offered.

"I shouldn't have come back here," Connor said.

"What nonsense." Marcello settled himself in the chair across from Connor, swirling brandy in one of the Waterford snifters. He brought the glass toward his nose and inhaled. "Ahh."

"I mean it. I should have stayed in California and let you and the girls come by yourselves. I don't belong here. All I do is screw up my life every time I come."

"And exactly how have you screwed up your life this time? You have been here almost no time at all."

Connor closed his eyes. He hadn't been here long, but it was long enough. Long enough to know that resisting Anne and whatever the hell she was doing for the rest of the summer was going to require a Herculean effort.

"Marcello, have you ever met a woman who had the power to turn you into your worst possible self?"

Marcello snorted. "I've never met one who hasn't."

"But one, just one, who made you do things you would never otherwise do?"

Marcello's smile was sad, his eyes understanding. "You are speaking of Signorina Anne, no? The one with whom you were going to be just old friends."

Connor sighed, then laughed slightly. "Right.

You were right. I was a fool to think we could ignore the past. What I didn't know was that we could so completely screw up the present."

"What has happened?"

Connor eyed him, wondering if the older man would be shocked if he were to tell him what had just happened.

"Do not forget, *sono Italiano*," Marcello said with a knowing half smile. "I know well the ways of *amore*."

Connor scoffed. "*Amore* had nothing to do with it. In fact, I don't even know what this had to do with. Lust, for the most part."

"You have slept with Anne?"

Connor chuckled wryly on an exhale. "Not exactly."

"I speak euphemistically."

"I know."

Marcello cocked his head. "And how do you feel? Do you want her back? Does she want you? What is the problem here?"

"The problem is she wants—well, honestly, I don't know what the hell she wants. All I know is I refuse to relive a past that is well and truly dead. Things ended the way they should have, whether or not I thought so at the time. But at this point in time I have no desire to change how things turned out."

"What you do now won't change how things turned out. You are both years older. You have both lived other lives. You could not recapture the past even if you wanted to."

"Well I don't want to."

"Good."

"But . . ." Connor ran a hand around his neck.

"But what?"

Connor shook his head, knowing that it was not as simple as that but unsure how to explain why. "But it's not that easy. For some reason—"

"You are afraid of what you feel for her."

"I don't feel *anything* for her." He felt the denial to his bones. And yet, he felt something. Fear, he thought, but that didn't make any sense. Maybe anger.

"So you just saw her, you . . . kissed her?"

Connor gave a noncommittal shrug.

Marcello chuckled low. "And now you are ashamed of yourself for your desire. This is foolish."

Denial rose up in him again. "This was not desire. This was revenge."

Revenge gone totally wrong. The last thing he'd wanted toward the end was to stop. It had taken every ounce of willpower he possessed to pull back and show her that two could play the game she'd begun. What he couldn't figure out was which outcome would make him the winner.

"Ah, this is different," Marcello said. "*Vendetta.*"

Connor looked at him.

Marcello swirled his brandy again, staring into the glass. He took a sip and licked his lips. "Revenge is complicated."

"You can say that again."

"But it is not necessarily of the baser emotions. You were hurt by this woman, and so you reacted. You are not a mean person, Connor. But you are much more emotional than you like to admit."

"No. The problem is that I'm *not* emotional, Marcello. I wasn't hurt, I have no feelings. I was pissed." And caught by a craving he could not resist.

"Hurt and anger are brothers, *il mio ragazzo*."

"So I'm reacting to being hurt *eleven years ago*? Could I possibly be that fucked up?"

Marcello chuckled. "We are all that fucked up, my friend. Lucky for you, you know why."

Connor shook his head. "No way. If I was 'reacting,' as you say, to anything I was reacting to what she's doing now, not what she did eleven years ago."

"What is she doing now?"

Connor pushed himself up in the chair. "I don't know! That's the hell of it. But she's doing *something*. For some unfathomable reason she's doing everything she can to seduce me." He looked up into Marcello's skeptical face. "I swear it. *She* came on to *me*. I had no intention of touching her."

"And you were powerless to resist her charms, eh?"

Connor dropped his self-righteous glare. "It

seemed more important at the time to make a point."

"A point?"

"Yes, to make the point that she shouldn't ask for what she doesn't want."

Marcello's eyes narrowed. "And did you make that point?"

"I don't know . . . No. Shit." Connor dropped his head onto the back of the chair. "The only point I made was that I have no self-control." He rubbed a hand over his face again and lifted his head. "And that I can be a complete bastard."

Marcello paused. "Maybe the point is that she's not asking for what she *doesn't* want."

Anne arrived at the house the next morning with the intention of seeking Connor out. She wasn't sure what she was going to say or do, but she wasn't going to let the momentum die with that trick he'd played yesterday.

Seconds after she stepped inside Sea Bluff, however, the drone of a buzz saw blasted through the air.

Anne's pulse jerked. It sounded as if someone were cutting a tree down inside the house. She pushed the front door closed behind her. It slammed with more force than she'd intended at the very moment the blasted grandfather clock in the hall sounded its discordant, jangling sound. Three chimes only, but it was enough to send her blood pressure through the roof.

Anne dropped her purse on the front table and looked at her watch. Eight o'clock. She started toward the grand salon when footfalls thudded in the hallway above her.

She stopped and turned her gaze to the ceiling, then to the steps to see Connor's thunderous face as he rounded the landing. He was dressed for the day but wore no shoes. She remembered summers when he'd never worn shoes, had never worn anything other than shorts. He'd been such a free spirit then.

Now he looked ready for a country club golf course. Except for his feet, of course.

"What in God's name is that?" he demanded, his gaze on the archway into the front parlor.

Anne slowly put two and two together. It had to be Dill, acting once again on their plan to make Marcello change his mind about buying Sea Bluff. If enough things were seen to be faulty, Dill reasoned, who would go through with such an expensive purchase? It wasn't a great idea, she thought, frowning, but it was the only one they had. "I'm not sure," Anne said.

His eyes shot to hers and he stopped midstep, clearly surprised that it was her standing in the front hall.

"Anne." He paused a moment, then continued down the stairs.

They stood looking at each other awkwardly. Connor pushed one hand in his pocket and ran the other one through his hair. It looked mussed afterward, as it would if he'd just come in from the beach.

"Listen, I, uh, I'd like to talk to you." He shot an annoyed glance in the direction of the saw, which had briefly shut off, then started up again. Louder, if possible.

"Of course." She balled her hands into fists, rubbed her fingers along her damp palms.

"Let me, though . . ." He extended a hand toward the noise. "Let me just deal with this first."

"All right. I mean, no. I will." She started toward the archway, but he had started there too. They both stopped and gestured for the other to proceed, until Anne laughed nervously. "You go ahead."

Connor strode through the door. She followed him through the front parlor into the grand salon.

There, above a tarp-covered settee, stood Dill on a ladder. He had a power saw in hand and was cutting a perfectly circular hole in the ceiling worthy of Bugs Bunny himself. Anne half expected to see Gabriella drop through on the round cutout to the floor. Her bedroom was the one overhead.

"What the hell are you doing?" Connor's voice cut through the noise, and Dill shut off the power tool.

He gave Connor a cheery smile. "Good morning, Mr. Emory. Hope I didn't wake you."

"*Wake me?*" Connor's eyes widened. "You're waking the dead with that racket. Not to mention ruining the only drywalled ceiling in the house. What I want to know is *why*."

Dill shook his head, unfazed by Connor's anger.

"Leak," was all he said.

Anne squinted at the ceiling, hoping to see some sort of pipe, but she knew Dill was nowhere near a bathroom or laundry room or anyplace else that might require plumbing.

"A *leak*?" Connor said. "From a *bedroom*?"

Dill, still unconcerned, shrugged. He was about to say something more when Marcello entered the room.

"What is this happening here, eh?" he asked. He held a bagel in one hand and chewed thoughtfully as he regarded the hole.

"Termites," Dill said this time.

Anne winced.

"Termites?" Connor repeated.

"I think what Dill means," Anne said, taking a step back as Connor turned abruptly toward her, "is that there was a leak from below the bedroom window, there." She pointed through the hole to the window. "And he thinks it was made by termites. But don't worry, he'll have it put back together in no time. Won't you, Dill?"

She gave him a significant look.

"Oh sure." He stuck a screwdriver into some of the ancient linty insulation between the ceiling and floor and dug around. "Oh yeah." He nodded as if the place was teeming with bugs. "Yep."

"Connor, you wanted to talk to me, isn't that right?" Anne touched his arm.

Connor jerked and stepped away from her, nearly tripping over Marcello next to him.

"*Attento*, Connor," Marcello chuckled.

Connor ran one hand along the back of his neck and glanced at Anne. "Come with me."

He led her to the library and moved straight to the desk at the back of the room before turning around. He wanted something large between them before he looked at her again.

She stood with her hands folded in front of her, her face passive. He templed his fingers on the desk in front of him and remained standing. Then he straightened and cleared his throat.

"First," he said, adopting the same impersonal voice he used with business associates, "I want to apologize for yesterday. It was—" He stopped and looked at the top of the empty desk, unable to stop thinking about her lithe body coming so willingly into his arms. "Inexcusable."

When he'd thought about this speech last night, he'd planned to suggest that she might want to leave Sea Bluff, to take the severance he'd offered her now and move on, away from him. But looking at her now, he didn't want to do that. If she wanted to leave, she'd have to quit. Not that he wouldn't still give her the severance, he just didn't want to be accused of asking her to leave.

Anne was silent.

Connor took another breath and continued. "Look, I don't know what's going on here. You and I have a lot of history and that's causing some . . . ah . . . inappropriate behavior. For my part, I regret . . ." He shook his head, forced himself to look at her. "I deeply regret my behavior."

She tilted her head.

"Connor," she said, her voice soft.

The intimacy of the tone made his muscles clench, as if he were about to drive head-on into a wall. He was glad he'd put the desk between them.

She clasped her hands together in front of her. "I should like to apologize too. I behaved . . . wantonly." She gave an embarrassed laugh.

He let his eyes linger momentarily on the unpartnered dimple, then dropped them. So they'd both apologized, so what? That didn't mean they weren't going to continue to make each other crazy. No, they needed a better solution. He wasn't going to play this game with her. It was too . . . dangerous? No, he rejected the word. It was too something else, something he wasn't going to think about. He just didn't want to get involved with her and that was that. The past was past.

"Listen," he said, businesslike again, "I think we need to talk about this."

"Well . . . yes." She kneaded her hands in front of her.

He took a deep breath. "I think you need to tell

me just what it is—uh—just what . . ." The wording suddenly eluded him. He didn't want to actually *accuse* her of anything.

Did he?

He started again. "I want to know what you—exactly what—oh hell, Anne, I just don't know what you're doing. Or who you are anymore. And you don't know me, either. So why do this? Why are you trying to—tempt me all the time?"

Her cheeks flushed and a spark lit her eyes. "*Tempt* you? Are you accusing me of playing Eve to your Adam?"

He laughed. "My Adam?"

She looked impatient. "Are you blaming *me* for plucking the apple from the forbidden tree, Connor? Because even if I did, *you're* the one who took it. Whatever else you can say, Connor—that you don't want to remember anything, that you want to sell the house, that you couldn't care less about *me*—" She let that hang in the air a moment before continuing. "You can't deny that you still feel it, Connor. Just like before. You still feel it."

His smile disappeared. "Feel it?" he repeated. "Feel what? *Love?*"

He was ready to deny it. Ready to argue the point as vehemently as he could. He'd spent years getting rid of his love for her, and he could tell her all about it. About the women he'd had that weren't her, the relationships he'd been in that had been nothing like theirs, the jobs he'd conquered, the trips he'd taken, the enormous quantities of time he'd spent actively *not* thinking about Anne Sayer.

Yes, he was completely willing, *and able*, to tell her about the millions of ways he'd forgotten about her, about that brutally painful loss so long ago.

"No. Not love." She leaned forward, her hands on the desk between them, her icy blue eyes locked on his. "*Desire*, Connor. You and I could never keep our hands off each other. Why should anything be different now? Obviously, it's not."

"But it is." His pulse tripped upward, as if someone were trying to rip him off. "It's completely different."

"How?"

"What do you mean, how?" He threw one hand out. "It's obvious how. Back then we were in love. Or thought we were, anyway. Now it's just, now it's just . . . been a while." He shrugged, wondering why, if he was so sure he felt nothing for her, he still worried about hurting her feelings. "Now it's just two single people enjoying . . ." He opened his hands, palm up, looking at her to supply the word.

"Enjoying?" She raised one brow.

"Sex."

There. They stood there in the aftermath of the word for a moment while his breathing accelerated.

Anne, on the other hand, appeared calm.

"But obviously," he said, pressing the point,

daring her to deny it, "that's not something you can handle. You want it to be more, to be tied to ancient history. Well it can't be, Anne. That history is dead."

You killed it.

He had her with that one, he thought. If she denied she wanted to re-create the past, she'd have to present herself as some kind of sensuality-seeking floozy, and she'd never do that. If she didn't, he'd stick to what he'd said all along—the past was over, irretrievable. He didn't want it anymore.

Besides, it seemed obvious they both had changed so much that they were now as different from their old selves as night and day.

For example, eleven years ago she'd been as pliant as a woman could be. Now she was someone with a spine of steel, a woman with an agenda, determined to get her own way. That in itself put her out of the running for him. He liked biddable women. Soft, feminine girls who were easy to please, and who liked to please him in return.

"If it was just sex," Anne said slowly, "then why did you call me in here to apologize? If it was just two single people enjoying each other, why was your behavior 'inexcusable'?"

She never used to do this to him, he thought sourly. Pin him, corner him, challenge him. Now he felt both compelled to defend himself and inadequate to the task.

"Because whether you want to hear it or not,

162 *Elaine Fox*

you're my employee. And because you obviously took our actions a different way," he said, disgusted to hear his voice emerge husky.

She moved to his side of the desk and stopped. "I may be employed by you, but I'm not *your* employee. And what if I told you I didn't?"

"Didn't what?"

"Didn't take our actions as anything but two single people enjoying sex. Or what might have been sex, if it hadn't been . . . interrupted."

He couldn't keep his eyes from her full lower lip, from the flash of straight, white teeth as she said *sex*.

He narrowed his eyes and raised them to meet hers. "I wouldn't believe you."

Her brows shot upward and her mouth opened. But before any words emerged, the door opened.

"*Not now*, dammit," Connor growled, his eyes not leaving Anne's face.

"*Connor Emory*," a voice tinged with equal parts Southern belle and Connecticut blue blood gasped. "How *dare* you speak that way to your mother."

Connor saw Anne whirl, a look of dread flashing across her face. He turned to his stepmother. He could practically see the electricity that arced between the two women.

At the same time, the insane clock in the hallway suddenly decided to chime again. The damn thing was loud even in this room. If it hadn't belonged to his great-grandfather Connor would have walked into the hallway this very minute and pitched it into the front yard.

He waited for the din to subside—through six boisterous, discordant gongs—then asked his stepmother, "What are you doing here? I thought you said you weren't coming."

Patsy Emory turned her gaze from Anne to Connor and swept into the room with all the command her five-foot-three-inch frame could muster.

His stepmother was the type to capture attention by volume rather than presence, and though her long flowing clothes were the sort to make taller women look regal, they were compromised by her short stature and sturdy gait. She'd been brought up a tough Virginia horsewoman and had been trying for the last thirty years—since capturing the illustrious Bradford Emory, his father—to reinvent herself as a delicate Southern belle.

"What am I doing here?" she repeated, stopping on the other side of the desk, where Anne had been standing. "What am I doing in a house that I own and have every right to visit whenever I wish?"

Connor studied her, familiar with this mood. He decided against correcting her about the ownership of the house. She owned only *half*, and it was a half she was desperate to get rid of.

"That's right."

"I came," she said, glaring at Anne again, "because Shirley Carmichael called, and said that I was desperately needed."

Connor closed his eyes briefly and exhaled.

"And I see," his stepmother continued archly, "that I arrived just in time."

Patsy directed a haughty glare down her nose at Anne.

Anne's face had turned to stone.

"Anne Sayer. How is your grandmother?" Patsy looked her up and down with insolent brown eyes.

Oddly, Anne did not appear surprised by the question, nor by the tone in which it was asked, which had been roughly the same one Patsy might have used to inquire about a relative imprisoned for murder.

"She's fine." Anne's spine was ramrod straight.

It struck Connor that in speaking to his stepmother Anne's voice no longer contained the quaver it had always had in the past. Funny, he'd forgotten all about that quaver.

"Still alive, then?" His stepmother placed her hands on her considerable hips.

"What kind of question is that?" Connor objected.

"Yes, she is," Anne answered. "She's quite well, in fact."

"I'm so glad to hear it."

And indeed, his stepmother did look glad, in an evil, pointy-smiled way.

"Just what did Mrs. Carmichael say you were

desperately needed *for*, Patsy?" Connor sat slowly in the desk chair.

"Why, to plan the party for Marcello!" She threw her hands out beside her with a clatter of gold jewelry. "I understand it's going to be carried on the Style Network."

Aha, he thought. Her presence suddenly made sense. She wanted to be on television. Back in Atlanta she'd been in the papers, and once or twice on the news, but an event like this party had brought her clear across the Atlantic Ocean. And Connor was sure she would have been willing to do even more than that.

"Anne's planning the party." He felt Anne's startled glance upon him.

"Anne!" Patsy glared at her again. "Connor, it's all well and good for the housekeeper to plan an afternoon tea, or even a dinner party, but this is a major gala. One that's to be on television. It's got to be *spectacular*. The right people have to come and the theme has to be perfect. A welcome for Marcello not just to Candlewick Island, but to *America*. Greeted by the very *best* of American society. I'm afraid Anne would be uncomfortably out of her depth. I'll handle it."

Connor leaned back in the chair, tilting it nonchalantly. Foiling his stepmother was almost as gratifying as surprising Anne with his support. "She's not the housekeeper."

Patsy laughed, then looked concerned. "What exactly *is* she?"

"I'm the events coordinator," Anne said.

Connor looked up at her. She was a strange amalgam of the Anne he used to know and the new one, the one who appeared so cool and direct. Maybe it was watching her in an old situation, or maybe it was just being able to look at her when she wasn't looking at him, but he thought he could see that the new Anne was simply the old one holding her self-possession before her like a shield.

He was surprised by a feeling of tenderness for her so strong he wanted to stand up, put his arms around her, and tell his stepmother to get back on her broomstick and ride back to whatever hell it was she'd come from.

He didn't, though.

"Events coordinator?" Patsy scoffed. "Well fine, then, you'll coordinate what I tell you."

Anne turned to him, her face stony. "Connor, I've got to go. Maybe we can continue this conversation some other time." She glanced at his stepmother. "And some other place."

Connor experienced an uncomfortable flashback. She was in the hallway, upstairs, outside his stepmother's sitting room, and she was telling him she couldn't talk to him, that his stepmother was too close. Shortly after that she met him on the beach and dumped him flat.

"Hang on a second, Anne." He turned to his stepmother. "That won't be necessary, Patsy. Anne's going to plan the party because that's what she does. And apparently she's good at it, even according to your Shirley Carmichael. Besides, we don't need any dancing bears or sequined Rockettes."

For a second Patsy looked like she was going to explode. Then she turned a cool smile on him and said, "Fine. I'll just stay and enjoy someone else doing all the work, for a change. I hope you'll at least keep me informed about what you're planning, Anne. It would be disastrous for Marcello if anything were to go awry. His very livelihood in this country depends upon this party's success."

Connor said dryly, "That might be overstating it just a bit."

But Anne inclined her head. "Of course I'll keep you informed."

They stood for a moment in awkward silence.

Anne looked at Connor. "Are we finished for now?"

He knew she was dying to leave. Even years ago she was never in a room with his stepmother longer than it took to leave it politely. And he always wanted to follow when she left.

"I am if you are."

She turned and headed straight out the door without looking at either of them.

Once she was gone, Patsy eyed him for a moment, during which time he knew something unpleasant was coming. Once again he wished he could have followed Anne out the door.

"You know, Connor, if you don't take a firm hand with the employees they'll walk all over you." Patsy fixed him with a scolding eye. "I know your father's will put you in charge of this place, but you're going to have trouble on your hands with that one. As I recall, she was trouble years ago. I can't imagine why we've kept her."

Connor put his fingertips together in front of him, his elbows on the arms of the desk chair. "She's not just an employee and you know it."

"Oh, Connor. Please. Don't tell me you haven't gotten over that schoolboy crush you used to have on her."

Connor kept his gaze steady. "I never had a schoolboy crush. I'm talking about the fact that Anne Sayer keeps this place running and has for years. God knows what would have gone on here the last ten years without her. She belongs in this house more than any of the rest of us."

Patsy scoffed and sat on the chair across from him, folding herself and her caftan into it. "Now you *are* being romantic. I know she's a nice girl, and attractive enough, in her way. But Connor, you've been out in the world now, not like when you used to come here. You know the caliber of woman you can attract. You don't have to settle for the only pretty girl on the island anymore."

Connor shook his head. "You don't know what you're talking about."

"Besides, wasn't there some . . . *issue* with her, years ago?" She put her hand on her chin.

Connor wondered if she was remembering the fight they'd had back then. He could recall it vividly when he wanted to, which was rarely. His father had sat in stony silence, letting Patsy do the talking for them both. Patsy, finally given free rein, had lectured him ruthlessly about how Anne wasn't good enough for him—wasn't good enough for *them*, the vaunted Emorys—how there were things about her that he didn't know . . .

"If you're talking about the fact that I was in love with her and she dumped me, then yes. There was an issue. But that's long over."

"In love with her!" Patsy laughed incredulously and waved the thought away with a bejeweled hand. "Don't be ridiculous, Connor. You liked the girl, yes, but you weren't serious. Your father was very against it, for one thing. She was unsuitable, he said."

"She was poor." Connor kept his eyes on his stepmother. "She didn't add to the Emory *prestige*."

"Well, that's certainly true. But I don't think it was the only thing." She looked at Connor, her fingertips tapping on the arms of the chair. "It was something else. I believe he thought she had a questionable character, though I'm not altogether sure what made him think so. You know how concerned he always was with character."

"A questionable character?" Connor repeated.

In the old days Patsy had harped on Anne being from "the wrong sort of family." This questionable character tack, at least with regard to Anne, was new.

"Yes, he told me once he caught her in some compromising situation." Patsy looked thoughtful.

Connor felt suddenly sick. He and his father had never been close, but they hadn't been enemies. They'd shared a distant, polite sort of relationship. Connor had always felt accepted and respected, if not exactly loved.

But Connor had no illusions about his father's character. He'd been a good businessman. Tough, but fair. And he'd been a generally kind man. But for as far back as Connor could remember his father had been a philanderer of the first order.

It had been a mystery for years whether or not Patsy had been aware of this, but nobody, least of all Connor, had been inclined to clue her in. Over the years, however, countless women had been let go from their employ in Atlanta, all because of questions about their "character." A questionable character, Connor well knew, was his father's euphemistic way of saying a woman had slept with him and now he was finished with her. Most of them left with handsome cash bonuses, but a few of the longer-term ones had been given cars, or, in one instance, a house, in addition to the money.

If Patsy was aware of his father's behavior, this sort of innuendo was disturbing only because she was not above using it to keep Connor away from an "undesirable element."

If she wasn't, however—and Connor had always believed her to be ignorant of his father's peccadilloes—she could well be relating much more than she realized.

Reluctantly, Connor thought about Anne's seductive behavior of the last few days. He also recalled Sean's story about Anne coming on to him.

What if Connor had always had Anne's character wrong? What if this new, sensual Anne wasn't in fact *new*?

What if she'd always had him fooled?

"Why don't you tell me exactly what Dad said," Connor said, as mildly as possible.

"Oh, goodness, I can't remember now." Patsy waved the subject off and stood up. "There's no need to revisit this, anyway. You've already decided she should plan the party. And it's not as if we're going to have to deal with her after the summer anyway, is it? Not with Marcello buying the place. So let's not argue, shall we, dear?"

"Were we arguing?"

"We were about to." She winked at him. "I can always tell when you're itching for a fight, Connor. I have since you were a little boy. Now, where is Marcello? Is he happy with the place so far?"

Connor stood, trepidation hanging like a stone in his chest. "What's not to be happy about?"

She took him by the arm as he came out from behind the desk. "Nothing, of course. I just want to be sure nothing stands in the way of this sale. I've got plans for that money, and it's about time we got rid of this old albatross. Everyone we want to see goes to Europe now anyway."

Chapter Ten

Candlewick Island Herald Press
July 31 edition
The Anonymous Observer

The Anonymous Observer feels compelled to report that during an anonymous lunch a day or two ago he spied the estimable Mr. "E" having lunch with the delectable Signorina "T" in the Black Fly Café. To describe this lunch the AO can only say that it appeared to be quite "cozy." Could the two have been making Plans of some sort? The AO distinctly heard the words "love" and "reception" as he passed by their table on the way out.

"They were probably saying how much they'd *love* to give Sean an ugly *reception* if he were to happen to actually stop at their table instead of just eavesdrop on it." Anne threw the paper down on the counter and bit the inside of her cheek. "You haven't seen Connor and Gabriella together much, have you, Prin?"

Prin held up a hand and kept her eyes on the

meat she was braising in front of her. "I'm not say-ing anything. I don't know nothing about it at all."

Anne stared at her. "You *have* seen them to-gether. Where? What were they doing?"

"They weren't doing nothing. Just walking up from the summerhouse, is all."

"The summerhouse!" Anne's stomach hit the floor. Could Connor possibly be toying with both of them? Not that he was, strictly speaking, *toying* with her. But maybe he really wasn't tempted by her, as she'd hoped. Maybe he was just teaching her a lesson.

She paused a moment and thought. How much of a threat could Gabriella really be if Connor had gone so far beyond his intentions the other day that he'd felt compelled to apologize to Anne?

No, she suspected it was Gabriella who wanted something from Connor, not the other way around. Still, it wouldn't hurt to make sure. Maybe she should have a little talk with the Evil Twin herself.

She left Prin and pushed out the double doors of the kitchen. As she marched out of the back hall into the foyer she found Dill taking the front door off its hinges.

She glanced around, peered in the doors to the front parlor and dining room, then moved closer to Dill. "What's the plan here, Slick? After the leak-termite thing I'm thinking maybe we need to discuss this a little more. The point is to make

Marcello think twice about buying the house, not force Connor to fire you."

Dill grinned at her. "Nah, don't worry. This'll be good. Trust me."

Anne shook her head. "We don't want it to be obvi—"

"I know, Ms. Sayer," he said in a suddenly loud voice. "I'm doing the best I can."

Anne glanced behind her to see—speak of the devils—Connor and Gabriella coming from the direction of the sunroom. Anne scrutinized them both. Was Gabriella's hair messed up? She stared at the offending locks.

"What is it now?" Connor asked as they neared.

Gabriella, noting Anne's look, raised her chin and brows simultaneously in an expression that instantly conveyed disdain.

Anne shifted her gaze to Connor, who was watching Dill with thinly disguised amusement.

Dill had hammered out the pins and was now jerking the door from the hinges. "The door," he said.

Connor obviously couldn't help smiling, but he did not take his gaze from Dill. He wasn't going to look at her, Anne thought.

"It keeps opening on its own," Dill continued. "Strangest thing. Even with no breeze, the door opens and closes just like someone coming in and closing it behind them."

Anne saw Gabriella's eyes widen and began to smile to herself.

"I haven't noticed that," Connor said mildly.

"Don't happen all the time." Dill leaned the door against the wall and took a level out of his tool chest.

"When does this happen?" Gabriella asked, edging closer to Connor. She placed a hand on his arm and stood slightly behind him, one breast pressed strategically into his side.

Anne studied Connor's reaction to this, which was, to her investigative eye, nonexistent.

"Welp." Dill slapped the level up against the doorjamb and peered at the bubble inside. "Hm. Perfect," he said as if to himself. He continued with an apologetic glance at Gabriella. "That's the strangest part. Only been happening on the full moon."

"At night?" Gabriella's haughty expression was gone, and her grip on Connor's arm was now white knuckled.

Anne felt like laughing. Dill was brilliant.

"Yep. Nighttime." He shook his head as if baffled. "Funny thing. Just like someone coming in the house. Like someone invisible."

"I'm sure it's just the wind," Anne said. No need to lay it on too thick.

"Nope. No wind." Dill dropped the level back into the tool chest and clattered around, finally pulling out a plane. He moved toward the door.

"It's opening on its own and you're going to plane it down?" Connor's voice was skeptical.

"Just gonna make the fit a little better. Might have to rough it up a little."

"Rough it up," Connor repeated.

Dill shrugged. "Might work."

"Might not," Connor chuckled.

"Connor," Anne said, worried he was catching on. Even if he wasn't yet, he would if Dill continued to offer more lame explanations. "I wanted to ask you about the guest list for the party. Have you got a minute?"

He finally looked at her, the amusement leaving his eyes. "The guest list?"

"Yes. There are some names missing. I'm sure you don't want to offend anyone."

He didn't move. "There are three hundred names on that list, Anne. What's a few more? Add them."

"But don't you want to know who they are?"

"Put them on the list. I'll look at it later."

He didn't want to be alone with her, she thought. Was that good or bad?

"There are other things we should discuss, too," she pressed.

He looked at her casually. "Like what?"

"Like the theme, decorations, and budget, and where you want the tents. Things like that."

"Anne, you're the party planner. Plan the party." He let the words sit there for a minute before adding, insincerely, she thought, "I trust you."

Anne sighed. If his plan really was to refuse to

talk to her, how would she ever get through to him? She glanced at Gabriella, who wore a smile, her dark eyes rich with satisfaction.

Clearly, it would do no good to talk to Gabriella about Connor. The woman had such obvious resentment for her—God knew why—she would never tell the truth. She'd just say whatever would bother Anne the most.

Anne looked at Dill. He was concentrating on the door as if it were a riddle containing the secrets of the universe. He ran his hands along one edge, searching for an imperfection.

"So you're telling me to do whatever I want?" she asked Connor.

"I'm telling you to plan the party."

She put her hands on her hips in frustration and glared at him. He looked back at her not coolly but with a significance that told her all she needed to know. He would not be alone with her again.

Anne wasn't sure what to say. She could plan the party. She'd done just that a thousand times. All by herself, with no input.

But she didn't want to do it this time. If she couldn't consult with Connor, when would she see him? In situations like this? In the hall, with Gabriella and Dill looking on? Maybe he planned to always be with Gabriella. Maybe she was a fool, Sean was right, and something really was going on between them. That might explain why Connor was so adamant about not revisiting the past with Anne.

She had to get rid of Gabriella somehow.

She turned to Dill. "Did you ever figure out why that rocking chair in Gabriella's room keeps moving?"

"Well I heard he was *Mafia*," the large woman behind the counter at the post office said.

The tiny place was strangely crowded, Marcello noted. He'd had to squeeze in the door and stand against the wall as two women—one young, large-boned and tall; one older, small and wiry— took packages, dispensed stamps, and told tales as if that too were an important aspect of their jobs.

Just now it seemed they were talking about himself, to his great amusement.

"But Little Helga," the gray-haired woman in front of the big-boned woman protested as she stuffed a roll of stamps into her pocketbook, "surely the Emorys wouldn't be involved in anything *shady*. And everything about the Mafia's shady, isn't it?"

Little Helga—who was anything but little— shook her head with a grimace. "These days the Mafia's into everything, Ethel. But still, I wouldn't put no stock in the idea. I heard it, is all I'm saying."

"He ain't Mafia," the wiry woman said.

Marcello remembered the women now. He'd heard about them. Little Helga was the tall, sturdily built daughter of the other, smaller woman, who was, ironically, Big Helga.

"He *says* he's a businessman," Big Helga continued.

Ethel, the gray-haired patron, was through with her business but didn't leave—she just stepped to the side of the room. That's why the place was so crowded. Everyone was staying to hear what the Helgas had to say.

"He's here to start a new business of his own," Big Helga continued.

"And you'll never guess what," Little Helga said.

"An amusement park!" an old man in a fishing vest called from behind the gray-haired Ethel.

Everyone laughed.

"Amusing to some," Little Helga said dourly. "He's *buying* Sea Bluff and . . ."

She paused as the room gasped. Marcello frowned.

"Using it for a TV show!" she finished.

The place went dead quiet.

Then it exploded into conversation.

"We could all be famous!" the teenage boy in front of Marcello said to his companion, another teenage boy.

Marcello saw an expression of smugness cross the face of Little Helga. "He just came from Hollywood!" she added into the din.

Big Helga shook her head as she straightened her drawer of stamps. "Burke did say when he picked 'em up from the airport, they'd just come from California. But . . ."

Burke had been the helicopter pilot, Marcello recalled. He hadn't seemed the chatty sort, but then these islanders only seemed to talk to each other and no one else.

The crowd noise died down a little.

"But a TV show ain't what I been told," Big Helga continued. She pulled out a stack of stamp books and straightened them, taking her time putting the rubber band around them and tucking them back into the drawer.

"What have you been told, Big Helga?" Ethel asked.

"Well, don't tell anyone I said so," Big Helga said in a voice loud enough to carry to the room at large while leaning forward confidentially. "But what I heard is, he's buying Sea Bluff . . . and turning it into a nudist beach club!"

The post office patrons emptied the room of oxygen with a simultaneous gasp, and Marcello had to laugh. The very idea was delightful; he was tempted to actually do it.

Marcello's laughter brought with it the attention of the teenager in front of him. An elbow or two later the whole place knew he was there. Seconds after that, the tiny room was empty save for Marcello and the two Helgas.

"Well, hello there," Little Helga said, as unabashed as if she'd just been recounting the weather and not spreading lies about this very man. "Don't suppose you'd care to clear up what you're here for, would you?"

He smiled broadly and put his envelope on the counter. "*Certamente!* You both had it all correct. I am with the Mafia and I am buying Sea Bluff for a TV show. In my spare time I will tend my colony of nudists."

Little Helga fixed him with an unamused glare, her blue eyes shrewd. Big Helga snorted once and stalked into the back room.

Little Helga watched her mother go, then picked up Marcello's envelope and studied the address. "Italy, huh?"

Marcello nodded. "That's correct. It is going to my future son-in-law."

Little Helga's eyes shot to his. "And which daughter would this fella be marrying, eh? Not the older one, she got her sights on Connor Emory, don't she?"

"Oh, now, Helga." Marcello shook his head, grinning. "You don't expect me to give it all to you at once, do you? Where is the fun in that?"

Little Helga stood a moment, considering. Then her mouth slipped into a mischievous smile. "That's *Little* Helga," she said, leaning close. "Mamma don't like it when people don't *distinguish.*"

Anne marched into the sunroom, where Connor sat having his breakfast at the round table by the front windows. She stopped a foot from his chair and put her hands on her hips.

Connor looked up, surprised, one hand holding an English muffin and the other frozen midswipe above it with a butter knife.

"Listen here, Connor," Anne said firmly. "Just because you can't handle being alone with me doesn't mean you can just throw this party into my lap without another word. We've got to talk about some of this stuff. Now, we're both adults. So if I promise not to stand within three feet of you do you think you can trust yourself not to compromise your integrity by attempting to kiss me again?"

Connor looked her up and down and said, "You're breaking that promise right now."

Behind her, a low chuckling erupted.

Anne whirled to see Marcello on the glider against the wall. He held a mug of coffee and the weekly *Herald*, and his feet were resting on the mosaic-tiled table in front of it.

"I . . . I'm sorry," she said to neither of them in particular. "I didn't mean to interrupt. I didn't realize there was anyone else in the room." She looked back at Connor, beet red. "I shouldn't have said all that."

Connor looked slowly from her to Marcello, a slight, wry smile on his face. "It's all right."

"It's all right with me, too, *bella*," Marcello said, the smile obvious in his words.

Anne looked back at him. Did Marcello think Gabriella was after Connor? Surely not, since he had essentially encouraged Anne to "fight for what she wanted," knowing full well that what she wanted was Connor. But then, maybe Gabriella's interest was new.

And Marcello was reading the paper. He must be aware of Sean's column.

"I just want you to know, Mr. Tucci, that I didn't mean anything. About the kiss, that is. It's not as if anything at all is going on between Connor and me. I just want to clarify that."

"To whom?" Marcello asked. "To me? To Connor? Or to yourself?" He took a sip of his coffee, keeping his eyes on her over the rim.

Anne hesitated. "To you, of course. I thought you might have concerns . . ."

"Concerns?" Marcello's brows rose.

"Yes." She looked uncertainly from Marcello to Connor. "About . . . you know, Gabriella."

"Ah." Marcello took his feet from the table and leaned forward, placing his mug on the mosaic surface. He cleared his throat, looking at neither of them. "No. No, of course not. No concerns."

"But you've read *The Anonymous Observer*?" she pressed.

"Well . . ." Marcello gave that nonchalant shrug that could mean anything.

"What *about* Gabriella?" Connor asked.

Anne felt relief flow over her like a cool breeze. If Connor didn't know what she was talking about, then he must not be reciprocating Gabriella's flirtation. And the pieces in the paper must be Sean's version of fiction.

"Nothing, nothing, *il mio ragazzo.* Signorina Anne must have misunderstood, ah, something." Marcello stood, puffing his chest out and adjusting his pants at the waist. "But I think I should leave the two of you alone. Clearly you have things to discuss amongst yourselves."

Anne looked at him in fascination. Marcello was flustered.

"Only the party," Connor said. "And your input would be welcome on that."

Anne turned to him. "I also want to talk to you about the employees."

Connor's eyes were on Marcello's rapidly retreating form. "What about the employees? Maybe Marcello should be here for that, too."

Marcello waved a hand behind him as he headed for the door. "You handle it, Connor. They are your employees. I will have my hands full enough in a few months, eh?"

"But—" Connor stopped, his eyes on the now-empty doorway.

Anne couldn't help smiling. "Quick exit." She pulled out the chair next to him and sat.

Connor turned his attention back to his English muffin. "He's slippery."

"You've decided to avoid me," Anne said.

Connor continued to butter the muffin, then angled the knife on the edge of his plate. He looked up at her and took a large bite, studying her a moment while he chewed. "No, I haven't."

Anne scoffed lightly. "No? Then why have you

brushed me off every time I've tried to talk to you about this party?"

He lifted a brow. "Because I thought party planners planned parties. I didn't realize I was going to have to supervise the operation so closely."

Anne straightened. "I can plan the party, Connor, but I need to know what you want. Unless you just want me to plan it however *I* want."

Connor reached across the table for the crystal-covered bowl of jam. He took the delicate silver spoon, dug it into the ruby mound, and slapped a large glob onto his plate with a casual look at Anne. "That would be fine."

She sighed. "Don't be ridiculous. This party's not for me. I need to know what you had in mind."

"So what do you need to know?"

She splayed her hands in front of her. "Well, I don't have my notes now. I thought we could arrange a time to sit down and sort everything out."

His mouth quirked slightly. "Will the three-foot rule hold for that meeting too?"

"Very funny."

He tipped his head in a thank-you.

"There was something else I wanted to discuss with you right now," she said.

"Yes, you mentioned the employees."

"Yes." She cleared her throat and sat forward, elbows on the table. "I think they should be told before the party. About their futures. Losing their jobs, I mean."

Connor's face lost its amused look. "Why?"

"Because you're planning to announce the sale of the house to Marcello at the party, aren't you? Don't you think it's a little heartless for everyone to have worked so hard, only to find out at the culmination that they're all losing their jobs? It's rather abrupt."

"Well, as *you* well know," he said slowly, "some news can only be delivered heartlessly."

She sat back. "May I ask what that's supposed to mean?"

Connor spread some jam on his muffin. "Only that you can't prepare people for some news. It'll be a shock no matter when it's delivered."

Anne got an unbidden image of Connor's face, pale and incredulous, after she'd told him she wouldn't continue their relationship, that summer so long ago. It had taken several tense minutes before he'd realized that she'd meant what she'd said. It was over, her feelings for him had changed.

She also remembered bleeding inside as she'd seen his disbelief turn to comprehension, then a devastation so complete he couldn't hide it from her. He hadn't even been angry, not then. He had simply been stunned past reaction.

The anger, it seemed, had come later.

She swallowed, an old, deep ache surfacing with the memory.

"But," Connor said lightly, taking a bite of his muffin, then a sip of his coffee, "people get over that sort of thing. Forget all about it, even."

Anne sat in silence a moment. "Apparently, they don't all forget."

He shot her a quick look, then dropped the last part of the muffin back onto his plate. "I—"

A clattering sounded at the door, and they both looked over to see Patsy Emory enter the room. She wore a fuschia kimono that flowed gracefully, though she marched into the room like a battle commander. Her hollow-heeled flip-flops clapped on the floor like castanets.

"I didn't realize the staff was eating with the family these days." She took the seat on the other side of Connor and glared across the table at Anne.

"I asked her to join me." Connor picked up his muffin again.

"We were discussing house business," Anne added, rising automatically.

"House business? Surely I should be included in that conversation."

"We're finished now. I'll tell you what we decided, if you're really that interested." Connor drained the last of his coffee.

"Of course I'm *interested*." She let her ire sink into the atmosphere a moment, then looked back at Anne. "But first I'd like some coffee, Anne. And as you probably noticed, Connor has just finished his, so bring us the pot, would you? Some orange juice, as well, and those wonderful blueberry muffins. Does Prin still make those? Surely there are some around. And please be quick about it.

I'm starving." She pushed her kimono sleeves up arms tanned dark as leather and reached for the bowl of grapes.

Connor glanced at Anne, and for a second she had the sense of conspiracy she'd always had with him when his parents were around.

"Just have Trudy bring it," he said. "You've got better things to do than wait on us."

"Better things to do than her job? Good heavens, Connor, what do you think we pay her for?"

"Party planning. What do you think we pay her for? Being a maid?"

"We pay her to do what we want when we come visit. And honestly, things used to be done a lot better around here than they are now. Breakfast used to be all laid out for us in the morning, for example." Patsy's kimono sleeve nearly took out Connor's juice glass as she reached for the sugar. She continued, spooning sugar onto the grapes. "We didn't have to *wait* or even *ask* for anything. It was all here, laid out like at the finest hotel in Europe. Things have obviously gone downhill since we stopped coming every year, don't you agree, Connor? Your father always forgot that employees out of one's sight can't be trusted."

Connor pushed his seat back from the table. "Some can. And no, I don't agree." His expression said clearly that he wasn't going to indulge, let alone join in, Patsy's complaints. "Things are being done exactly the way *I* want them to be done,

Patsy. If you've got a problem with something, you can come to me. Don't blame Anne."

Patsy's expression was startled. Anne had a hard time containing a smile.

Connor started to rise. Anne hoped he planned to walk out with her, but Patsy stopped him with a hand on his arm.

"Connor, I need to talk to you." Her gaze flitted to Anne, and she jutted her chin toward the door. "Go on, then, Anne. I just asked for some coffee and muffins. If it's not too much to ask, I'd appreciate it if you'd at least find that other girl and let her know."

"Fine." Anne's brows rose and she started to turn, only too eager to escape.

"Anne." Connor's voice made her turn back to the two. He was always her best refuge when she was in Patsy's company, and when she looked into his eyes, she thought she saw that he still was. "Get your notes together and we'll go over that stuff tomorrow. No, wait, Thursday's better—after lunch."

"What stuff?" Patsy demanded. "I should be included if you're going over anything about the house. Or the party."

"Thursday's fine. Shall I come to your office?" Anne asked, ignoring her.

Connor's glance slid Patsy's way but didn't quite reach her. "No. Ah. I'll find you. About one o'clock. Is that convenient?"

"I demand to know what you're talking

about." Patsy's voice rose an octave. "I demand to be included."

Anne kept her eyes on Connor's, as if she could pretend Patsy wasn't real, and then she wouldn't be. Besides, no matter what Patsy said, Connor was obviously in charge of the house now. And they were all fired at the end of the year anyway, so why should she even try to be polite?

Because . . . she reminded herself.

"Of course. One o'clock." Anne nodded once and turned to leave.

As she exited the room, scraping Patsy's hateful glare off her back onto the doorjamb as she rounded it, she heard Connor say, "I don't want to hear you speaking to her like that again. You don't need to concern yourself with every little thing that goes on here."

Anne stopped in the hall just outside the room and took several deep breaths. She loved that Connor was standing up for her, but it made her nervous.

Because one thing was certain: her troubles hadn't died with Bradford Emory.

Chapter Eleven

"Patsy, my dear!" Marcello stretched one hand out toward Connor's stepmother as she emerged from the sunroom. He descended the last few steps and approached her, thinking how reminiscent of a bantam rooster she was in her flowing red caftan. "Where is your charming son, eh? We are supposed to meet with Mr. Crawford this afternoon, and I have lost the dear boy."

Patsy's face opened up when she saw him, and she took his hand in hers. "Why, Marcello, I don't know. I had breakfast with him this morning, as usual, but he left for town right afterward. I believe he had a fax to send, but he should have been back by now."

"Ah, a fax." Marcello scowled and shook his head, hoping the fax story was a lie and instead Connor had gone off somewhere with the pretty Signorina Anne. "You should talk to that boy, Patsy. He struggles too much and for what? He needs to learn how to relax."

Patsy wagged a finger at him. "He's a very important man now, Marcello, with important responsibilities. We mustn't keep thinking of him as a boy."

Marcello waved her words away. "To me, he will always be a boy. Except perhaps today, when he will be a tough businessman." He laughed, wishing Patsy would fall off her high horse once and for all. As far as he was concerned the woman didn't know how to enjoy life.

"Connor is always a tough businessman. That's why it's such a shame he left his job at Emory Enterprises. He was a natural. *Such* a success, everyone said so. And so in demand. He was always invited to all the most important functions, and he frequently took me along, you know." She laughed lightly. "Yes, I was getting quite well known in the media. Those society columns just can't get enough of the Emorys, it seems."

"*Ah, sí,* one never knows what the papers will find interesting, eh?" Marcello gave her a sidelong glance.

"They never get tired of the rich and famous, I'll tell you that." Patsy sighed with the burden. "But now that Connor's left Emory, I wonder if they'll still find him interesting. Such a shame, as I said. He was getting to be quite the celebrity. The most eligible bachelor in town, you know. By far." Her brow furrowed. "He hasn't said anything to you, has he, about why he left the job?"

"To me?" Marcello drew his head back and placed his fingers on his chest as if the idea were preposterous. "What would he say to me?"

Patsy pursed her lips. "I suppose you're right. If he wouldn't tell me, what would he say to you? I try and try to talk to him about it, but whenever I ask why he quit he only says, 'It was time.'" She shook her head, obviously annoyed. "Time for what, is what I'd like to know. Failure?"

"Pah! That boy couldn't fail if he tried to. He simply needed to be his own man. To do something without the family crest on it." He made a stamping motion with his fist and chuckled. "Surely you can understand that, can you not?"

Patsy stopped, a hand on Marcello's arm, and looked at him intently. "Is that what he said? That he wanted to get away from the family name?"

Marcello shrugged, uncomfortable. He never divulged any confidences, but something about Patsy always made him feel as if he had. "No, no. That is my own conjecture, *cara*. Come, walk with me. I want to see the gardens this fine day."

He took her arm and looped it through his. Perhaps she'd be more interesting outside.

"*You're* certainly seeming to relax here," she said. Her tone was almost accusatory. "Are you enjoying Sea Bluff so far?"

Marcello smiled and flung his free hand out to encompass the house. "Of course! Who would not? The place is a palace, a paradise. Though I confess I will feel much better when all of this legal finagling is over with. Nothing can ruin a vacation faster than paperwork."

Patsy smiled indulgently and patted his arm. "You'll have plenty of vacations here without paperwork once the sale is complete. I know you'll love this place as we did for so many years."

"Yes, I believe I shall. Your son, he seems particularly to love it here, eh? And I think I know why!" He laughed and sent Patsy a conspiratorial look. "It is good for the boy, don't you think?"

Patsy's smile froze on her face. "What is? What do you mean?"

Marcello pushed open the back door and gestured for her to precede him into the garden. She did, then immediately turned back to him in expectation.

He had to squeeze out between her and the door to be able to close it behind him. "I mean he is enjoying himself. He is remembering who he is." Marcello thought of the look on Connor's face when they'd talked about his latest encounter with Anne. He'd been upset, yes, but he'd been alive. More alive than Marcello had seen him in a long time.

He took Patsy's arm again and started walking her toward the garden.

"Connor has always known who he is." Patsy's tone rejected the idea like a parent ignoring the suggestion of a child. "He's an Emory, and he's taken that responsibility quite seriously. Up until now, that is." She shook her head. "I wish I knew what's gotten into him."

Marcello sighed. Tiresome woman. "I think it

helps him to return to a place he was happy in as a boy. He changed so much when he left school, do you not agree? He became . . . how do I say? Heavyhearted. Very serious."

Patsy looked up at him, her expression almost offended. "Oh, I disagree completely," she said firmly. "I think he really came into his own once he started working. Before that, he had so many foolish dreams. So many unrealistic expectations. That youthful idealism can be quite destructive if taken too far, you know."

Marcello sighed again.

"I just hope nothing's going on with that wretched woman again." Her tone was venomous.

Marcello looked over at her, at her pinched face and her tough brown eyes.

"What wretched woman?"

Patsy looked up at him, her face bulldog determined. "That maid. That Anne Sayer."

Marcello didn't try to hide his astonishment. "What is the matter with Anne?"

Patsy stopped and leaned toward him. "Don't you know? She broke his heart years ago. Just used him and dropped him. Took the poor boy months to get over her. And now she's trying it again."

Marcello nodded slowly and looked at her slyly. "But we mustn't call him a boy any longer. He is a man."

"That's right." She nodded, clearly not realizing he was parroting her own words.

They resumed walking.

"And so we must let the man make his own decisions," Marcello added. "If Anne is his decision, then perhaps things will work out differently this time."

Patsy stopped in her tracks again.

Marcello realized it two steps later when her hand slid out from his arm.

"Oh, no. No, no. That's not going to happen," she said adamantly. "Not again. She's completely unsuitable. Isn't it obvious?"

"Ah." Marcello's eyes widened in understanding. "You disapprove."

Patsy looked scandalized. "Of course I disapprove. She's a *maid*, for heaven's sake. Connor can do so much better than that." She paused. "You don't think there *is* something going on between them, do you? You haven't seen them together at all, have you?"

Marcello touched a rose on the bush in front of him and leaned over to smell it. "Only every now and then. They discuss the house, the party, that sort of thing." He grinned at her. "You must be very excited to be on the television soon, eh, *cara*?"

His calculation was correct. Patsy's hard eyes were suddenly agleam.

"Oh, yes. It *is* exciting, isn't it?" she gushed. "Of course, I've been on the television quite a bit in Atlanta."

"Ah. Well then. It is boring for you."

"But that was mostly local television. This is much bigger. I've told all my friends about it, and they're all green with envy. Why, the Style Network is about the only thing anyone ever watches these days. At least among those in my circle. Leslie Drummond told me just last month it was the only thing she watched anymore. You know who Leslie Drummond is, don't you?"

Marcello straightened and offered his arm to her again. Finally, a subject to wean her off her obsession to control Connor.

"Tell me about her, *cara*," he said, walking her down the garden path. "Tell me about all these society friends of yours. Who are they, what do they do? . . ."

"All right," Anne said into the phone, "don't worry about it, Trudy. Just make sure you get lots of rest, and feel better in the morning."

Anne rolled her eyes at Prin, who smiled and continued unloading the bags of groceries that sat on the long wooden counter.

"No, I told you when you left that you don't need to come back," Anne insisted. "We'll be fine. I can change the sheets. Yes, and the wastebaskets. Trudy, I know how to do your job." She laughed. "Yes, all right. The nursery? What's it doing in there? Oh. Okay, don't worry. I'll pull it up and put it in the bathroom. Good idea. Now drink some orange juice and go back to sleep. I know, honey. Good-bye."

Anne hung up the phone, laughing.

"I guess what that girl lacks in normality she makes up for with dedication," Prin said.

"That's for sure. I had to beg her not to come back after her nap and give us all her cold."

"What was that about pulling something up and putting it in the bathroom?" Prin shoved a large bag of rice under the bottom shelf of the pantry.

"Oh, the vacuum cleaner chewed up the bathroom rug in the Galleon Suite, so she was going to take the one from the nursery and put it in the bathroom."

"Hunh. Guess it ain't as if that nursery's gonna be used for anything any time soon."

"Yes, she seemed quite concerned that it be done right away." Anne grabbed a bag of pretzels protruding from one of the grocery bags and opened it. "Afraid Connor'd slip getting out of the shower and knock himself senseless on the sink or something, I guess." She laughed and popped a pretzel into her mouth.

"Maybe it'd knock some sense into him," Prin said.

Anne's brows rose. "Think he needs that?"

"Sense of humor, maybe. You noticed how serious he is? I swear I don't remember him being so sour. Used to be he had a grin for anyone and everyone."

Anne felt herself blush. "Hm. Yes. I think I know what you mean."

"Well, guess I better go move that rug before Trudy calls back," Anne said, crinkling up the top of the pretzel bag and tucking it back into the grocery bag.

Prin stopped and put her hands on her hips. "Now why are you putting that back in there? Would it have been so hard to stick it in the cupboard where it belongs?"

Anne laughed as she headed for the double-doored exit from the kitchen. "Sorry, Prin!"

Connor had gone into town that morning after breakfast, Anne knew, so when she passed his room she paused in the open doorway and looked around. The place was neat as a pin. None of his clothes graced the furniture, nor were there shoes or other paraphernalia lying about.

She did spy a novel on the table by the bed and wondered what it was, but she figured she could surreptitiously look around once she'd retrieved the rug from the nursery. That way, in case anyone caught her in there, she'd have an excuse. Not even an excuse—a valid reason for being in his room. Besides, it wasn't as if she was going to rifle through his things. Much as she might want to.

Trudy had stripped the beds that morning and had left the sheets and towels in a pile on the floor in the hall. Anne glanced at them and decided to pick them up for the laundry once she got the bathroom rug.

She made her way down the hallway, past the rooms Deborah and Astrid, Connor's sisters, used to occupy, to the nursery at the end of the hallway. The only thing beyond this room was the linen closet, where dozens of shelves full of towels resided. Anne used to love hiding in that closet as a child. It had always smelled so clean and fresh, and no matter which way you turned you were greeted by the rich fluffy softness of snowy white towels.

Anne entered the nursery, reflecting on the attitude that had built the room so far away from the master suite. It had once been part of the room next door, but it had been divided into the nursery and a room for the nanny with a large, strategically anchored piece of plywood and drywall sometime in the sixties. Both of them far enough away from the rest of the house that the manor-born child wouldn't disturb its own parents. The nanny's room was now the smallest of the guest rooms.

The rug was a small, rubber-backed Persian that would actually look quite good in the Galleon Suite bathroom, Anne thought. She had to remember to compliment Trudy on her resourcefulness. She bent down and began to roll it up.

Her eyes strayed to the crib in the corner. Who had been the last baby in that crib? she wondered. She couldn't remember a time it had ever been used, and no doubt by now it would be considered unsafe. But it was a beautiful piece, made of dark wood with ornate carvings of ducks and bunnies on the head and footboards.

Her eyes trailed up the wall to see a long crack extending the width of the room, all the way across the crease at the ceiling. She rose, leaning the rolled carpet against the wall by the door, and approached the perpendicular wall, the plywood one between the nanny's room and this one.

Oddly, the picture above the crib seemed to be leaning toward her. There was a definite space between the bottom of the frame and the wall. She glanced at the ground. Dust covered the floor and lay in a fine film on the railing of the crib.

Anne took hold of the child's bed and pulled it into the middle of the room.

Instantly, the entire wall tilted toward her.

For a second she felt dizzy, as if the whole room were moving, but her reflexes were quick. She lurched forward, catching the wall with her palms and pushing it upright. It crunched upward, sending more dust to the floor, but would not go completely back into the space from where it had come.

Her eyes trailed around the edges. The joints had been cut.

She started to laugh, then closed her eyes on a heavy sigh.

She had to talk to Dill. He was going about this the wrong way, taking it way too far. The wall was obviously not load-bearing, and neither this room nor the one next to it was being used, so he must have decided it was the perfect place for more evidence that the house was falling apart.

Unfortunately, *she* was the one who had discovered it, and not Marcello or one of the girls. If Dill was going to do this right, he needed to make sure the right people witnessed it, and he needed to make sure it was convincing. All he was doing with tactics like cutting holes in the ceiling and knocking down walls was pissing off Connor, and that wouldn't get them anyplace.

She slowly backed away, hoping the wall would stay where she'd pushed it, but as soon as she took the pressure off her hands it immediately leaned toward her again. She stepped forward and caught it again, grunting with the effort. If the room had been any bigger, she thought, she might have been in real danger here. As it was, the wall was just sizeable enough to be unwieldy.

Glancing behind her, she wondered why she'd had to pull the crib so far away. If she could have reached it, she might have been able to prop the wall up with it. That must have been what had been holding it up before.

She again tried pushing the drywall back into the space it had been, but she was afraid to push too hard for fear it would sail right through into the other room. And she happened to know there was an antique washstand, complete with pitcher and bowl, on the other side. Not to mention a painting of Julia Emory—Connor's great-great-grandmother—as a child.

She sighed, turning to look around the room and leaning her back against the wall. She braced her feet on the wood floor, thankful she'd worn her sneakers today. There was very little heavy furniture in the room. She was unsure whether the crib would hold the cumbersome wall up now that it had come loose.

She supposed she could just let it go, but it could well destroy the floor when it came crashing down.

She started to laugh again. What a predicament! She was stuck. And she could be here for hours unless she figured something out.

She was about to start calling for help when she heard footsteps coming down the hall. Sturdy, masculine footsteps.

Oh God, don't let it be Connor, she prayed.

She pushed her back solidly against the wall, glancing up to be sure the gap at the crease wouldn't immediately be obvious. Then she glanced down at her pants and brushed the dry-wall dust off them.

She looked at the door just in time to see Connor pass by it. She sighed. Just her luck. Of all the people in this house, it couldn't have been Lois or Dill or even Marcello.

Connor hadn't seen her, as he'd been heading toward the linen closet, but he was bound to notice her standing there when he turned around. She took a breath and pushed off the wall, leaning one palm against it and crossing her legs, trying to look nonchalant.

Sure enough, two seconds later Connor stopped

in the doorway, a pair of fresh towels in his hands.

"Hi," Anne said with a brilliant smile.

Connor's brows rose. "Hi. What are you doing?"

"Oh, just holding up the wall." She laughed, hoping he'd think it was a joke. Who in their right mind *wouldn't* think it was a joke? "Actually I was thinking about rearranging this room. Just standing here, trying to picture it."

He leaned against the doorframe and glanced around the room. "Somebody going to be using it?"

"No, not that I know of. Just thought I'd think about it now, before someone decided to."

He nodded.

Anne sighed inwardly. *Just go*, she pleaded silently. *Don't be interested in talking now, of all times.*

"Taking a shower?" she inquired gaily.

He glanced at the towels in his hand. "I was planning on it. Listen, Anne."

"Yeah?" The wall seemed increasingly heavy, and her wrist was getting sore. She tried to twist gracefully so she could lean her back against it again without letting it move. But almost as soon as she had, she thought she felt the wall shift. She stayed still.

"I wanted to apologize for my stepmother," Connor said. "The way she was at breakfast yesterday morning. I know she can be a real bitch sometimes, but I want you to know that's just her way of doing things. Don't take it personally."

"Oh, don't worry." Anne waved her other hand. "I know how she is, it doesn't bother me anymore."

He smiled slightly. "Yes, you do seem to handle it better than you used to."

Anne cursed the wall behind her. Connor was finally remembering something from the past on his own and she was not in a position to push him a little further, perhaps into a good memory.

"Well, it makes a difference that you're the one in charge now," she said, attempting a shrug. She felt some drywall dust drift to the back of her hand and froze.

"I hope you know that I really do appreciate all you've done, and still do, for the house." Connor's eyes were sincere, his expression kind. "You're really the glue that holds this place together, you know."

Anne bit her lip against a wave of hysterical laughter. *Little does he know*, she thought.

"Thank you," she said in a choked voice.

"Prin, Franklin, they've been here for years, but it's you who keeps the place running. And you've done a great job of it." He cocked his head. "Even Marcello talks about it. He's quite impressed with you."

Anne smiled. She was losing sensation in her fingers. "I do like him," she said. "And not just because he's said nice things about me."

Why, oh why, Anne thought, did Connor have

to seem so accessible *now*, when she was about to be crushed by a large portion of the house?

"Well, he likes you too." Connor's eyes narrowed, and he seemed to study her face. "What *are* you doing in here?"

"Just . . ." She glanced around. "Like I said, trying to figure out how to rearrange it. Connor, would you do me a favor and go get Dill for me?"

"Dill?"

"Yes, you know, the handyman." She was nearly gasping with pain now. It was shooting up her forearm and into her shoulder. She wondered if she could be doing serious damage.

"Anne." Connor stepped into the room, his eyes scanning her face.

Sweat was popping out on her brow, and she was probably beet red by now.

"Are you all right?" He neared her.

"Oh God," she gasped, yanking her hand from the wall and shifting quickly to press her back up against it. She moved fast, but not before the crunch of the shifting structure had thrust a cloud of dust billowing into the room.

"What the—?" Connor pushed against the wall himself, looking at Anne as if she'd lost her mind. "What in the world is going on here?"

Anne expelled a breath. "I don't know. I came in here to get that rug." She gestured toward the one leaning against the other wall. "And I noticed this wall leaning. Unfortunately I didn't notice how serious it was until I moved the crib, and then the whole thing threatened to come down."

"Why in God's name didn't you tell me? You just let me stand there chatting." He started to laugh. "While you were literally holding up the wall."

Anne couldn't help the laughter that bubbled up inside her. They stood there, backs against the wall, laughing. It felt so good she wished it could go on forever. It was the closest she'd felt to him since they'd broken up.

If this had happened eleven years ago, they'd have been coconspirators, she'd be willing to bet. And he would probably have had much better ideas about what kinds of things to do to convince the interloper not to buy the house.

But this was now, and Connor was the one trying to sell. Anne tried desperately to regain some semblance of sobriety. She had to at least appear concerned about a wall suddenly dropping over in the middle of the house.

"I didn't want you to worry," she said, trying to think fast. "Dill can take care of this—"

"And you were just going to wait until he happened by? How long have you been here?"

"Just a little while. Maybe twenty minutes. I was hoping somebody other than the owner of the house might venture into this wing."

He looked at her as if she were nuts. "That could have taken days."

She shot him a sidelong look. "I'm sure I would have gone ahead and dropped it before the end of the week."

He looked as if he was trying to stop laughing, but he couldn't keep the smile from his face. "Anne, did you think I'd blame you? I mean," he glanced around, "I don't see a hacksaw or anything, so I'm pretty sure you didn't do this."

"No, of course not. Nobody did it," she said, searching for a reason that might be obvious. "It must have been the termites Dill was looking for the other day."

Connor gave her a look of profound skepticism. "Termites, you say."

"Well? Doesn't it have to be? I mean, why *else* would a wall just suddenly fall over?" She could barely get the words out with a straight face. She put a finger under her nose and pressed, as if she were about to sneeze.

Connor looked at her a long moment, his eyes both amused and amazed. "Oh, I don't know. Maybe if somebody cut all the joints and sawed all the studs in half, that might do it."

She tried to look quizzical. "Why would someone do that?"

Connor's eyes didn't leave her face, but his expression gentled. "I don't know, Anne. You tell me."

She looked away, down at her feet, then at her hands, which she then thrust out in a helpless gesture. "I don't know. I can't imagine."

He was silent a long moment.

She glanced at him from the corners of her eyes.

"There's some weird stuff going on here,

Anne," he said finally. He looked at her. Her eyes shot forward, away from his. "Termites and leaks. Ghosts. That sort of thing. You know I have to get to the bottom of it."

"Of course," she said, but the words lacked the conviction out loud that they'd had in her head.

"Listen," he said, "why don't you go get Dill and I'll wait here with the, uh, wall." His eyes trailed upward to the rough edge of the drywall. He looked back at her with a small smile. "He and I can figure out what to do about this. I think we've probably got a thing or two to talk about, as well."

Anne pushed herself slowly off the wall and looked at him worriedly. "Have you got it?"

Connor nodded. "If you could hold it up with one hand during an entire conversation, I can hold it up until you find Dill."

Anne kneaded her fingers in front of her. She hoped he wasn't planning on firing Dill, at least not before the time he was firing all of them, but she didn't want to ask. She knew he saw right through her, but if she admitted that she knew what was going on she'd end up giving it all away. At least if they both pretended she was ignorant of the situation, then she couldn't be tempted to confess anything to him.

"He's a good worker, Dill is," she said finally.

Connor glanced up at the wall again. "Clearly."

"And a really nice guy."

"I'm sure he is."

Anne gripped her fingers. "There's not a lot of

work on the island, you know. Especially for people without references."

Connor tilted his head and smiled slightly. "I'm not going to fire him, Anne. Well, at least not today."

She breathed a sigh of relief, wanting to thank him, but even that seemed too confessional.

"Though I have no idea why not," Connor added, shifting his weight and treating himself to a shower of drywall dust.

"Because you're a really nice guy, too, Connor," she said impulsively. Then she turned swiftly and headed for the door. "I'll find him as quickly as I can!"

Chapter Twelve

Connor knew the moment he went looking for her on Thursday that Anne would not be in the house at one o'clock. If he was honest with himself, he'd admit that he'd known it when he'd left their meeting place up to her. All he'd told himself then, however, was that he didn't want his stepmother barging in on the meeting, as she surely would do if they had told her where they would be.

He could have brought it up yesterday when he'd found Anne holding up that damn wall, he thought with a private chuckle. But he'd been so astounded at the circumstances that the thought hadn't occurred to him.

Then Dill had come back, alone, to help him shore up the space, offering some wild excuse about how he thought they'd decided to turn the two rooms back into one since both were too small to really be useful and there weren't any babies around anyway, least of all nannies.

When Connor had asked who had decided this, Dill had then launched into a long story about a conversation he'd had with Nicola, complete with

Italian phrases and dead-on imitations of her gestures and accent, including some creative theories about how and where the misunderstanding might have occurred. He'd then segued into similarities between English and Italian words that really have quite different meanings.

He finished up by asking if Connor himself spoke Italian, not bothering to hide his delight when Connor said no.

Why Dill thought nineteen-year-old Nicola might have been speaking for the owners of the house regarding remodeling remained a mystery throughout the conversation, however.

As he made his way across the front foyer, Connor was pretty sure he knew where Anne would choose to meet. Either the summerhouse or the old chapel— both of which were rich with their shared history. She wouldn't have chosen the boathouse, he knew, even though that was the place most of their intimacy had taken place in the past. That atmosphere—while being patently unsuitable for discussing party preparations in any case—would have been too charged with memories.

If he could have arranged it gracefully, without arousing Patsy's notice or interest, he'd have tried to get Marcello to join them. But Patsy and Marcello had been breakfasting this morning, and Connor didn't, under any circumstances, want Patsy getting into another conversation with Anne. He couldn't stand seeing what his stepmother did to her. Belittling her, making sure she knew she was an employee—no, worse; a *servant*—with every word she spoke.

Anne bore it well these days, though. Much better than she used to. In the old days he would see her practically shrink before his stepmother, her eyes casting downward, her hands gripping each other with such force that he'd worry that the delicate bones would snap.

Still, though she stood strong before Patsy's degradations, Connor thought he could sense the same frustrated impotence Anne used to feel in her presence.

Maybe, he thought as he made his way to the kitchen and Prin, who knew everything and everyone's whereabouts most of the time, maybe he still knew Anne well enough to know she felt helpless before Patsy. And helplessness was a terrible feeling, Connor knew.

He stopped, thinking about the one time he had felt truly helpless in his life. The moment Anne had ended their relationship, when his whole life, his whole *world*, had taken on a terrifying unreality.

He remembered thinking even then that the moment was going to change his life in ways that were incalculable. And it had. It had changed the way he'd seen the world from that moment on. Never again would he feel as sure of himself, as sure of anything at all, as he had prior to the day she'd let him go.

Now, however, he had the opportunity to find

out just what had gone wrong back then. She obviously had things she wanted to tell him; why couldn't he let her say them? What harm would it do to understand what had happened?

"She's in the summerhouse," Lois said, brushing past him in the narrow hallway.

Jerked from his thoughts, Connor focused on Lois's retreating back. "What?"

But Lois was by then too far to hear. He continued down the back hallway toward the kitchen.

Trudy emerged from the double doors bearing a large watering can.

"Oh! Mr. Emory," she said, her eyes trailing suspiciously around his perimeter. He hoped to God she wasn't planning to say something about his aura. "Miss Sayer's in the summerhouse. She said to be sure to tell you, if I saw you."

"Yes, I know. Thank you," he said, walking past her. He felt her eyes on him—or rather, just next to him—as he continued down the hall. He turned as he reached the double doors and saw her squinting at him.

She refocused on his face and spun away when his eyes met hers.

He pushed backwards through the doors, chuckling despite himself. Behind him and down the hall, the grandfather clock began to chime. Amazing how annoying the sound was, he thought, even at a distance. It was one o'clock and the clock had already struck three by the time he entered the kitchen.

"There you are, Connor," Prin said, thrusting a

basket handle in his hand before he had a chance to think. "Take that to Anne in the summerhouse. She's waiting for you there."

Connor looked down at the basket. The wickered weight of it felt distantly familiar. "What's this?"

"Lunch," Prin said, in the tone of one surprised by another's stupidity.

"For who?"

"You," she answered in the same tone. "And Anne. And whoever else happens to show up. There's plenty there."

Connor hefted the weighty basket a couple of times. "Seems to be."

Had Anne planned this? A picnic in the summerhouse? He hesitated. It was too familiar.

He shook his head. Not a good idea. If they were going to resolve whatever was going on between them, it would have to be done without sentimental journeys to those long-gone summers.

He set the basket on the counter. "We're going to be talking business, Prin. We won't be needing lunch."

Prin turned, hands on her hips. "Won't be needing lunch! Everybody needs lunch."

Connor walked toward the back door and shot her a grin. "That's right. And I'll be back for mine in about an hour. Put whatever's in there on ice."

"But Anne'll be hungry. She ain't had nothing since breakfast."

"She can have lunch later too." He opened the door. "I won't stop her."

He heard Prin's *harumph* of indignation as he closed the door behind him.

The walk through the grounds was so quiet that Connor felt peace descend upon him like a blanket. The day was sunny, almost hot, and birds trilled from the trees. A soft breeze made branches and flower heads tilt and sway, and lifted the warm scent of soil and grass into the air.

He neared the summerhouse door and felt trepidation weigh in his chest once again. Seems he could not encounter Anne alone without that dread. Of what? he asked himself. Of her tempting him again?

No, of her getting her way. Of her snapping her fingers and getting him right back where she wanted him.

Anger flashed through him at the thought, and he realized just exactly where his problem lay. His pride. She'd gotten rid of him years ago for whatever reason, and now she seemed to want him back.

Well, it wasn't that easy. There was a lot of water under that bridge, and it wasn't going to flow back upstream.

This time, he thought, *he* was the one who was going to make the decisions. Things would either go his way or they wouldn't go at all. Either way was fine with him.

He pushed open the sticking door.

Anne sat on the couch, papers splayed on the low table in front of her. The place had been cleaned up, he noted immediately. The dust of the other day had been swept away and the windows opened. The honeysuckle that draped across one side of the screened building whispered its sweet scent into the room.

Connor shut the door behind him.

Anne looked up, blue eyes clear and bright in her lightly tanned face. "Hi."

God, but she was pretty, he thought. He nodded curtly. "Anne."

Instead of going to sit with her on the couch, he crossed the room, took a chair from the dining table, and took it over to set it across the low table from Anne.

She watched him with a questioning expression.

He sat.

Anne exhaled. "Well. I guess you took that three-foot rule pretty seriously."

"Someone has to."

She chuckled. "You're a tough nut to crack, Connor." She looked back down at her papers.

"And yet you keep trying to crack me." With one foot on the table he pushed the chair onto its two back legs.

She looked back up at him and tilted her head. A smile played around her lips. "I'm not trying to 'crack' you, Connor. Why do you say that?"

He shrugged. "No reason. So what do you need to know? About the party, I mean."

She gazed at him a second, then put her pen in her mouth and started shuffling through papers. After a minute, she took the pen from her lips and said, "I have several estimates here for you to look at, the first one's for . . ."

"I think I can save us some time," Connor interrupted. "I don't care much what anything costs. Go with what you think is the best quality. We're kind of last minute on this, so things are bound to be more expensive. Next?"

"Okay." She tucked the pen behind her ear. "I was talking about the tents, but I guess you mean for that to hold true across the board."

"Right."

"So, we're going with an Italian theme, naturally. The classic, romanticized version, nothing too pretentious. Red-and-white checked table-cloths, lanterns, torches, strolling violinists outside, string quartet playing Vivaldi and the like inside the house. I was thinking of more of a pan-Mediterranean menu, however, rather than straight Italian."

"Fine."

She looked at him suspiciously a second, then went back to shuffling her papers. "There'll be seven bartenders, tending four separate bars. The one by the gazebo will be small. What do you think about having one more in the boathouse? For the people arriving by yacht."

"Fine."

"Good. I've hired thirty-two extra servers and bus people."

"All right." He rocked the chair back and forth on its back legs.

"Two coat check girls, five valet parkers, and a cigar roller from Havana."

"Fine."

"I've also rented a carousel and arranged for swans in the reflecting pool."

"Fine."

"At about the midpoint of the party Maria Garibaldi will sing select opera songs, perhaps with Marcello accompanying her." She looked up at him through her lashes.

He continued to rock the chair. "Fine."

"And then the Flying Karamazov Brothers will perform a routine on the front lawn, using tree branches and tire swings as their trapezes. A special request by Patsy."

Connor dropped the chair's front legs to the ground. "What?"

Anne's face burst into a grin and she laughed. "Just making sure you're listening."

Connor shook his head, but he couldn't help smiling with her. She looked so beautiful. Carefree. Even her eyes were laughing.

She had, he thought suddenly, turned into the very woman he'd thought she would when he'd fallen head over heels in love with her all those years ago. Beautiful, confident, capable, and as bright and warm as a burst of sunlight after a storm.

"Anne."

She gazed at him, the smile lingering on her lips.

"I . . ." He hesitated, wanting to hear how her life had shaped her but reluctant to ask how it had happened without him. "Have you been happy?"

She looked startled. Her cheeks turned pink and her eyes searched his face a moment before answering. "I—I—yes, I think so."

"You *think* so?" His lips curved slightly.

"Well, what do you mean? Lately? Or . . . or since we last . . ." She flipped a hand out.

He understood her awkwardness. He'd been avoiding talking about anything personal since he'd gotten back, and now he was diving in head-first. No wonder she was disconcerted.

He almost couldn't ask the question, for fear her honesty would tell him more than he wanted to know. But something inside of him wanted to make sure she'd been happy in the intervening years, even if he didn't want to know exactly how or why.

"Since we last saw each other." He kept his voice even, his hands loose on the arms of the chair.

"Well . . ." She looked down. "It's . . . complicated. But I suppose, well, I've loved my job. I've loved being able to stay on the island. So many people have to leave, you know, to find work."

He didn't answer. He didn't want to get into a conversation about her job or the state of employment on Candlewick Island. What he wanted to know were the personal things—like how she'd really *felt* all these years, about him, about her life—but he didn't know how to frame the question.

He cocked his head. "Why have you never married? I thought sure you'd have a couple of kids by now."

It was only because she *didn't* have a couple of kids that he was able to ask her about it, he acknowledged to himself. If they'd been sitting here discussing her family—well, they wouldn't have been sitting here discussing her family. Call him shallow, but he wouldn't have been able to stand that.

Her cheeks were red now, and she looked flustered. "Goodness!" She laughed nervously. "That's . . . that's hard to say, I guess. I've dated." She glanced at him, then away. "Mostly summer people, of course. But nobody . . . nobody special."

"I guess there aren't that many men on the island, not year-round anyway," he said, feeling more relieved by the minute. "And not in the right age group."

"No." She laughed again. "None. Unless you

count Sean Crawford. Which most people don't."

Connor should have known Crawford had been lying with that business about Anne coming on to him. It would have been so unlike Anne, for one thing, and Crawford was such an arrogant windbag.

"What about you?" she asked. Her eyes met his this time, their expression guarded but curious. "Why haven't you gotten married?"

He took a deep breath. "I was engaged once."

She looked surprised, then tried to cover it. "Really?" The word emerged softly, almost as more of a statement than a question.

Connor grinned. "But it didn't take."

She tried to smile but didn't quite accomplish it. "What went wrong?"

He shook his head. "I don't know. I guess after a time it became obvious to both of us that we weren't in love."

She looked skeptical. "Neither one of you?"

He glanced down. "Mostly me, I suppose. It wasn't a very long engagement, at any rate. Nobody was left heartbroken or anything."

Unlike when I left here, he thought.

"Connor, I . . . ," she began.

Connor's pulse accelerated, and a cool sweat threatened to break out on his brow.

"I'm glad you've been happy, Anne," he said quickly. For some reason, he didn't want to hear what she had to say, didn't want to have to deal with it once it had been said. "I'm sure someone will come along soon and sweep you off your feet."

She looked at him, her eyes savvy. "I wouldn't be too sure about that. There hasn't been anyone even remotely interesting since . . ."

Connor pushed the chair onto its back legs again and looked at the papers spread across the table between himself and Anne. He shouldn't have made this conversation personal. It was just . . . he really wanted to know how she'd been.

He really wanted to know that she'd never been in love with anyone after him.

Selfish, yes. Impossible to ask, certainly. But true.

"Since?" he asked. His mind was at war over wanting to know and wanting to change the subject.

He kept the chair rocking casually and his eyes cool.

"Since you." She turned both hands palm up. "Is that what you wanted to hear, Connor?"

Yes.

"It's what I thought you might say."

She laughed slightly. "How modest of you."

He smiled and looked down. "No. I only meant—I just thought you'd say so because of the way you've been looking back."

"Looking back?"

He lifted his shoulders. "To me. To a time when things seemed simpler."

She took the pen from behind her ear and placed it carefully on the papers in front of her. "That's not what I'm doing, Connor."

"No?" He stopped rocking. "What *are* you doing?"

She took a deep breath, seemed about to say something, and stopped.

"All right. Maybe you don't want to say, but I think we both know." He looked at her intently. "And Anne, I'm asking you to stop. Stop trying. Please."

She didn't say anything for a minute, kept her eyes on him, then let her gaze drop to the table.

Against his will, he remembered how she'd looked pressed up against the door of this very room a few days ago. Her hair messed up, her eyes sultry, and her lips reddened from the roughness of his kisses. He felt a tightening in his groin.

Damn her, he thought. Damn her for being so pretty. No, more than pretty. She was desirable in a way he'd never encountered before or since. But he didn't want her, or rather, didn't *want* to want her.

"Connor, tell me honestly." Her candid gaze fixed on him again. "Is the only reason you're saying that because you're still holding a grudge?"

"A grudge?"

"Yes." She leaned back in the couch. "For breaking up with you. Can't we forget about that?"

He laughed. "Forget about it?"

Forget that she'd ripped his heart out and tossed it to the wind one arbitrary day? Forget that she'd led him on the entire summer, let him think she felt as strongly about him as he did about her, let him blather on about how things would be when they were married and living in the same place the whole year around? Forget that it was all a game to her? A *lie*?

He laughed again. "You forget about it, Anne. It seems easier for you."

"Connor, I haven't forgotten anything. But we can't change what happened. Don't you understand that circumstances were different then?"

"Different? Sure, I believe they were different. They were different than I'd ever dreamed they were even at the time." He stopped himself and took a slow breath.

She sat forward on the couch. "What I really mean is, can't you believe that circumstances are different *now*."

He sighed. "That, I can believe. And circumstances are different for me too. This isn't about any grudge. I'm not trying to punish you. How petty do you think I am?"

And he wasn't. If anyone was being punished, it was himself.

She looked at him steadily, her expression clearly doubtful.

He made an incredulous sound. "All right, so you think I'm pretty petty. Sorry to know your opinion of me has sunk so low." She started to protest, but he wouldn't let her. "Listen, I'm telling you the truth, this has nothing to do with me teaching you a lesson or getting back at you for anything you did in the past. I was hurt, sure, we both know that. But it's over. All I'm saying now is that I do not want to be taken in again. You took me by surprise before, yes, but I won't be taken by surprise again now."

"What do you mean? Are you—are you *bracing* yourself against me? Because of what happened eleven years ago? Because of something I—as a *much* younger, less experienced, more confused woman—did?"

"No, I just said it has nothing to do with the past. I just don't want to renew anything."

"Fine. I don't want to 'renew' anything either. But when you say you're not punishing me for what I did, then say something about how you're not going to be taken in by me again, I have to think the past is what's at the bottom of it all. Why, Connor? Why can't you let go of all that and let us live in the present?"

He spread his arms out to his sides. "That's just what I've been saying. Let's forget it. *You're* the one who's not letting it go, Anne. I want us to encounter each other now as adults and professionals, but you don't seem willing or able to do that."

She made a frustrated sound and looked at the ceiling. "Oh! There's that word again. *Professionals.*" She nearly spat it. "What about *friends*, Connor? Is your grudge against me so ingrained that you can't allow for that?"

He shook his head, willing the adrenaline in his system to stop making his heart race. "I keep telling you, it's not a grudge, Anne. It's a decision."

"A decision." She looked at him steadily. "You made a decision not to be friends with me."

Connor hesitated, looking at her clear blue eyes, her determined face, then said, "Yes."

The reality of it struck him as he said the word.

Her mouth dropped open. "Why?"

He shook his head. His eyes dipped to the table between them. He felt as if the door to an entire roomful of understanding had just opened up before him. "Because I can't trust you."

The truth of it was momentous. *That* was the source of the dread he felt when he saw her alone, he realized. Not that she would kiss him, or that he would want her physically. If that were the case he'd just take her, physically, and be done with it.

No, the danger was that he'd begin to think she was the old Anne. That he'd begin to trust her again. And that he'd be wrong about her. Again.

For a long moment it appeared as if she didn't breathe. Then she took a long inhale and said, "Well."

She leaned forward on the couch and reached out for the papers, stacking them up. Connor thought her hands were shaking as the pages fluttered slightly in her grasp.

"I guess that would be a problem." Her voice emerged nearly breathless.

The moment stretched taut as Connor debated what to say next.

Maybe things *could* be different, if they never talked about the past, never talked about their feelings, never expected each other to *have* any feelings. If they encountered each other as adults who desired each other and nothing more, then yes. Things would be different.

Then maybe he could get her out of his system.

"Are we finished talking about the party?" He kept his gaze steady.

"If you can't trust me, Connor," she said, "surely you can't employ me."

"You know that's not what I meant."

Her eyes flashed to his, and she held the papers in her lap. "What *did* you mean, then? Trust is trust, isn't it? I'm either a trustworthy person or I'm not."

"I have faith in your integrity, Anne. In your honesty. In your work ethic."

"My work ethic?" she repeated, as if she couldn't believe what she was hearing.

He leaned forward. "That's right. I believe you're a trustworthy person. What I'm talking about is different. It's . . ." He searched for the words. "It's only your heart I don't trust."

The look she gave him was so bewildered that it stabbed him to his core. For a split second he contemplated stepping around the table and taking her in his arms, but that would be foolishness, of course.

He didn't mean to hurt her, or even insult her. Didn't she know that? Couldn't she see what he meant?

"Maybe," she said finally, looking him dead in the eye, "it's *your* heart you don't trust, Connor. Did you ever think of that?"

Chapter Thirteen

"*My* heart," Connor repeated.

"That's right." She leaned back, chin tilted, and looked at him, suddenly sure. "It doesn't seem to me you'd worry much about what was in *my* heart if your heart wasn't involved somehow."

Connor laughed and stood up. "That's an interesting analysis." He circled his chair and stood behind it, hands on its back. "But I know what part of my body's involved and, trust me, it's not my heart."

Her lips curved. "Which part is it?"

To her surprise, he laughed. "Are you sure you want to know?"

She raised her brows and did not relinquish his gaze.

He shook his head. "Not a good enough answer, Anne. Tell me, is that what you want? Would that be enough for you?" he asked. "Because if it is . . ."

She paused, confused. "What do you mean?"

"I mean, you've teased me since the day I got back here. Is a physical relationship what you want? The physical and nothing else?"

Anne stood up, too, her heart racing. "Is that what you're offering?"

He was silent a long moment, but their eyes held across the table.

Anne's pulse went into overdrive. She was suddenly hot. What if he meant . . . What would she say? Could she really . . .

"I'm not offering anything, Anne."

She expelled a breath.

"I'm just trying to figure out how we can work together," he continued. "We obviously have a lot of chemistry. And you're right, that's always been true. But we don't have to indulge it. We don't have to turn it into something it's not."

"Like what?"

"Like what we had before. We were kids, Anne." He stepped around the chair and toward her, intent. "We thought in terms of grand passions, poetic destinies. But we're adults now, and I think we both know that what we had was just a youthful, idealistic attachment. It was best that it ended when it did. But now . . ."

Anne rounded the coffee table as he spoke and stopped near where he stood. "Is that really all you think it was? Or are you just saying that because we ended up with nothing afterwards? Nothing but a lot of leftover hostility, anyway."

He leaned one hip against the side of the chair and crossed his arms over his chest. "Does it really matter what I think it was? It's been over since the end of that summer. As a matter of fact, I seem to recall those being your very words, Anne. 'It's over.' "

Outside, a mourning dove cooed. The quiet call sounded lazy and lonely in the trees, giving the summerhouse an even more remote feel than usual.

"I remember what I said." She approached the chair against which he leaned and put a hand on the wing back, inches from his hip, breaking the three-foot rule by half. "And I remember why I said it."

His eyes, looking down at her, appeared sultry. Standing this close, she could see the tender sweep of his lashes. He loosened his arms, moved his hand to hers, and let his fingers rest on her wrist. His thumb moved on her wristbone.

She dropped her eyes to where he touched her, studied the familiarity of his tanned hand. The square nails, the limber knuckles, the tendoned back. She turned her hand over and their palms met.

"Tell me, Anne, honestly," he said, his voice low.

She raised her eyes, feeling the warmth of his palm all the way up her arm.

He continued, his expression sober, "If we were to sleep together once, twice, even the whole summer, are you saying you wouldn't see that as a renewal of that old relationship?"

Anne felt a thrill in her stomach, imagined

touching him, kissing him, feeling his hands upon her with no contests, no challenges, no arguing. "What if I said I wouldn't?"

He studied her, then raised his other hand to touch her neck, just below her ear. Her nerves rippled like water to the tips of her toes.

"*Are* you saying you wouldn't?" he asked. "Because I'm not going backwards, Anne. I'm not willing to say let's try it again."

To Anne, he suddenly seemed much closer than he'd been, though neither one of them had moved.

"What *are* you willing to say?" What was she willing to accept?

"I can say . . . let's indulge this chemistry. Let's get rid of this tension between us the only way we know how."

Anne caught her breath.

"So if you can tell me this would be nothing more . . ." He let his hand trail to her collarbone, just inside the scooped neck of her shirt. ". . . than two adults . . ." His thumb traced a light line on her skin. ". . . enjoying . . ." He tipped his head just fractionally toward her. ". . . sex . . ." His lips touched hers so lightly that she might have dreamed it. He pulled back, his gray eyes impaling her where she stood. ". . . then I can do that."

She stood stock-still as he touched her. If she said yes, she could have him again, at least physically. She could experience his arms around her, feel his skin against hers, his body loving her even if his heart didn't.

Yet.

Her body quivered under his touch, her nerves reaching out for more, like a million tiny birds crying for food. She seriously believed that something inside of her might snap if she denied herself this opportunity. Her longing for him was as palpable as her need for breath.

Was she a fool to think it would lead to something more even though he was telling her straight out that it wouldn't? Was it possible that she could know him better than he knew himself?

No. It wasn't possible. Too much time had passed. Too many experiences had changed him into someone she could no longer predict.

And yet, she wanted to take the risk anyway. She wanted to throw her body and soul into making this man hers again. Though it scared her to think about losing, if she didn't take this chance, if she let him walk away and avoid her for the rest of the summer, she'd always wonder if she could have convinced him their love was still alive.

Wouldn't she?

"What do you say, Anne? Are we ready to be grown-ups?" His fingers were warm against her skin.

She caught her breath. "Grown-ups?" she asked. "Is that what hopping into bed would make us?"

One finger slid under her bra strap, caressing

the skin there. "Not hopping into bed," he said, his eyes downcast, scanning her neck, her hair, the place where his hand lay, creating shivers along her skin. "Satisfying this need. Getting past our physical response to one another."

She looked at the side of his face, at the fineness of his cheekbones, the way his eyes sloped gracefully at the corners.

Another finger dipped under her bra strap, and she had to fight an urge to pull his hand completely under her shirt, to feel that hot palm against her naked breast.

"Anne . . ." His voice was husky. "We could quench this once and for all. We could get rid of this tension."

She swallowed hard. "No." Her voice emerged as nearly a whisper.

He didn't move. His thumb just kept tracing her collarbone, his body mere inches from hers.

"No?" he repeated. His breath brushed her cheek. His voice was raw silk, his eyes as potent as a hypnotist's watch.

She dropped her gaze to his lips. So close.

"No," she said again. "It wouldn't quench it and you know it. We would just want more."

A tiny smile curved his lips, and his eyes, under those thick sensual lashes, slid to hers. "Then we take more, until it's gone."

Her heart thrummed in her chest and her limbs felt like butter. "Without emotion," she said, "without feelings."

"Without commitment. Without responsibility." He gave her a sidelong look. "Surely that appeals to you, Anne."

She licked her suddenly dry lips. "Why would that appeal to me?"

"Because it's what you said, years ago. That it could never go anywhere, *we* could never go anywhere. That I was just another summer person."

She closed her eyes.

His other hand touched her side, then slid to rest on her hip. She wondered if he could feel the throbbing that seemed to pulse through her entire body at his nearness. She felt like a giant glowing ember, burning hotter and brighter every place he touched her.

"I told you, that was a long time ago." Her voice was low with desire. She had to force the words from her throat. "Besides, I know you, Connor. You could never separate your head from your heart."

He bent his head, his cheek grazing hers, and let his lips linger just below her ear. "I've changed."

She shuddered. Her hands reached up and took hold of his elbows to steady herself.

She held her breath. "I haven't."

The hand at her hip rose up her rib cage, his thumb skimming the underside of her breast.

Her head dropped back as his lips trailed down her neck. "Connor, I'm serious."

He kissed the hollow between her neck and

shoulder, his teeth biting softly at her skin, sending spiraling shivers up and down her spine.

She shook her head. "I can't . . . I can't have just a sexual relationship with you."

She swallowed as the hand at her neck moved down over her shirt.

"Are you sure?"

She was about to answer, but the moment she opened her mouth to speak his lips captured hers.

As if of their own volition, her arms encircled his neck and she opened her lips to his.

Objections swirled in her head like angry bees. She should stop, she should be firm, she should stand for her convictions. But if she didn't pick one and pursue it, it couldn't sting her.

If she just concentrated on her body, she would be happy, at least for the moment.

She pulled herself against him. His arms held her tight, his mouth hungrily devoured hers. She felt his desire through her skin and knew she radiated it right back into him. They were two flames that fed each other, flaring higher the closer they got.

His hands moved across her back, hot through her shirt, and she imagined herself giving in, telling him she would take whatever he could give. In her mind's eye she saw them heading back up to the house, walking up the stairs, hand in hand, her body alive in a way it hadn't been in years.

His tongue caressed her lips. She answered

it with hers, and imagined him taking off her shirt, her skirt, her underclothes . . . imagined him kissing her breasts as he lay her down on the huge sleigh bed in his room . . . his bare chest on hers . . . skin against skin . . .

She pulled him tighter with the erotic thoughts, flattened her body against his and felt his erection rise up to meet her, pressing into her hip.

A low sound came from Connor's throat, and one of his hands cupped her head, his fingers threading through her hair. She opened her mouth under his and felt her resistance taking flight, a suddenly vaporous, elusive thing.

She imagined Connor above her, shoulders and chest broad, arms flexed and sinewy as he moved his hips against hers, and she felt the hot lava of desire between her legs.

She could have it. She could have it right now.

Connor's other hand pressed against her lower back, urging her into him, and Anne's knees went weak.

He moved his mouth to her cheek, her ear, her neck, and she bent her head into his chest, breathing hard.

She imagined them lying in bed afterward, her head on his bare shoulder, his arm around her and his hand caressing her with light, loving touches.

Then she imagined him saying, *Same time tomorrow good for you?*

Her body stiffened. She opened her eyes.

Always in tune with her shifting thoughts, more attentive to her body language than anyone else she'd ever known, Connor pulled back, his gaze intent. His arms were still tight around her, their torsos melded together.

"I can't do this," she breathed. Her hands were flat on his chest.

"Yes you can." He kissed her cheek again, then his tongue traced a path to her ear.

She felt tingles all the way up her spine, felt the heat of intense longing flood through her again.

Is a physical relationship what you want? The physical and nothing else?

She pushed him away, nearly stumbling as she left the security of his embrace. He reached out with a hand and grabbed hers, steadying her.

She nearly thanked him, but she pressed her lips together. Her other hand rose, her fingers against her mouth.

He wanted sex, that's what he'd said. He was being honest, and she was dreaming.

Sure, she could go with him, satisfy that part of her desire and his, then feel as confused about his feelings and their future as she did now. Would that really help? What kind of idiot would she be if she believed she could convince him to love her by sleeping with him? How many desperate, foolish women through the ages had attempted the same thing and ended up alone, worse off than before because they'd lost their self-respect? Too many to count.

"No," she said, shaking her head. "I can't. I won't. Do this."

His face was forbidding.

"Don't look at me that way, Connor," she said, emotion suffusing her face with heat.

"What way?" His voice was rough, hoarse, and his breathing was accelerated. His cheeks were flushed, too, but his eyes sparked with something that looked like anger.

"Like I've done something horrible to you."

"I never said that." He turned away from her, running a hand through his hair.

For some reason her eyes caught on the back of his neck, and she felt a wave of longing for the vulnerable, sweet boy with that same nape, the one who apparently didn't exist anymore.

"No, I know you didn't." Thwarted desire made her words sharp. "And you wouldn't *say* it. You just wear it on your face—a look . . . the same look as a high-school jock who's just been told by his girlfriend she won't 'go all the way.'"

He turned back to her, his hair mussed from his hand and his lips quirked in a wry smile. But his eyes were still shuttered, unreadable.

"You like to make me the villain, don't you, Anne?" He stood behind the chair again, his hands on its back.

She straightened her spine. "No more than you like to make me one."

He gazed at her consideringly, then cocked his head. "Maybe, but what have I ever done to you?"

*   *   *

"Signorina!"

Anne stopped by the piano in the grand salon and turned to smile at the man. She couldn't help it. Try as she might to blame Marcello for buying Sea Bluff and ruining her life, she really liked him.

Then again, she thought, maybe he hadn't ruined her life. He had, after all, brought Connor back here. Only time would tell what difference that might make.

She and Connor had left things unresolved the day before. Just after she'd turned him down, she'd beaten a hasty retreat, afraid she would change her mind if given a second chance.

While there was no doubt in her mind that she wanted Connor back, she wasn't going to do it with the understanding that it meant nothing.

"Mr. Tucci, what can I do for you?"

"I have been thinking about the party." Marcello's bushy eyebrows drew together over his nose. "And I think it is important to have some very fine Italian wines. Old wines, you understand."

"Sure." Anne raised the clipboard she was holding and flipped through some pages to the back. She pulled the pen from under the clasp. "I'll make a note for the caterer. Have you got a specific vineyard or year in mind?"

"Actually . . ." He took her elbow and steered her back toward the door through which he had just come and she had passed through moments before on the way to the back parlor. The topic seemed quite important to him, however, so Anne changed her course, even though she was to meet the florist in the back parlor in half an hour to discuss the arrangements.

Marcello's head was bent, and his eyes were on the floor as he continued. "I was in the wine cellar earlier and spied some bottles that would be perfect for the occasion."

"In this wine cellar?" she asked, surprised. The collection was extensive, but Anne had believed them to be primarily French wines, with a generous helping of California thrown in for good measure.

"*Sí, sí*, here in this very place." Marcello laughed and squeezed her arm with his hand. "I thought you and I should go down there and look, make some notes, make sure with Connor that these can be used."

"Oh, I'm sure he wouldn't have a problem with it." Anne nodded and smiled at Nicola, who passed the two of them with a broad smile—deaf to the world in her semipermanent headphones—on her way into the parlor they'd just left.

A second later she yanked the headphones off and drew her arm up in a big wave. "*Dill!*" she called, the name coming out as *Deal* with her accent.

Anne turned to watch her run toward the handyman, who'd paused as he'd passed the double doors in the back parlor. He was no doubt back there to repair the drywall hole he'd made looking for leaks and termites.

"That girl," Marcello said with an indulgent smile, looking after his youngest daughter.

"She's lovely," Anne said.

"She's—how you say—boy crazy." He laughed, the sound echoing in the hallway as they emerged from the front parlor. Marcello paused a moment and looked up at the chandelier. "Is this not a lovely foyer? Such light and space."

Anne looked up, smiling politely. "Yes, it is. People always remark on it."

He stood a long moment, hands in his pockets, looking up at the ceiling.

Anne waited a minute, then cleared her throat. "Uh, Mr. Tucci, I don't mean to rush you, but I do have the florist coming shortly. Would you like to discuss the wines later, or shall we go make a few quick notes now?"

Marcello started. "Oh! Now, most assuredly. I want to be sure we can use these wines, that it is all right with Connor, or we shall have to have someone do some searching, *sí*? The best wines are not always so readily available, *capire*?"

Anne put a hand on his arm, hoping to urge him toward the basement. "If there's something down there you like, I'm sure Connor will be fine with using them. Most of those wines have been sitting untouched for years. With the family gone, it's not as if anyone else was raiding the collection."

Marcello took a step, then paused again. "But I

do want to be certain, you understand."

Anne stopped and looked at him oddly. "Of course. We'll check with Connor. But first let's make a list of what you want."

"*Sí, sí*, of course." He took two steps, then stopped again. "But, ah, you don't think . . ." He paused, his hand at his chin, apparently deep in thought.

"I don't think what?" she urged.

"Well, I am just concerned . . ." He looked up at the ceiling again.

Anne looked up too. What in the world was going on with the man? He was acting as if he'd forgotten what they were talking about.

"Mr. Tucci, are you all right?"

He snapped to attention. "*Naturalmente!*"

Footsteps sounded on the stairs above and behind them, and with a broad smile Marcello whirled.

"Connor!" he boomed. "Just in the nick of time. We were going to the wine cellar."

Connor rounded the banister at the bottom of the stairs and approached them. His eyes flitted from Marcello to Anne. She felt his gaze like a touch.

He was freshly showered, his hair slightly damp, and he wore a white shirt that offset skin that was increasingly tanned. She could smell the fresh scent of his soap and couldn't stop her mind from straying to the idea that if she said the word they could, as Connor put it, *get rid of this tension.*

Connor's eyes returned to Marcello, and he gave the man a suspicious look. "Marcello, I thought you wanted to go down to the—"

"To the wine cellar!" Marcello interjected. "Exactly, *il mio ragazzo*. I have just been telling Anne that I have found the most delicious collection of wines down there that I think should be served at the party."

Connor shrugged. "Whatever you want."

Anne smiled. "I told him you wouldn't mind using anything that was down there."

Connor's eyes grazed her face, his lips curving slightly as they did.

Anne's body fairly sizzled with the look.

"But these are very *old* wines," Marcello insisted. "A lovely but valuable collection. I truly believe we must look at them to be sure."

"Nothing down there's worth all that much now, I wouldn't think," Connor said. "Seems to me Dad had all the good stuff shipped back to him a few years after we stopped coming."

Connor's gaze found Anne's face again. She met it, her pulse pounding in her throat. She remembered the day the owner of the Cork & Curd had come to package up those bottles. It had seemed to her the most concrete sign yet that the Emorys weren't planning to return.

"But I believe he missed a corner," Marcello insisted, one finger in the air as he strode down the corridor.

Anne and Connor shared a dubious look and followed behind.

As Marcello marched down the basement stairs ahead of them, Connor stood back and gestured for Anne to precede him. She grasped the narrow railing and started down.

The steps to the back basement were ancient stone, worn smooth by a hundred years' worth of footfalls heading for the wine cellar. This part of the house was the oldest, the wine cellar dating back to the early eighteen hundreds.

Anne used to avoid coming down here because it gave her the creeps. Between the musty smell and the wine cellar's thick, iron-hinged wooden door the whole place felt like a dungeon.

These days she didn't like it only because it felt dangerous coming up those smooth, hard steps with bottles of wine in her hands. She usually sent Dill down to get them, when necessary.

They reached the bottom of the stairs and ducked through the low doorway into the darkened hall that led to the old oak door. Marcello was leaning down, peering at the lock with the metal hoop that held the basement keys—a collection of skeleton keys that looked for all the world like a jailer's ring.

As they stood in the dank air, Anne folded her arms over her chilled skin, too aware that Connor, with all his soap-scented body heat, was standing just behind her.

Marcello finally found the right key and pulled the heavy doorway back. He entered the room first and pulled the string for the overhead bulb.

Dim light cast long shadows from the rows of shelved wine bottles. Many of the shelves were empty, but there were enough bottles to glow dully in the muted light. At the end of each shelf a piece of curling yellowed paper was tacked, with names and dates written on each in various hands.

Some of the writing was her own, Anne knew, and some was her mother's. But most was Prin's, or the previous cook's, a man named Rayeaux, who was reputed to haunt the place for no good reason.

"Ah! *Ché idiot!*" Marcello exclaimed, actually hitting himself on the forehead with the palm of his hand as he reached the middle of the wine cave. "Excuse me. I forgot my own notes. Let me go get them."

"But the bottles are right here," Anne said. "Can't we just make new notes?"

"No no." Marcello waved a hand over his head as he made for the doorway. "I must remember what I was thinking before. I will only be *uno momento.*"

He moved quickly toward the door and grasped the iron handle behind him as he passed through.

"Marcello, *wait*—"

But Connor's words were cut off by the slamming of the heavy portal.

Anne's mouth dropped open, and Connor stood stock-still a moment, staring at the place where Marcello had been.

Then, as if poked from behind, Connor strode toward the door and laid his hands upon it.

There was no handle on this side, Anne quickly noted, wondering if there ever had been. She moved next to Connor, searching for signs that a handle had been removed. She didn't remember that getting locked in was one of the risks of coming down here, but then it had been a number of years since she'd been here.

Connor's fingers searched the edge of the door, as if he might be able to get some kind of grip and pull it open that way, but the futility of that hope was immediately obvious to Anne.

"I think it's useless, Connor," she said, stepping back to allow the dim light to shine on the door. "We're just going to have to wait until Marcello comes back."

Connor turned slowly and leaned his back against the door. He shook his head. "I can't believe it." He looked at the ceiling, expelled a breath, and started to chuckle. "The old devil locked us in."

Chapter Fourteen

"Surely he didn't do it on purpose," Anne said, looking at Connor doubtfully.

This wasn't good. This was *not good.*

It had been hard enough resisting Connor yesterday, when she'd had an open door behind her. Now, here, in this dark silent room, with no way out . . .

Connor looked at her with heavy-lidded eyes. "I wouldn't be so sure about that."

"But why?" Anne asked. "Why would he do that?"

Or, more to the point, why would Connor *think* he'd do that? Anne knew from her conversations with Marcello that Marcello knew how she felt about Connor. But what did he know about Connor's feelings? And was it knowledge of those feelings that had led him to lock the two of them in together?

Connor studied her a minute, then turned back to the door. "There's got to be a way to get this open. It's not as if he locked it, right? You didn't hear him lock it, did you?"

He looked over his shoulder at Anne. She shook her head.

"Me neither. He wouldn't lock us in here. He may be devious, but he's not demented. I don't think." He squatted and tried to work his fingers under the door. But there was not enough of a gap to get any kind of hold.

"Do you think we could run out of air?" Anne looked around the cellar, at the smooth cement floor, the stone walls of the foundation, and the thick-timbered ceiling. She wrapped her arms around herself in the chill air.

"We're not going to be in here long enough to find out."

Connor turned from trying to get his fingers under the door and let his eyes scan the room. After a second, he rose and moved to one of the shelves. Pushing aside the yellowed paper on the end of one shelf, he slipped one finger under a string and pulled it toward him. On the other end was a corkscrew.

He turned to her with a triumphant smile.

Anne raised her brows. "Thirsty?"

Connor laughed. "Watch this."

He cut the corkscrew from the string with the small foil knife on one side. Then he took it to the door and began screwing it into the wood.

"What on earth are you doing?" Anne stepped closer to watch him twist the implement into the wood.

He really had to work at it, angling his shoulders and pressing as he turned. Finally, with the coil about two-thirds of the way in, he turned to Anne.

"Ye of little faith," he said with a smile. Gripping the handle of the corkscrew in his palm, his fingers on either side of the coil, he stepped back from the door as if it were about to swing wide, and pulled hard.

The handle popped off in his hand. He took several stunned steps backwards.

The door hadn't budged.

Anne's gaze went from his fingers to the sharp glint of metal protruding from the wooden door, and she began to laugh.

"Nice going!" she crowed. Seeing the look on his face, she laughed even harder.

"Well, shit." He looked at the broken tool in his hand.

Anne doubled over, laughing. She couldn't help it. Maybe it was the tension of the last couple of days. Maybe it was the tension of being alone again with Connor, but she couldn't stop. Her eyes teared, her stomach hurt, she tried to get an apology out—at least he'd tried something—but couldn't.

Seconds later a reluctant smile grew on his face, and before long they were laughing together.

"It *was* a good idea," she choked, swiping away tears of laughter.

"Yeah, but now we're screwed." He ran a hand through his hair, still chuckling.

"Well, the door is, anyway," she said, and they both started laughing again.

Eventually, their laughter died down, and Connor looked at his watch. "What in God's name is keeping Marcello?"

"How long's it been?"

"Nearly twenty minutes."

"Really? Shoot, I'm going to miss the florist. She was supposed to meet me here around now."

"Maybe when she arrives she'll remind Marcello that we're missing."

Anne strolled to one of the shelves of wine and started looking at labels, brushing the dust off with a finger to look at the years. "Do you think he's forgotten us?"

Connor sat down on the floor, his back against the wall. "I doubt it."

Anne shivered. She was dressed for a summer day, not for a room that was engineered to keep a steady temperature of fifty-seven degrees.

"I wonder if there's any brandy down here," she said idly. "I wouldn't mind having something that might warm me up."

"No brandy." He shook his head. "Dad took all the good stuff. I can't even believe I fell for that stupid ruse of Marcello's, that there was some great stash of old wine down here."

"I don't know . . ." Anne brushed some dust off

another label. "It looks as if he's right. There's some old stuff down here. Nineteen eighty-four. Nineteen seventy-eight."

"That's not old. I'm talking about stuff from the forties and thirties." He rubbed a hand down each one of his arms for friction heat. "It is cold down here."

Anne looked over at him and nodded.

He stood up and joined her. "Maybe we should open one of these. A nice Bordeaux would probably warm us up."

He picked up a bottle and held it in both hands, reading the label.

"That would be a good idea," Anne said, "if someone hadn't embedded the corkscrew in six inches of oak planking."

He shot her a sidelong glare. "I have other resources."

She laughed. "Oh, really?"

He pulled a Swiss army knife from his pocket and flipped out a tiny corkscrew. "You game?"

She smiled. He smiled back.

An hour later they were sitting side by side on the cold cement floor, opening a new bottle. They'd tried pounding on the door, the ceiling, and yelling through the walls, but no one had come. The florist had apparently not alerted anyone to the fact that Anne was missing, and Connor hadn't had any appointments all day.

He'd been planning, he said, to go sailing with Marcello. Something he'd like to try to do again tomorrow if only to throw the manipulative little man overboard.

Anne rubbed her arms again as Connor pulled the cork from the new bottle. It was actually kind of relaxing, knowing she couldn't go anywhere even if she wanted to. Of course, it helped that she was stuck in this situation with the man she'd fantasized about being alone with for the last eleven years.

"Still cold?" Connor asked.

She nodded. "It's just so damp."

Connor scooted closer to her on the floor and put an arm around her shoulders. "Just business," he said with a grin.

It was probably the alcohol, but Anne giggled. She *never* giggled, but right now she felt as giddy as a twelve-year-old at her first dance.

She sank back against his shoulder, her arm alongside his chest. He rubbed a hand up and down her upper arm while he tilted the new bottle back and drank.

He lowered the bottle, swallowed, and held it up to the light of the lone bulb. "Ah, a full-bodied, *fleshy* wine . . . exuding a ripe, velvety, oaky fruit flavor . . . echoing with refinement, that explodes into a lingering finish."

"*Explodes* into a *lingering* finish?" Anne laughed.

He handed her the bottle. "See for yourself."

She took it, tipped it back, and, forgetting that the bottle was now full, ended up spilling it down the front of her shirt. She gasped and sat forward.

Connor laughed and brushed at her shirt with his hand. "I know the wine experts say you should let a wine coat your mouth before swallowing it, but I never knew anyone who let it coat their shirt too."

"Yeah, that's it. I like my fleshy, fruity wine to have a lingering *fabric* finish."

They laughed, their fingers bumping as they absently brushed at her shirt, and their eyes met. Connor's arm was still around her. The warmth he shared gave the wine in her blood plenty of circulation.

She let her lips stay curved in a smile as she looked into his eyes, thinking that maybe a physical relationship *was* a good idea. After all, being so close, performing an act of love could regenerate an old *feeling* of love, couldn't it? Didn't people always say if you force yourself to smile when you're depressed, you actually begin to feel happier?

For a second she lost the train of her own thought, and wondered why she should be smiling at him.

Connor's hand stopped brushing her blouse and rose to her cheek, turning her face more fully toward him. His gaze was exploratory and intent, his eyes focused on hers until the moment his lips touched her mouth.

Then she didn't know if he still looked at her or not, because she closed her eyes and shifted so that her arm went around his neck.

The kiss was long, deep, and slow, both of their mouths tasting richly of wine. She remembered this level of comfort with him, this feeling of getting lost in his kiss, awash in the sensation of his mouth on hers.

Her hand moved to his neck, half-cupping his cheek as their tongues slid over one another and their lips caressed each other.

This wasn't a challenge, like the other kisses they'd shared. It wasn't even a hunger like the other moments they'd experienced. There was no emotional frenzy here, just the slow delicious pairing of two bodies that cried out for each other whenever they were near.

Anne wasn't sure whether Connor eased her back or she lay herself down, but they slid together to the cold, cement floor, her back flat with Connor on his elbows above her. Their mouths never lost each other and both of Anne's arms rose to encircle Connor's neck. The fingers of one hand dove into his hair, relishing its softness and the feel of his head in her palm.

His mouth left hers to travel down her neck. His fingers worked the buttons of her shirt, fumbling slightly so that she chuckled softly.

"Hey, no fair laughing at the drunk guy," he murmured, his lips moving down the skin of her chest as he undid first one button, then the next, then the next.

Anne's head arched back as his kisses followed his hands, and when he pushed her blouse away,

the cool air of the room made her nipples stand
hard.

Connor moved his head to take one nipple in
his lips through the silk of her bra.

Anne gasped and arched toward him. His other
hand pulled the bra cup away from her breast,
and suddenly his lips were on skin.

"Oh God," she breathed, pulling his head into
her breast.

His tongue, teeth, lips, all moved over her nipple, causing waves of glorious sensation to cas-
cade down her body. She clutched at his back, felt
his hips crush into hers. She could feel his erection
and shifted herself so that it hit just where she
wanted it to.

"Anne," he murmured, his voice a near gut-
tural moan. He pushed himself up, tasting her
throat, her ear, her cheek, and then her mouth.

One of his hands pulled at her skirt, and he
shifted his weight so that he could drag the mate-
rial to her waist. His fingers found her panties,
traced the line of them at her hip bone and down,
until they could dive under the fabric and into
the spot where she was melting with desire for
him.

She pushed into his hand, felt his fingers slide
deftly inside, and she expelled a long, trembling
breath.

"Oh, Connor." She raised up her hips and
pushed at her panties with one hand.

Connor grasped them with his, and in one motion whipped them off down her legs.

She reached for his belt buckle, fumbled with the leather flap, finally loosened it and reached for the button. But Connor was impatient and his hand covered hers, flipping the button open and running the zipper down.

Her hand was on him as soon as his pants opened.

He inhaled sharply, then pushed into her hand. Without a second thought, she widened her legs and began to draw him to her.

He stopped, pushed his pants off, then rose up above her. His eyes locked on hers, he slid inside.

The moment he entered her they both exhaled in relief. Hearing the other, they each uttered a low laugh.

"My God," Connor murmured as he slowly eased himself deeper within her.

"I've missed you so much," she whispered, pushing her hips upward to draw him even further inside.

As soon as she moved a fire seemed to ignite between them. Desire raced through her body and she clung to him, pulling him ever tighter to her.

Connor pushed deeply, then he eased back and thrust again, and again, moving faster and with greater purpose. "Oh *Jesus*," he said softly, raising up on his hands to pump even further, harder, deeper.

Anne's hands were everywhere, along his chest, down his sides, up his ribs, down to his hips. She met him thrust for thrust, felt her soul turning inside out to take his body into hers.

She wanted to crawl into his skin, taste his very essence, feel him up, on, around and within her. She pulled his face to hers, and his tongue dove into her mouth just as his body dove into hers below.

They were frantic now, their bodies moving as one. Anne could not get enough, could not feel close enough, could not take him deep enough. She moved her head to the side with a cry as her entire being shattered into a thousand tiny pieces with the power of her orgasm.

Seconds later Connor plunged into her one last time, arching his head back with a low sound in his throat as his muscles shuddered beneath the grip of her fingers.

"My God, Anne," Connor breathed, lowering himself beside her but not leaving her body. They lay there, joined from lovemaking, no longer feeling the cold cement floor or the dank chill of the air.

Connor shifted first. His movement away from her created a cold spot on Anne's side where his body once was.

He took a deep breath. "Maybe you should tell me what those circumstances were now."

Perhaps it was the wine exaggerating her emotions, but Anne's entire body stiffened. She knew what he meant, those "circumstances" about their breakup that she'd alluded to so cavalierly, thinking if he wanted to hear about them she could doctor them so they wouldn't seem like the sabotage of a dead man.

But her mind was fuzzy now, and all she could think about was the ugliness of the situation that had led her to break up with him.

"It was your parents," she began, thinking she could skirt the truth.

"What about my parents?" His hand was on her stomach and he lay on his side, up on one elbow.

"They . . ." *Threatened me? No, then he'd ask with what.* "They hated me, as you know."

Connor said nothing.

"They called me into their room, that morning—"

"Which morning?" Connor asked.

"The morning of—of that last day. The day after the carnival."

He nodded. "Go on."

She swallowed, suddenly thirsty. "They told me they didn't want me to continue to see you." She looked at the wall beyond him, picturing the scene. Patsy Emory's hard face; Bradford Emory's supreme indifference.

"That was an easy one," he said mildly, "considering I was going back to Atlanta the next day."

She met his eyes. "That's just what I said. I told them I wouldn't write to you, or call, if they didn't want. But there was no reason I should break up with you. Why should I hurt you, when you were leaving the next day anyway?"

Connor's expression was closed, deceptively calm. "So why did you?"

Anne swallowed again and turned her head. "Where's that wine? I'm so thirsty."

They both sat up then, and took the opportunity to find and straighten their clothing. Anne was sorry to lose the intimacy, but she didn't think she could continue feeling exposed on so many levels.

Anne grabbed the bottle that stood against the wall and took a long gulp.

"You were saying?" Connor pressed as she handed him the bottle.

She inhaled deeply and sat back against the wall. She remembered that a lot of what they had said had rung true to her. "They . . . they told me all about your life there, in Atlanta. They told me about your new job, how it would develop. They said you'd be part of a huge, multinational conglomerate. You'd meet with congressmen and ambassadors. Captains of industry, I remember Patsy saying. I'd never heard the term before."

Connor looked unimpressed. "You knew all that."

She nodded. "Yes, but I'd never heard it the way they said it. The way it sounded in my head. They voiced all of my fears, confirming them. They told me I'd never fit in, that I'd hold you back, that you'd resent me. And they pointed out that, after all, it wasn't as if you were ever going to marry me."

Stupidly, she felt a lump grow in her throat, remembering how she'd hoped she was wrong, though she'd known that what they had been saying was true. Their assessment had just been the last nail in the coffin of her dream.

They were both silent a long minute. Anne shifted her gaze tentatively to his face.

Connor's eyes were downcast, his hands still in his lap. As she looked at him he swallowed, and she followed the motion with her eyes.

"So they said, why drag it on?" she continued, looking away from him again. "Why hold on to something you know you're going to lose? Let him go."

And I did. The unspoken words hung in the air.

"That doesn't," he paused, "really explain it, Anne." He turned his head, fixed her with a look. "That doesn't explain why you told me it was over, you didn't love me. I was nothing to you."

"I didn't say that," she said, quietly aghast.

"Yes, you did. Maybe not in those exact words, but that's what you said." His voice hardened. "But you went out of your way to tell me we were finished, Anne. Why? Why didn't you just tell me your concerns? Why didn't you tell me what my parents had said? I could have helped you."

"What could you have done, Connor?" she

asked heatedly, her own frustration making her words strident. "Stood up to your parents? Made them hate me more? For what? So we could have been pen pals another year and had a two-week affair come summer? We had no future—"

"*No,*" Connor interrupted. He rose to his feet. "You don't know that."

She rose too, heart beating frantically. "Of course I did. I wasn't stupid, Connor. We were young, I was nobody, a maid! I wasn't leaving the island for some high-powered job. You weren't going to—"

"*How do you know?*" He turned on her fiercely, enunciating each word with force. "Did you believe even then I was as pretentious as my parents? After all I said, all we did together, everything we planned—did you really believe I thought you weren't good enough for me?"

"But Connor, what future did we—"

"I had a *ring* in my pocket, Anne."

Anne's breath left her. "*What?*"

He took another deep breath and ran a hand through his hair, looking away from her at the ground. "That day, on the beach. I had a ring." He looked back up at her. "Two-carat, emerald cut, white gold, sized for you with that blade of grass I'd tied on your finger weeks before."

Anne's mouth dropped open. She thought she might throw up.

He laughed cynically at himself, shook his head, and looked back at the floor. "But we were just kids. You weren't even twenty. And I was just a fool."

A pounding sounded at the door.

They both jumped, Anne nearly out of her skin, then they separated even further than they already were.

Anne's heart felt as if it were going to blow right through the top of her head, it was pumping so fast. She glanced at the floor for any signs of their lovemaking, saw none, and looked back at Connor.

The pounding sounded again, only this time it wasn't a knock. It was someone trying to open up the door.

"Anne? Are you in there?"

Anne expelled a breath. "It's Lois."

She went to the door, smoothing her hair and touching her lips with one hand.

"I'm here, Lois. We've been locked in." She stepped to the side of the door, and a second later it jerked open, slamming against the inside wall.

Lois and Anne looked at each other in the startled aftermath of the sound. Then Lois's eyes traveled over Anne's face. "Are you all right?"

"Yes, I'm fine." Anne's hands rose involuntarily to her cheeks. "Where's Marcello?"

"He had to go to town suddenly, some business thing." Lois's gaze must have caught sight of Connor, because she looked suddenly aware.

"How did you find us?"

Lois refocused on Anne. "Mr. Tucci called from

the post office, said he suddenly remembered he'd left you all in the wine cellar. He said he'd come down here with you, had to go back upstairs because he'd forgotten something, and then he got distracted. He wanted me to apologize to you, though he didn't know why you hadn't come up yet."

"We were locked in!" Anne exclaimed.

"So you said." Lois's expression was all too savvy. "I wish Mr. Tucci'd remembered earlier where he left you. By the time he called I'd already searched practically the whole damn place. For both of you."

Anne heard Connor approach, felt him stop just behind her. She could almost believe in Trudy's auras, so strongly did his presence touch her without any sort of contact.

"Your mother's on the warpath," Lois said to Connor, tilting her head back toward the stairs. "She's been interrogating everyone about where you all are. Apparently she wanted to talk to you first thing this morning, Connor, but someone took all of her clothes to the laundry while she was in the shower."

Anne's mouth dropped open. "Really?"

"*All* of her clothes?" Connor repeated.

"Every last stitch," Lois confirmed. "They even took the sheets from the bed. She was stuck in her room all morning, with no options but to emerge naked or wait for a maid."

Part of Anne wanted to lean right back into

Connor's chest, but the other part told her to thank her lucky stars that Lois had shown up. She needed to digest what he'd just told her, figure out what it all meant.

"And which did she choose?" Connor asked.

Anne looked up at him sideways. He had a slight smile on his face.

"She called Shirley Carmichael and had Shirley call the house to send the maid to her room."

"Wow," Anne said, impressed. "I don't know that I'd have thought of that."

"Pretty resourceful," Connor nodded.

Lois grimaced. "Yes, well, the rest of us have been paying for it ever since she got out. And she's looking for either one of you, with—and I'm just guessing here—every intention of tarring and feathering one of you."

"Probably me," Anne said.

"You seemed to be the one she preferred," Lois concurred.

"But I guess it ought to be me." Connor stepped around Anne, turning back to look at her before descending the short stoop. "We'll continue this discussion later."

Anne tucked her hair behind her ear. "Yes," she said, clinging to him with her gaze. "Yes."

He turned and took off up the hallway to the stairs.

Lois turned slowly to Anne, brows raised. "Well, well . . ."

The flush on Anne's face was apparently permanent. She couldn't even dim it. "Yes, well . . ."

Lois smiled. "I guess Sean's column was wrong again."

She focused on Lois's face. "What do you mean?"

"I mean, he said Connor Emory was seen shopping for Gabriella-sized diamonds earlier this week." Lois chuckled and started back up the hall. "Something tells me maybe they were Anne-sized."

Chapter Fifteen

Connor entered the upper hallway in time to hear his stepmother demand of Trudy, "I know you know and I insist you tell me, where is Miss Sayer?"

Trudy cocked her head to one side and answered, "Don't know, ma'am. I haven't seen Miss Sayer all day."

"Haven't you, really?" Patsy inquired. "I was told by the cook that the two of you had been washing draperies just this morning."

Trudy ignored his stepmother's pointed question and said, "Has anyone ever told you you're ruled by your third chakra?"

Connor stopped, interested to see his stepmother's reaction to this.

Patsy laid a hand on Trudy's arm and leaned slightly toward her. With a scathing look, she said, "Honey, you ever bring that nonsense up with me again and you'll be out of a job. And if you're smart you'll keep it to yourself around everyone else, too. You'll never get a husband coming off like the loony you are."

Connor watched Trudy's face for signs of intimidation, but she simply nodded. "A little of the first chakra, too, but no sign of the fourth at all." With that she walked off.

Patsy spotted Connor. "*Well!* Just who I was looking for." She beckoned him toward her. "You have *no idea* what kind of day I've had. It's been intolerable. And here it is nearly dinnertime. This place has gone to hell in a handbag. As far as I'm concerned we can't get rid of it fast enough."

Connor walked slowly across the hallway, thinking her day couldn't have been any stranger than his. Though, he had to admit, there'd been some truly sublime moments in his.

He pictured Anne's face, her hair fanned out around her on the cement floor as he'd taken her for the first time in eleven years. Just thinking about it nearly caused him to rise up again with desire.

Their conversation had been less sublime, but certainly more necessary. He wasn't sure, but he was beginning to believe they might actually be able to get past what had happened all those years ago. The expression on Anne's face when he'd told her about the ring had been one of pure, unadulterated shock. There was no way she'd believed he was going to propose before he left that last summer.

It was even possible for him to believe that his parents had intimidated her into turning him away.

But something still niggled at the back of his mind. She'd been so adamant that day on the beach—he remembered it with perfect clarity. She'd been more than clear, she'd been resolute, determined to convince him that she did not want him anymore. Didn't love him. Didn't want to be tied down. Didn't want to think about him the coming year.

Why—and how—would she have done that if she had merely been scared? Why hadn't she talked to him about the future, if that was what had been making her so afraid? Why, if she'd loved and trusted him, had she believed his parents' opinion of her over his?

"I suppose you've been off with that *Anne* again," Patsy said. Her back was ramrod straight as she led him into the formal front room.

The windows in this room were tall and long, bathing the airy space in sunlight. A grand piano sat in the back corner, and several richly brocaded settees were scattered amongst sculptures and plants, delicate armchairs and small tiptoeing side tables.

Connor walked straight for the windows and looked out over the expanse of front lawn. *"That Anne?"* he repeated, easily imagining Patsy telling Anne she wasn't good enough. It was something she'd done all the time back then. Something she was still doing. Why had Anne finally fallen for it?

Patsy joined him at the window.

"You know," she began, "by this time I thought there'd be grandchildren scampering about on that grass."

He looked down at her, remembering how it was she—and not his father—who used to take them out on the lawn as children and set up games of baseball and croquet. Once upon a time, she had been a mother to him. The only mother he'd ever known, really.

She was a powerhouse of energy, Patsy Emory was, and when she was using it for something she wanted she could create marvelous things.

At the same time she could be downright evil.

She shook her head. "But you're not even married, and your sisters . . ." She huffed a laugh. "Well, they're so busy traveling and furnishing vacation homes of their own that a pregnancy would only get in their way."

Connor gazed back out the window. He had the strange sensation of having been set free. As if he'd held onto something for too long and letting it go had relieved him of an enormous weight.

"Don't worry. You'll get your grandchildren. I'd be willing to bet Deborah, at least, is pregnant within a year." He looked back down at her.

She stepped away from the window and settled on one of the formal sofas. "Come sit down for a minute, Connor."

He strolled across the room, noting the way the high ceilings made him feel as if he could breathe easier. Between his office and his condo, he hadn't realized how constrained he'd felt by his surroundings. Sea Bluff was working its magic on him, it seemed.

Sea Bluff or Anne. He never could separate the two.

"A situation has arisen that I need you to take care of." Patsy sat forward on the sofa, her hands on her knees. There was always a sense of urgency about her when she spoke, with the leaning in, the intent look, the assertive body language.

"A situation?" He wondered if he and Anne qualified as "a situation."

"Yes, and it's rather . . . ugly. I'd have liked to spare you this, but it needs to be dealt with, and I . . ." She paused, looked at the floor, and shook her head. "I just can't do it."

Connor watched her and said nothing.

Patsy's jaw clenched a moment before she spoke. "There's a woman in Atlanta, named Diana Bell. She used to work for us."

"I remember her. Dark curly hair. She cooked for you, didn't she? A few years ago, maybe five?"

Patsy nodded. "That's right. Well, we had to let her go. Because of character issues."

Connor closed his eyes, a sinking feeling in his chest. He knew what was coming.

"And now," Patsy continued, voice heating with ire, "she's going to the press. She said your father . . . She said she's going to reveal that they had an affair—and she's claiming that he promised to leave her seven million dollars at his death."

Connor opened his eyes. "Seven million dollars? Where did she get that figure?"

He watched a vein on Patsy's forehead rise as she searched for words. "I don't know. She said your father was in love with her. That he knew he was dying . . ."

Connor's brows drew together. "He died of a heart attack. How could he have known?"

Patsy scoffed and threw up her hands. "That's what she says! She claimed he was going to give it to her, then said when he realized he was sick he would bequeath it to her."

"His will was dated six months before he died. When did this grand affair supposedly take place? Does she have any proof?"

"I don't know." Patsy shook her head. "But she says she's going to the press, so proof doesn't really matter, does it? It'll be out there, true or not, and whenever anyone sees the name Bradford Emory they'll think sex scandal. That's just how it works."

Connor laughed once, without mirth. "Maybe."

Patsy's hard brown eyes met his. "What I need you to do is go talk to this woman. Convince her not to go to the papers. Offer her whatever it will take, Connor. I will not have the public memory of your father besmirched like this."

He wondered if Patsy realized that "whatever it will take" could amount to the whole seven million, depending on what sort of evidence the woman had. Patsy was no skinflint when it came to herself or her daughters, but he had a hard time believing she'd be one for giving away money to women who claimed to have slept with her husband.

"Where is she?" he asked. "Atlanta still?"

Patsy nodded.

Connor hesitated. "If we give her a settlement and the press finds out, her claim will seem that much more substantial."

"It doesn't matter. You have to do it, Connor," Patsy said urgently. "Go talk to her. You'll be able to convince her, I know it. We just need her to keep quiet."

Connor studied her. Was she this afraid of damage to his father's memory? Or was she worried that it would make her look bad? Probably both.

"You believe her, don't you?" he asked gently.

Patsy was still for a long moment. Then she looked up, her expression hard. "I believe she had the affair. I don't believe he offered her seven million dollars."

Connor nodded slowly. Maybe Patsy wasn't as clueless about his father's "character" as he'd believed.

"So will you go?" She raised her chin as she looked at him.

"I probably don't have to go," he said. "We can find out what proof she's got, then whatever settlement we reach can be dealt with through our lawyers."

"No." Patsy was adamant. "I don't want the lawyers involved. I don't want this getting out.

And the more people who know about it, the more chance there is it'll be leaked."

Connor shook his head. "Not with our attorneys. They're required by law to keep quiet."

Patsy sighed and leaned back on the couch, apparently defeated.

Connor began mentally planning whom he needed to call and what he needed them to do. He was about to excuse himself to get on it when his stepmother spoke again.

"I also wanted to apologize for the other morning."

Connor tried to remember what "other morning" and what had happened, but failed. The apology in and of itself was remarkable, however.

"With Anne," she clarified. "At breakfast. I know you think I'm hateful to her."

Connor sighed. He'd just begun to believe Anne's name might not come up in the conversation. "You are hateful to her. But you should be apologizing to Anne about that, not me."

Patsy shook her head, dropping her intent gaze to her lap. "No. I can't speak to her, not without . . . remembering."

Connor studied her downcast eyes. He thought he noted an unusual pallor to her face. "Remembering what?"

She looked back up at him, her coffee brown gaze intent again. "That's the other thing I wanted to talk to you about. Because I see you falling back under her spell—"

"I'm not falling back under her spell." But he knew he was lying.

Patsy watched him shrewdly. "If that's true, I'm glad to hear it. But I'll tell you, it's not for lack of trying on her part. Now Connor." She scooted forward on the settee and put a square hand on his knee. "I have one more thing to tell you that might shock you, but I really feel you ought to know this."

He looked at her impassively.

"You see . . ." She paused, her gaze drifting past him, and he thought for one astounded moment that tears were welling in her eyes. But she blinked and refocused on his face. "This situation, with Diana Bell . . . well, it isn't the first time something like this has happened."

No kidding, Connor thought.

But her eyes were too intent on him. It wasn't possible that what she had to say might shock him; he could see that she was calculating for it to shock.

"Years ago," she continued, "I caught your father in a . . . well, something of a tête-à-tête. With Anne Sayer."

A bitter taste rose in Connor's mouth. "A tête-à-tête?"

The vision of Patsy playing croquet with them on the lawn was now long gone, replaced by a memory of her using every nasty word in the book to describe Anne to him years ago.

He narrowed his eyes at her.

Her gaze steadfastly met his. "Yes, and you must believe me. There was no mistaking what was going on between them. Afterwards, your father confessed to me all about it. He said it wasn't a full-blown affair and he didn't want Anne to be fired. But still—"

Anger straightened Connor's limbs and made him stand up. Patsy's hand dropped from his knee. "That's impossible."

Patsy shook her head, looked at the floor, and seemed to have a hard time swallowing. Connor watched her throat work, feeling his entire perspective dip like the deck of a storm-swept ship.

"You'd say anything to keep me away from her," he said, anger turning his words sharp as razor blades. "But I never dreamed you'd sink this low. To accuse Anne of . . . That's about the most repulsive thing you've ever said."

"Connor, it's true. Her shirt was open. His hands were—they were—" She put her own hands out in front of her as if demonstrating, but her face was tragic. "And he was kissing her on the—"

"When did this supposedly happen?" he demanded. *And where were* her *hands?* he wanted to add. But he didn't want to give credence to anything Patsy said.

Because he didn't believe it. He couldn't. He *wouldn't*. This was just one more example of Patsy's self-serving manipulation.

She looked up at him, and for all the world he thought she might cry. She dropped her hands to her lap. "That last summer we were here. Why do you think we never came back?"

Connor's blood froze. He'd thought it was because of *his* heartbreak, *his* trauma; but that couldn't have been the case. Nobody had known about his heartbreak except himself and Anne. And even Anne hadn't known the extent of it.

People had known about their relationship each summer, naturally, but the breakup had occurred just as he would have left anyway. And he had not been in any mood to share his shattered feelings with any member of his family. So how would they have known?

"I have a hard time believing that if this story were true," he said, his voice flinty, "you wouldn't have just fired her." He paced away from his stepmother, then turned back. "You, of all people, Patsy, would never turn tail and run from a mere nineteen-year-old girl."

Patsy's eyes shot to his, her expression cold as a shark's. "She wouldn't go."

"Of course she wouldn't." He threw his hands up. "Because nothing happened."

"Connor, listen to me." Patsy lowered her voice, but it was strong and sure. "It happened. Your father didn't want to tell you because he knew how you felt about her."

Connor opened his mouth to speak, to ask why, if that was the case, his father supposedly touched her in the first place. But he didn't believe it, and he didn't want to hear her explanations.

Still, she continued, and he was powerless to make himself stop her. It was like looking for the bloody bodies in a car wreck, even though you knew you didn't want to see them.

"We tried everything to get her to quit, but she wouldn't go. And if we'd fired her we'd have opened ourselves up to a sexual harassment lawsuit. We consulted the lawyers."

"What are you talking about? Anne wouldn't have *sued*, for God's sake."

It was impossible for him to think Anne, especially the old Anne, would have stood up to pressure from people as powerful as his father and stepmother at all. That she would actually have threatened them with a lawsuit was absurd. As far as he was concerned, the assertion exposed the lie.

"Your determination to put her down has always been unbelievable," he continued, "but this takes the cake. To invent such—"

"I have *proof*." Patsy stood as she said the words, her tone peremptory. "And it wasn't Anne who threatened the lawsuit. She was even more of a mouse back then than she is now. No, it was her grandmother. Delores Sayer."

Her grandmother. Connor remembered meeting the steely old bird early on that last summer. Anne had had the surprising optimism to believe that if her grandmother actually met Connor, she wouldn't be so dead-set against him.

It hadn't worked out that way. The old woman had eyed him like he was bacteria under a microscope and had let him know in no uncertain terms that was just what she thought of him.

Connor had always cut Delores Sayer some slack when Anne had told him the things she'd say, believing she was only trying to protect her granddaughter. It was understandable that she'd fear he was just toying with the pretty local girl.

But Delores's hatred had sprung from something else entirely, something he hadn't understood but could see without a doubt, and it had run deep.

"What proof?" Connor asked.

Patsy marched across the room to a briefcase on a round table near the wall. She flipped open the clasps to reveal an accordion file full of manila folders. She pulled one out.

"Bring them all here," Connor said. His skin felt suddenly icy.

Patsy pulled the accordion file from the case and came back to him. She handed him the files, keeping the one she'd pulled out.

Connor glanced at the folder headings. *Augusta Williams. Emily Robinson. Margaret Moore. Jane Newell. Clara Brock.* And many more.

He remembered them, most of them. Gussy and Emily. Maggie, Jane . . . They'd all left their jobs at the Emory household without warning. As he'd gotten older, Connor had realized why.

He would see them surreptitiously leaving his father's bedroom in the mornings, or making special trips to his office in the afternoons, or bringing him coffee or brandy to the den, then closing the door and locking it behind them.

Patsy then, as now, was a society belle, rarely home and always on the go. There'd been plenty of time for his father to indulge himself with the desirable employees—of which there always seemed to be a surplus.

Connor opened up Margaret Moore's folder and saw cancelled checks. Clara had been the one to get a car, he remembered, and opened her folder to see paperwork from Bob Merritt's Mercedes dealership.

He looked at Patsy and held out his hand.

She placed the last folder in it. The label said *Anne Sayer*.

There was only one cancelled check, made out to Anne. The ink of the endorsement had partially bled through the paper. Backwards, he read, *Deposit only*.

The amount was $50,000.

Chapter Sixteen

A bloodcurdling scream rent the night. Connor jerked bolt upright in bed. He hadn't been asleep—the way he felt he doubted he'd ever sleep again—but adrenaline shot through his veins nonetheless.

He jumped out of bed, pulled on his pajama bottoms, and swung open the bedroom door. From down the hall he heard the sound of female voices raised several octaves above normal in terror.

He took off in that direction, but before he'd gone five steps Gabriella and Nicola, babbling excitedly and incomprehensibly in Italian, came bolting toward him.

"Hold on, hold on!" He raised his arms out to his sides as if to catch them.

They stopped before him, chattering like birds—Italian birds—their eyes wide with panic.

"What's going on?" he asked in his loudest calm voice.

"Th-th-there—" Gabriella pointed down the hall with a violently trembling finger.

Connor's gaze traveled the hallway, looking for flames, an intruder, anything.

"Calm down, Gabriella. What is it? Is something on fire?"

She shook her head no, impatiently, and said something rapidly in Italian to Nicola.

"She say she saw someting," Nicola said, helpfully. It was the first time in days he'd seen her without her CD player. He realized he'd actually forgotten what her voice sounded like.

"What did she see?" He looked from Nicola to Gabriella questioningly.

"Fantasmi." Gabriella breathed the word.

Connor looked to Nicola.

"Ghosts," she said and nodded.

Connor closed his eyes and exhaled. Just what he needed.

He opened his eyes. "Was someone in your room, Gabriella? Is that what happened?"

"No, no, nel giardino."

Connor turned to Nicola.

"In the garden," she translated.

"All right, then. Come on." He took Gabriella's hand, her fingers closed tightly around his, and he started down the hall. They were halfway down the stairs when Gabriella stopped dead, nearly yanking Connor's arm out of its socket.

"No, no," she protested. "I doan go . . . outside."

Nicola hovered behind them, looking excited.

"You'll be all right," he promised. "Both of you. We're just going to go see what's out there. Sometimes the trees can look ghostly in the moonlight."

"Not a tree!" Gabriella spat.

"Well, let's go see." He started up again. She came with him, reluctantly.

They crossed the hallway and Connor opened the front door, which, he noted, was just as snug in its frame as ever.

They stepped out into the night, crossed the porch, and went down the stoop.

"Where did you see them? Out your window?" Connor asked.

"*Sí, sí*, outa my window." Gabriella clutched his arm in both her hands and held it close to her body.

He had trouble walking with her so close, and he was suddenly aware that she wore only a short baby-doll nightdress. Her breasts pressed against either side of his arm.

They rounded the corner of the house to the large expanse of lawn that lay outside Gabriella's window. A cool breeze blew the trees, and the grass looked white in the light from the three-quarter moon.

"Where did you see the, ah, ghost?" Connor turned to her. She did not relinquish his arm.

Her brow furrowed, and she pointed vaguely in the direction of the garden, wagging the finger from potting shed to hedgerow—a good thirty-yard differential.

"What was it doing?" He pictured something possibly caught in a tree, something that might have looked like it was flying.

"It was . . ." Gabriella made a shoveling motion with her hands.

Connor did a double take. "It was what?"

She made the motion again, her expression annoyed.

"It was digging?"

She stopped. "*Si, si*, it was deegging. Deegging a hole."

Connor didn't even know what to say to that.

"Well, do you see it now?" Connor looked down at the top of her head. Her hair fell in riotous curls around her shoulders and down her back. He saw her head shake.

He glanced back at Nicola, who stood just behind her sister. "Did you see it too?"

She shook her head. "No, no. I no see. But she . . ." She pointed at her sister. "She tell me about it. I believe her. She very, very 'fraid." She giggled.

"Sure, sure." Connor nodded. "But you don't see it now, neither of you." They shook their nearly identical heads.

Gabriella looked up at him, frowning prettily. "You no believe in me?"

Connor smiled wanly. "You, I believe in. Ghosts, no. I'm sure it was something else, something that just looked like a ghost."

She pouted and looked at his chest. After a second she raised the hand that wasn't gripping his to his pectoral muscle, as if noticing for the first time he was shirtless. She touched the hair on his chest with her fingers and looked up at him through her lashes. She smiled.

He took her fingers in his other hand and removed them from his chest. She was beautiful, she was unattached, and she was not part of any painful past. It would be so easy if he were attracted to Gabriella the way he was attracted to Anne.

Well, not easy. She was hell on wheels.

But he wasn't attracted to her. Not in any way. And he could not get Anne out of his mind. Even with all he now knew about her.

"Come on," he said. "That's enough of that."

"No," she said in a babyish voice. "No enough."

"Yes," he said decisively, thinking about how exhausted he was going to be the next morning. How exhausted he was already. "Enough. Now let's go wake your father up and tell him about the ghost."

"Ah, *sí!*" Nicola said, and ran ahead. "*Papa!*"

Gabriella dropped Connor's arm and stalked off after her sister, baby-doll pajamas flaring over her pretty legs like a bell.

Anne arrived at her job the following morning with such a deep sense of well-being it almost scared her. She was still losing her job. She was still losing this house that had been practically home for most of her life.

But the fact that Connor had planned to *propose*

to her—even though it was eleven years ago—that he'd been that much in love with her, made her feel light as a feather. Connor had wanted to spend the rest of his life with her. Surely there were more than just remnants of that love left inside him.

She paused for a moment and remembered the look on his face the previous day as he'd entered her. That hadn't been a quick roll in the wine cellar, she thought with a private smile. Granted, they'd been a little drunk, but they'd been there, in the moment. They had *both* felt something in their hearts, she was sure of it.

Was this intuition? she wondered. Was everything going to work out the way she hoped? Or was she fooling herself?

Either way, she thought, tossing the mail onto the little desk in the kitchen and hanging her purse on the hook in the closet, she felt good today.

Even the sound of Patsy's voice outside the kitchen doors couldn't disturb her sunny mood. Patsy had no power over her anymore. Connor was running the show, and Anne was no longer a young girl afraid of her own shadow.

Add to that the fact that Bradford Emory was dead, and she felt positively immune to Patsy's machinations.

For a second she thought about Bradford Emory, testing herself, as she sometimes did, to see if there was still a bruise where the memory lay.

She thought of the last time she'd seen the man—in the upstairs master sitting room, with Patsy—and her palms began to sweat.

The meeting had been horrendous. Scary. Threatening. She'd left the room more shaken than she'd been the morning Mr. Emory had cornered her in the conservatory. He'd actually waited for her to go to the music room, he'd pointed out, because the sound wouldn't carry.

Shame scalded her cheeks.

Bradford Emory's amorous excesses were legendary. There wasn't a maid in the house who hadn't known to avoid being caught alone in a room with him—and at that time there had been a lot more maids than there were now.

But it had happened to her anyway. And she'd handled it so badly. So very, very badly.

So badly that everyone involved had gotten the wrong idea, and it had given Patsy and Bradford the ammunition they'd needed to keep the impoverished maid away from their golden son.

Prin bustled into the kitchen and stopped when she saw Anne.

Anne shook herself out of her reverie, her mood dampened, and made a mental note not to test that memory again any time soon.

"Morning, Prin," she said, then looked at her oddly. "What's the matter?"

Prin had stopped dead in the center of the room, as if surprised to see her sitting there. She planted her hands on her hips. "Connor's fixing to fly back to Atlanta this morning. Mrs. Emory just told me. Did you know that?"

"Figlio." Marcello stood in Connor's doorway with his hands outstretched, wearing a blue silk dressing gown over blue paisley pajamas. "You are not leaving?"

"Well, if it isn't the puppetmaster himself," Connor said with a scowl. "Nice work yesterday, locking us up. Pretty subtle."

"I don't know what you mean," Marcello objected, his face the picture of innocence. "But what is the meaning of this, eh, *figlio? Dove li pensate state andando?"*

"I'm going to Atlanta, if that's what you just asked." Connor shoved a pair of shoes into the side pocket of his duffel bag.

"Ma perchè?"

Connor stopped, straightened, and gave him a look.

"Why? What is the point of this?" Marcello came into the room, arms out, shoulders hunched upward, his entire body asking the question. "Have you told Anne?"

"Huh," Connor scoffed. *"No."* He turned back to his packing.

There were circumstances you didn't know. Things had happened . . . The words had run through his mind all night, like a song he couldn't escape. The words Anne had used that day he'd run into her at the harbor, when she'd tried to tell him why things were different now. She'd said the same thing that day in the summerhouse.

He understood now what circumstances she'd been talking about. Things had happened, all right. Things she wouldn't tell him about yesterday, when he'd asked. Things she would probably never have told him about.

"I see," Marcello said, but his tone said anything but. "Is she the reason you are leaving?"

Connor expelled a deep breath. She sure as hell was. "I'm going because some woman is threatening to go to the papers with a story about an affair she had with my father."

Marcello's body relaxed. "Ah. Your father. And what are you supposed to do about this?"

Connor threw his belt into the bag with more force than necessary. "I don't know. Talk her out of it, I guess."

Marcello snorted.

"Give her money, if I have to. And I suspect I'll have to. Apparently we have an entire foundation set up for this kind of thing." He pushed his toiletry bag into the rapidly filling duffel, forcibly flattening the pile of clothes beneath it.

"Who does? What foundation?"

"We do. The Emorys. For years we've apparently been funding women who would sleep with my father." He threw a ball of socks at the bag. They bounced off and landed on the floor. He threw three more, grinding out words as he tossed them. "We're just—that—kind—of family."

"Il mio ragazzo." *My boy.* Marcello put a firm hand on his shoulder. "Sit down a moment and talk to me. You are upset."

Connor moved away from the hand, picked up the socks on the floor, and punched them into the bag. "I'm not upset."

Marcello shrugged. "All right. I am upset. Sit. For a moment."

Connor gave him an exasperated look.

"Your father," Marcello began, seating himself on the edge of the king-size bed, "he was not a bad man. He was a man of great charm."

Connor scoffed, something like rage bubbling just below his breastbone. "Apparently."

"But he had what we call a wandering eye."

"And hands. And—"

"Yes, well. When one is as charming as your father, wandering eyes are frequently indulged by those upon whom they fall."

"You mean," Connor said through clenched teeth, "when one is as *rich* as my father."

Marcello tipped his head. "Perhaps. Yes, some women are attracted for that reason."

Connor looked him in the eye. "You'd be surprised who's been attracted for that reason."

Marcello chuckled. "You're not trying to surprise me with Patsy, are you?"

Connor sat heavily on the bed, across the suitcase from Marcello. He looked at his hands, fatigue washing over him. "No."

"It was a joke, *figlio*." Marcello looked at him in concern.

Figlio. Son. How Connor wished he *were* Marcello's son.

"I know," Connor said.

Silence hung between them.

"Tell me," Marcello said. "What is it upsetting you? You knew about your father before, yes?"

Connor nodded slowly. "But . . . not everything."

Marcello waited.

"My stepmother," Connor began, choosing each word with care, "has a check, for a great deal of money, made out to—"

He stopped. Did he really want to reveal this to anyone else? Wouldn't that make it more real? Right now it was just between him and Patsy— and Anne, though she didn't know it. If he told Marcello, it would mean he himself believed it. Hell, maybe he did believe it. There was certainly no disputing the check.

Still, it seemed to him that repeating the story would somehow make it true.

Marcello cleared his throat. Connor looked at him; his eyes were on the floor.

"Your father," he said again, "was a good man. A kind man. But he was the sort of man who . . . how shall I say? He could not control his desires. Oftentimes he did not even try to control them. He did not think until later what were the repercussions of his actions."

Connor shook his head. "It's not my father's actions I'm upset about. At least, not entirely."

"Ah, then it is someone connected to your father? Perhaps someone who is . . . Ahhhh." Marcello's eyes widened in comprehension.

"I don't know. I don't know." Connor shook his head and looked at the floor, feeling as if the truth had morphed into something alien and unknowable.

"Let me tell you this," Marcello said, looking at him significantly this time, "and I do not tell you this to hurt you. But Bradford Emory was the kind of man I would not leave my own daughters alone in a room with."

Confused, Connor looked up at him. "What are you saying? He *attacked* these women?"

"I'm saying, *figlio*, that maybe he did not always know when his attentions were not desired."

The look on Marcello's face was compelling.

"Do you—did you *know* about Anne?" Connor asked, his voice a hoarse whisper.

Marcello gave a self-deprecating shrug. "I suspected that is who you were talking about. But no, I know of nothing between Anne and your father."

Connor put his head in his hands, rubbing his palms back along his scalp to his neck. He looked over the suitcase at Marcello. "She took a check, Marcello. Why? Why would she take the money if my father's attentions were not desired?"

Marcello frowned. "You saw this check? You know for a fact this check existed?"

Connor looked at him and nodded. "I saw it, all right. Made out to her, endorsed, cancelled and everything."

Marcello attempted a flippant look. "So how do you know what this check was for? Perhaps it was some sort of bonus. A Christmas present."

Connor laughed cynically. "It was for fifty thousand dollars. That's one helluva bonus."

"*Cinquanta mila . . .*" Marcello repeated softly.

"Yeah. Rationalize that." Connor dropped his head again, closing his eyes.

He thought again about that day, the day she'd broken up with him. They'd gone to the carnival the night before, and he had given her a cheap glass ring he'd won at one of the booths. *Until the real thing comes along*, he'd said, placing it dramatically on her left-hand ring finger. She'd even been wearing it when she'd broken up with him.

What a fool he'd been. She'd probably been laughing at him the whole time. A cheap glass ring or fifty thousand dollars? Tough choice.

"I don't know, *il mio ragazzo*." Marcello's brow was etched with concern, his kind eyes calm but not convinced. "But *she* will."

"She will what?"

"She will know everything. You should ask *her* why she took the money."

Connor sat still a moment. Then he stood up and zipped his duffel bag. "Marcello," he said, hefting the bag onto his shoulder, "right now Anne Sayer is the last person I want to talk to."

*   *   *

Anne spotted them as they disappeared into the copse of pines. Marcello and Connor. Connor had his duffel bag slung over his shoulder, and the staccato sound of the helicopter's blades peppered the air above them.

She ran along the path behind them, whipping aside lolling branches and kicking up pebbles as she went.

She caught up with them in front of the old chapel.

Marcello heard her coming and turned. A step later, Connor turned too. She halted a few feet away.

The look he gave her could have frozen fire.

"Are you *leaving*?" she gasped.

"Yes."

She gaped at him. "For how long? Are you coming back?"

He didn't answer right away, and her stomach plummeted to the ground.

"Were you going to *tell* me?" Her voice was reflexively quieter in the face of his coldness.

Connor's gaze flitted from the garden behind her to the ground, then up to her face.

"No, I wasn't," he said, with a brief flick of his brows. "I guess I wanted to have a secret of my own, Anne. Just like you have."

"What secret? What are you talking about?"

He laughed, looking disgusted. "Nothing." He turned away.

"Connor—"

He slowed, turned back.

She glanced at Marcello. She didn't want to end up getting personal in front of him again, but what did that leave her?

"What about the party?" She grasped at the one straw she had, and felt foolish doing it. "It's just a couple weeks away now."

Connor scowled. "I don't give a damn about the party. You do whatever you want with it."

He started to turn again.

"You can't do that." She took another step toward him, her body so charged with adrenaline that she nearly grabbed his arm and jerked him back to face her. But she stopped at the forbidding expression on his face. "You can't just take off and tell me to do whatever I want. For one thing you know Patsy'll turn the whole thing into a circus. You think she'll listen to me without you here?"

"Make it a goddamn circus then," Connor said, turning fully away.

"Connor!" She reached a hand out, but again did not touch him. "What's going on? I thought— I thought we were . . ."

She glanced again at Marcello.

Connor stopped and looked at her.

Marcello cleared his throat. "I will leave the two of you alone *uno momento.*"

"There's no need—" Connor began, but Marcello stopped him with a raised hand.

"Talk to her, *figlio.* I will tell the pilot you are

coming." He took two steps away, then turned back, scratching thoughtfully behind one ear. "But if you're going to argue anyway, at least argue about the right thing. Tell her, Connor. Tell her you know about the check."

Chapter Seventeen

"What check?" Anne asked. Could all this be about some financial mix-up at the house? Surely he would have questioned her if he didn't understand one of her purchases.

His face was drawn, as if he hadn't slept. "The check, Anne. The fifty-thousand-dollar one."

Relieved, Anne laughed. It *was* some sort of misunderstanding. "Connor, I've never written a check for fifty thousand dollars in my life. You must have read something wrong. Tell me what you're talking about."

"I'm talking about the check," he said, watching her, "that my father wrote to you. I'm talking about the fact that my stepmother apparently"—here he paused, brows raised—"walked in on the two of you, in the middle of . . . something."

Anne felt the blood leave her head in a wave. For a second she thought she might stumble.

So Patsy'd finally told him. The witch had seen that Anne wasn't afraid of her, so instead of threatening Anne again she'd gone straight for Connor.

Maybe Patsy sensed that he'd believe her now.

One thing was certain, she obviously didn't care how much the story would hurt Connor. Connor, who had only just lost the one true parent he'd ever known, would now have to discover that that parent was a reprobate.

Unless Anne kept the truth to herself. And gave him up.

But if she decided not to tell him the truth about that day, would it really preserve his memory of his father? How could it? Surely he wouldn't be better off thinking his father had actually had some kind of affair with her.

"Should I take from your silence that you know the incident I'm talking about?" Connor's voice was quiet and more tired than accusatory.

"I know the incident," she said, but her voice emerged almost too low to be heard. She cleared her throat, clasping her hands together in front of her. "But Connor, it wasn't how it looked. I know what Patsy believed, what she no doubt told you, but it wasn't true. It wasn't like that."

God, how many times had she gone over and over this in her head? How many times had she wished she'd done everything differently?

Connor's face was ashen. "It wasn't *like that*? Are you trying to tell me that you actually—that you cared about my father? That you weren't just after the money?"

"*No!*" She couldn't have been more shocked if he'd hit her. "Connor, I was in love with *you*. I *still* . . ." She stopped, and swallowed over the lump in her throat. "Your father just—he just—it was *nothing*. Not really."

He laughed skeptically. "It was nothing? A whim? An impulse? A bad joke?"

She heard how it sounded. Blood rushed to her face. "I mean, it wasn't an affair. It wasn't even— *nothing happened*. It was like an accident. God, I can't even believe I'm having to tell you this. I never wanted to. I knew how hurt you'd be. But not because there was anything to it. Just because . . . because of the misunderstanding."

His expression was skeptical.

"He was your *father*, Connor. I didn't want to have to tell you what he'd done, the kind of thing he was capable of."

"So you're saying you kept it from me to spare me?"

"Yes! You were trying so hard with him, to get closer, to be the son he wanted. How could I tell you—this? How could I tell you that he wasn't the father you wanted?"

"You couldn't have. Not without also telling me you weren't the girl I wanted."

She closed her eyes briefly. "It wasn't me. I swear to you. How could you think I'd do anything with him? *He* came after *me* one day. He caught me alone in the conservatory and—and just—latched on."

She looked away, feeling the same panic she'd felt the day it had happened. She hadn't known what to do. Mr. Emory had been her employer.

He'd been her boyfriend's father. He'd been belligerent and stubborn and a little bit drunk, she remembered, and she'd been only nineteen years old. She hadn't known she could be indignant, hadn't known she could throw him off, hit him if she had to, and he wouldn't be able to fire her or whatever else it was she'd feared he'd do.

She'd known his reputation, just like the rest of the girls on the staff, so she should have been prepared for something like that to happen. She should have known what to do.

But she had been his son's girlfriend. She'd thought she was protected, immune. She'd been astonished when he'd approached her.

And stupid.

She'd frozen. Like the proverbial deer in the headlights. She'd stood stock-still for several minutes as he'd kissed her and told her how beautiful he thought she was. She'd been repulsed, but she'd thought that if she did nothing to encourage him he would stop. She'd told herself she should push him away, but it had seemed—rude somehow, and disrespectful.

She flushed even now to think how stupid she'd been.

Then he'd tried to open her shirt, and her reflexes had taken over. She'd shoved him away. His hand had caught in her blouse, and the shirt had ripped. She'd been so horrified and ashamed that she'd fled from the room, near tears, and had run smack into Patsy.

Anne regulated her breathing, wondering just what and how much to tell Connor about that day. The man had died not six months ago. How could she tell Connor what a despicable sort he'd been? Even at the time she hadn't wanted to ruin Connor's relationship with his father. His stepmother showed so much favoritism to her own children, Connor's half sisters, Astrid and Deborah, that Anne hadn't wanted to destroy the respect he'd had for his father.

Besides, he'd needed his father's love, she'd thought then. And if she'd told Connor what had happened, he'd have confronted his father, perhaps even fought with him. Nothing good would have come of that.

Just as nothing good would come of sullying the man's memory any further now.

"Connor, it was a misunderstanding. He, I guess, didn't know I wasn't . . . interested. I'm sure it was my fault." The words tasted bad on her tongue. She had a hard time getting them out, but she had to tell him something. And she couldn't tell him that his father—an otherwise distantly nice man—was a frighteningly persistent lecher when he'd been drinking.

"Patsy said she watched you for some time before coming in." Connor's gaze was steady. She could feel it upon her like a weight. "She said you weren't resisting. I asked, Anne."

She raised her eyes to his, aware that she was crimson with shame. "And are you asking *me* now,

Connor? Are you asking me for the truth, or are you simply telling me what you already believe?"

"I think I can tell by your face that the truth I've been told isn't so very different from yours."

She laughed, a strangled sound. It was true, in a twisted way. "So your mind is made up. You believe her story and not mine. Who'd have thought you'd end up trusting Patsy over me, huh, Connor? How we would have laughed at that idea back when we were together."

Connor shook his head. "I didn't believe her, Anne. I believed the check. When I saw that, her story got a great deal more . . . credible."

Anne's glare shot back to his face. "*What* check?"

His expression turned angry, and he took a step toward her. "The fifty-thousand-dollar check, Anne. Or is it just one of so many that you can't remember it?"

She instinctively drew back. "I don't have any fifty-thousand-dollar check!"

He nearly rolled his eyes. "No, not now you don't. Patsy's got it, and believe me, she's keeping it."

"Connor—"

"Do you think I'm an *idiot*?" One hand clenched into a fist at his side, the other, white-knuckled, held the strap of his bag. "It was made out to you. Endorsed, cancelled—you took the money, Anne. You cashed the goddamn check. Why don't you just admit it?"

Anne's heart pumped frantically, fury and fear

surging through her veins like fire. "Connor, I don't know what you're talking about. I didn't take any money. Are you saying I *stole* from you?"

"I never said you *stole* anything," he said impatiently. "In fact, it sounds to me as if you earned it."

Anne put her hands to her head. "Jesus, Connor, just tell me what the hell you're talking about. *What check?*"

"The check my father gave to you as a kiss-off so you wouldn't sue him for sexual harassment."

"*What?*"

"You heard me."

"You think your father gave me fifty thousand dollars?" Her voice rose an octave or two with the question. It was ludicrous. "*When?*"

Connor sighed. "I don't remember. Seems like it was dated a few months after you dumped me. Eleven years ago, Anne, but I can't believe it was so long ago you can't remember. You seem to remember everything else pretty vividly."

Alarm made her limbs go weak. Her mind spun wildly. It had to be something Patsy had cooked up. Something false. Something convincing.

"Connor, you have to believe me. I never took a check from your father. I never had fifty thousand dollars. For god's sake, if I had, what do you think I did with it?"

Connor shrugged elaborately. "Oh, I don't know. Bought a car? Paid off your house? Went to college?"

She felt breathless. All of that was true. Her life was a minefield of things like that, but none of it had been funded by Bradford Emory.

"Connor, I did those things. You obviously know I did. But I paid for the house and the car from my own salary. And college—my grandmother saved and paid for that."

His face took on a frighteningly satisfied expression, and he stretched his hands out to his sides. "And that brings us to your grandmother."

Anne crossed her arms in front of her stomach. Her skin felt cold to the touch. "What about my grandmother?"

"The very one whom you sent to threaten my father with a lawsuit." He cocked his head. "Just too shy to do your own dirty work, weren't you?"

She laughed again, a desperate, hysterical laugh. "*I* threatened *your father?* Try it the other way around, Connor. They threatened me. He and Patsy together. They said they'd tell you everything—"

"I can understand why you'd be afraid of that."

"But it wouldn't have been the real story. Don't you see? Not the one I'm telling you now. Your mother—stepmother—Patsy—I'm sure she believed what she told you. But your father!" She stopped, swallowed hard, and shook her head, gritting her teeth against the awful things she could have said about him.

"I have no illusions about my father's character. But I do know he wouldn't attack anyone."

"I never said he did! He just didn't know when

to stop. And I didn't know how to stop him." She felt tears gathering behind her eyes. "You knew me, Connor. You knew how shy I was, how . . . how deferential. How unassertive. Surely you can see how he might have intimidated me."

Connor laughed once. "Sure. But there's one thing more. The most convincing thing of all. If I know anything about you at all, Anne, it's that you wouldn't take money for nothing."

Anne stood in stunned silence a moment, then started to laugh. "How flattering. Your faith in my integrity is touching, even in the face of your colossal misunderstanding of my character. Think about it, Connor. Who do you really think is lying here? And why? And if you think it's me, then you go ahead and get on that helicopter. We obviously never knew each other at all."

Before the angry tears could drop, she turned on her heel and left.

Anne stalked back down the garden path and slammed into the kitchen. Above the house, the helicopter whirled away into a postcard blue sky.

He'd gotten on the copter. She'd seen him in it as it had lifted over the trees.

"Have you seen Mrs. Emory?" she demanded of a wide-eyed Prin.

"She was in the sunroom, last I looked." Prin turned fully toward her, a shrewd expression on her face. "What's going on, Anne? This have something to do with Connor leaving?"

But Anne was too upset to talk. She gritted her teeth, held her hands up, and kept walking, up the back corridor into the front hall. She turned to look in the sunroom, walked through to the dining room, looped around to the front parlor, then the back parlor and the grand salon.

Nicola walked past the library door as Anne was coming out.

"Excuse me, Nicola," Anne said, enunciating each word clearly for the girl. "Have you seen Mrs. Emory?"

But Nicola, wearing her headphones, didn't hear her. She just smiled when she noticed Anne standing there and kept on walking, nodding her head in time to the tinny rhythm Anne could hear emerging from the headphones.

She took a deep breath and started up the staircase. Her heart thundered in her chest. Years ago she had made this very same trip. Up the stairs, down the long hallway, to the master suite. She'd been summoned there by Mrs. Emory. One of the maids had told Anne in a trembling voice that Mrs. Emory had demanded to see her without delay, she didn't care what Anne was doing.

The maid had looked frightened, Anne remembered thinking. Apparently Mrs. Emory had impressed upon her that if Anne wasn't found immediately heads would roll.

Anne had felt powerless then, as she'd knocked on the door to the master suite sitting room. She'd been certain the summons had had to do with Mr.

Emory's moral lapse in the conservatory. And it hadn't taken a great deal of intuition to know that she was about to be blamed for it.

For a moment, Anne found herself reliving the scene that had changed the course of her life.

"Enter." The word was issued with senatorial solemnity by Mrs. Emory.

Anne slowly opened the door.

The two of them were sitting there—Mr. and Mrs. Emory—in identical armchairs, facing the door like an angry parole board.

"Close the door behind you." Mrs. Emory's face was a thundercloud, radiating hostility with an ugliness that shocked Anne.

She closed the door, feeling sweat break out of every pore on her body. If she'd been unsure of what this meeting was going to be about, she would have figured it out quickly by the way Mr. Emory wouldn't look at her.

Anne thought first of her grandmother, of how angry she would be. She'd warned Anne something like this would happen. She'd told her to be careful around the rich folks, that they took what they wanted and didn't care who paid for it, as long as it wasn't themselves.

But Anne had thought she'd been referring to Connor. And she'd been young, in love, and naïve enough to think her grandmother was too old to know what she was talking about.

Connor. What if he were to find out what his father had done? How would he ever look at her the same way again? His father had *kissed* her! How disgusting was that? How *perverse*. Surely he would blame her a little, just as she blamed herself. And even if he didn't—even if she explained everything and somehow managed to believe herself that she wasn't at least a little responsible for not heading off the situation—he would never be able to *forget* what had happened. Would he?

She wanted to cry when she thought of hurting him that way. He was trying so hard to get closer to his father. They'd even gone fishing last week, though Mr. Emory had shown up for the trip in pressed slacks and Italian leather loafers. There'd always been a distance between them, Connor had told her, that he hoped they could overcome that summer, before he began working for Emory Enterprises.

"I'm sure you know what this meeting is about," Mrs. Emory began, eyeing Anne as if she were a convict caught trying to escape.

"I—I suppose." Anne felt Mr. Emory's eyes upon her and glanced at him, but he looked away.

Neither of them said anything for a long time. They just sat there, Mrs. Emory looking at her with dagger-filled eyes, Mr. Emory sitting stoically, as if required by law to be in attendance.

"I want to know," Mrs. Emory said, "what you think we should do about this?"

Anne started. "What I think?"

"Yes, dear," Mrs. Emory said slowly, "I imagine

you do think every once in a while, don't you?"

Anne's spine straightened. "I—I'm not sure what you mean. I . . ." She looked at Mr. Emory, who had picked up a book from the small table between the chairs and was leafing through it. "I don't think anything should be done. It was just a mistake."

"A *mistake*, you say?" Mrs. Emory's chin lowered, her eyes still on Anne.

"Yes. Nothing happened, really. I—I'm . . . all right. I've nearly forgotten about it." She laughed lightly, threw her hands out to the side.

Mrs. Emory looked at her as if she were even more stupid than previously imagined.

Anne knew the Emorys weren't worried about her—they were worried about her telling someone, exposing Mr. Emory. They'd want to be sure she'd be discreet, and she was ready to tell them she would.

"Forgotten!" Mrs. Emory managed to laugh without even a bitter semblance of a smile. "You throw yourself at my husband and now you claim to have forgotten about it?"

"No! That's not what I meant. I didn't—"

"That's what you just said." Mrs. Emory glanced at her husband. "We both heard it. Didn't we, dear?"

Mr. Emory cleared his throat and answered without looking up from his book. "That's right." His tone was bored. Not ashamed. Not upset. *Bored.*

Anne gaped at him.

"Anne." Mrs. Emory's curt tone drew Anne's attention back to her. "You know we could fire you for this."

Anne had trouble breathing. How would she support her grandmother? How would she *ever* save enough to go to school?

"God knows, that's what I wanted to do. But my husband is more forgiving." She took his hand from where it lay on the arm of the chair. Anne wondered just how tight her grip was. "He says we should let you stay."

Mrs. Emory looked at her expectantly.

Anne clasped her hands together. They were damp with sweat. "Th-thank you." The words emerged as a question.

"However," Mrs. Emory drew the word out, seeming to relish it. "We have conditions."

Another silence.

"Conditions?" Anne asked. If they wanted her participation, repetition was the best she was going to be able to do.

"You must—and there is no negotiation on this. None. You must give up Connor. Let him go."

Anne exhaled. "What?"

Mrs. Emory sat forward in her chair, speaking with bared teeth. "Break things off with him. Tell him it's over. Break his heart if you must, but *end it*. Today."

Anne looked desperately from one to the other of them. "But you're leaving tomorrow. There's no need. You'll be gone, and I'll be here. I promise I won't write to him. I won't call." She stopped and tried to swallow, but her mouth was parched. "Surely you don't want me to hurt him."

Anne's chest ached at the very thought.

"Anne, listen to me," Patsy said sternly. "You know as well as I do that you don't belong with a boy like Connor. He's a blue blood, in the truest sense of the word. His ancestry goes straight back to the Mayflower. He is an American aristocrat, a cut above everyone else, now, isn't he?"

Anne blinked rapidly. "Yes."

And he was. More than a cut. He was head and shoulders above anyone else she had ever known.

"And you . . ." Patsy looked almost sadly at Anne, shaking her head. "Well, you're a working girl, aren't you? Who were your parents? Working people. There's nobility in that, Anne. Nobility in knowing and sticking to your place in the world. Surely you didn't think that anything would ever come of your relationship with Connor." Mrs. Emory's brows rose.

Anne blushed. "Come of it?"

"I mean, you couldn't honestly believe that Connor would ever, for example, *marry* you." Mrs. Emory laughed at the idea.

Anne shook her head. "No," she answered honestly. "No, I've never believed that."

But oh, how she'd wanted to. How she'd dreamed of it.

Mrs. Emory sat back, apparently satisfied. "All

I'm asking you to do, then, is give him up now. Before he breaks your heart. Because you know he will. He'll be going out into the world this fall, working for Emory Enterprises. He has a very prestigious future ahead of him. A future that you would never fit into." She laughed again lightly and looked at Anne as if she might join in. "My goodness, can you imagine yourself at a charity ball, Anne? Having a closet full of cocktail dresses and drawers full of diamond jewelry? Can you imagine chatting with senators and congressmen? Ambassadors from other countries? Can you imagine representing Connor to other captains of industry at society events?"

She laughed again and shook her head.

"Anne, you've seen the kinds of parties we have here," she concluded. "They're nice, aren't they? But these are nothing like the ones we have in Atlanta. My goodness, this is our *country* home!"

Anne could not even pretend to laugh along. It was all too true for her. She *couldn't* imagine charity balls and cocktail dresses. Speaking to congressmen and ambassadors. When she'd dreamed of marrying Connor, it had always been here that it had taken place, and this life that they'd lived.

Mrs. Emory brushed each of her cheeks with one hand, as if tears of mirth had leaked from her eyes. "Ah well. Chances are he'd never come back here anyway."

Then why are you so worried about me? Anne

wanted to ask. She gripped her fingers so hard that they hurt.

Mrs. Emory frowned. "But I want to be sure he doesn't waste any time thinking about you. I want to be sure he knows that you understand it's over. That there is no coming back. You must tell him you do not want him."

"But why—"

Mrs. Emory stood up. Mr. Emory's eyes jerked from the book to his wife, as if awakened from a nap.

"*What?*" she demanded of Anne.

Anne felt as if her insides were melting, as if her brain was dripping down into her body, unable to form a coherent thought.

"I was just going to ask," she began.

"Speak up, girl, I can barely hear you!" Mrs. Emory walked toward her slowly. When she reached her, standing too close for Anne's comfort, she began walking around her, looking her up and down.

"I was going to ask," Anne said, in a louder voice that quavered nonetheless, "why we can't just let it die naturally. He's leaving anyway, why do I have to hurt him?"

Mrs. Emory rounded her other side and fixed her with a hard, cold stare. Anne looked away.

"Because if you don't," Mrs. Emory said, standing so close that Anne could smell her breath, "we will fire you. And we will blackball you from here to New Hampshire. How will you live then,

Anne? How will *your grandmother* live? How? In addition I will tell Connor everything that went on between you and my husband. That you threw yourself at him. That you even took off your shirt. Don't you think *that* will hurt him more?"

"But—Mr. Emory—*you* know what happened . . ." Anne reflexively extended a pleading hand in his direction.

Mrs. Emory walked through it, pushing it aside with her own.

"My husband will corroborate everything I say, of course. He will tell Connor what you've really been after, Anne Sayer. Money. And Connor will believe us. Why wouldn't he? We're his parents. And when he understands what your character really is, he'll have no trouble believing you capable of figuring out who you might get more money from, the father or the son."

Chapter Eighteen

Anne's hand shook as she knocked on the sitting room door. She didn't know if it was from rage, or fear that she'd revert back to the frightened young girl she'd been. Part of her fully expected to see Patsy in the armchair facing the door when she entered, the ghost of her dead husband beside her.

After her knock, Anne heard a rustling behind the door, then the voice of Patsy Emory, unchanged over the course of a decade, came through the heavy portal. "Enter."

Anne steeled herself, fixed Patsy's lie firmly in her mind, and opened the door.

Patsy stood by her dresser, one drawer open, folding what looked like a silk nightgown.

"Why, Anne," she said, smiling coolly. She dropped the shimmering pink fabric into the drawer. "I didn't expect to see you."

"Didn't you?" Anne asked.

She stood just inside the door with her hands clasped before her. She was determined not to show her anger, determined to be the calm, rational, *sane* one in this war of wills.

Still, she would not leave this room until she saw this mythical "check" for fifty thousand dollars. She wanted to see her endorsement, the bank upon which it was drawn, and the account it was deposited into. She wanted each and every piece of evidence she could get her hands on that Patsy Emory was a conniving liar.

Patsy pushed the drawer closed and turned fully to her. "Of course not. Come in and have a seat." She motioned toward the armchairs by the dormant fireplace.

The chairs were situated in their normal, friendly arrangement, angled toward each other, facing the hearth. They'd been re-covered since that long-ago day, too, but Anne remembered well how they'd borne the weight of the Emory's condescension.

Anne waited until Patsy sat, then said, "I'd rather stand, thank you."

Patsy's brows lowered in an expression that was no doubt meant to convey concern, but Anne could tell she was irked. She didn't like having to look up at Anne.

"However you're most comfortable."

"I'm sure you know why I'm here, Mrs. Emory." Anne's voice was steady, as was her gaze.

Patsy raised her hands, palms up, and shook her head. Her expression was all innocence. "I'm afraid I don't, dear. What's on your mind?"

Dear?

Anne took a deep breath. "What's on my mind

is fifty thousand dollars. Specifically, a check you have made out to me for that amount. As it would come in quite handy right now—I'm sure you know I'm about to lose my job—I'd appreciate your giving it to me." She held out her hand.

Patsy's face darkened, and she dropped all pretense of a friendly demeanor. "I only have one check for that amount, and I'm afraid you've already cashed it. As you are perfectly aware."

Anne's limbs began to tremble with anger. "Why don't you save us both some time, Mrs. Emory, and at least speak the truth when we're alone together. Connor's gone, you managed to chase him off pretty neatly so he won't hear you expose your own lies. What did you show him that made him think I'd taken money from you?"

Patsy stood, her little body a cannon tilted toward Anne. "I showed him the money you *took*, Anne. If either of us is playing games right now, it's you. I wouldn't be surprised if you had some sort of hidden tape recorder, hoping to catch me saying something you could twist to your own ends. You always were clever at pulling the wool over the Emory men's eyes. But the fact remains, missy, that I have the check my husband wrote to you and that you cashed. The *payoff* for your disgusting behavior."

Anne had expected her to play dirty, but she hadn't expected this. Outrageous, outlandish lies spoken straight to her face. She didn't even know how to respond.

Anne took a step toward her on wooden legs, her entire body shot through with astonishment. "Mrs. Emory, you and I *both* know that I did nothing wrong that day. Your husband cornered me—the way he cornered countless women in your employ, and out, for all I know—and you just happened to walk in as I was attempting to fend him off."

"Oh, please—"

"And you *also* know that I never, ever, in my wildest dreams—or yours—took money from you or your morally reprehensible husband. Least of all fifty thousand dollars!" Anne threw a hand out with the words. "I wouldn't even know what to do with such a sum."

Patsy's lips curved into a cool smile, and she sat down again. Anne felt her stomach plummet. In the war of *calm* wills, Patsy was already winning. Anne had to get hold of herself.

"Are you *trying* to get fired, Miss Sayer?" Patsy held her hands together in front of her, fingers tented and elbows resting on the chair. "Because you're coming awfully close. To accuse my husband—to denigrate him when he's barely six months in his grave—"

"I've said nothing that isn't true."

"*That* is a matter of opinion."

"Show me," Anne said through gritted teeth. "Show me what you showed Connor."

"What I showed Connor?" Patsy's brows rose fractionally. She didn't try very hard to look ignorant, but she obviously wasn't going to give anything away.

"I want to see the check," Anne said. "I demand to know exactly what you've concocted to manipulate Connor away from me again."

Patsy drew herself slowly out of the chair, her eyes like bullets. "How dare you demand anything of me. I have never been spoken to like this in my life."

"I'm sorry to hear it. You'd have been the better for it." Anne held herself rigid.

Patsy glared at her, then swept over to the closet, threw open the door, and reached in. As she bent toward the floor, Anne briefly envisioned herself pushing the hapless woman in, locking the door, and keeping her there until she confessed.

But it was just a fantasy. A really, really tempting one.

Patsy emerged from the closet with a burgundy leather briefcase, which she took to the bed and threw upon its surface. It bounced lightly on the plush mattress. With a swift click of the clasps, she pulled the lid up and yanked from it a file folder. Then she strode the four steps toward Anne and thrust the thin folder at her.

Anne's name was typed neatly on a label at the top. The sight of this sent a chill through her. It was like an FBI file. She wondered what other names were typed on the files in that briefcase.

With shaking hands, she flipped open the cover

and saw a long blue check, covered with the stamps and faded inks of cancellation. The top left corner read *Bradford R. Emory, Personal Account*. The Pay To line read *Anne Sayer* in a bold, masculine script. Below that, the words *Fifty Thousand and no/100* were slashed. The signature was definitely Bradford Emory's.

Her first thought was, How long ago was this ruse devised?

The date of the check was October 2, 1992. The cancellation marks all read October 3.

Anne's second thought was to turn the check over.

There, at the top of the check, in her grandmother's unmistakable spidery scrawl, were the words *Deposit Only*.

The breath left her in one fell swoop. A chill swept over her skin, making her feel hot and cold at the same time. She thought she might pass out.

"Any questions?" Patsy drawled.

Anne felt like screaming, like ripping the check up and throwing it in her face. No, like throwing something heavier, one of the armchairs maybe, in her face.

Her head spun and her heart raced. "This check is real."

She'd meant it to be a question. But there was no question. She'd been paid, all right, and her grandmother had taken the money.

More importantly, Connor had seen this check. And Connor had thought *she'd* taken the money.

"Of course it's real," Patsy said impatiently. "And you can play dumb all you like, but you were compensated, and compensated quite handsomely, for your little affair with my husband."

Anne fixed her with a hard look, desperation clouding her vision. All she could see was Connor's tired face as he'd headed for the helipad.

This had hurt him. He had begun to believe in her, and he'd been betrayed, by the same woman, again.

But that woman was not Anne.

"You know perfectly well I had no 'affair' with your husband. You're not stupid, Patsy," she said in the most scathing tone she'd ever used on another human being. "You knew what your husband was like. And yet you put up with it because what else were you going to do? Divorce him? Give up all that money and status and prestige?"

"That's *enough*." Patsy slashed a hand diagonally through the air with the words.

Anne glared at her, then continued in a low voice. "He even, in this instance, did you a favor, didn't he? You needed a way to get rid of me, and he gave you one. How fortunate for you. Or did you plan it together?"

Anne nearly gasped as her own deduction rang true. *Of course.* Why had she never thought of this before? She'd always been baffled by the fact that Connor's father would go after her, knowing she was Connor's girlfriend. It hadn't made any sense.

But now . . . What perfect faith they'd had in her, Bradford and Patsy. How well they must have known her, in a twisted sort of way, to be so sure that she would never in a million years tell Connor what his father had done.

Bradford Emory had been safe making a move on her, and he'd known it.

"You knew it wasn't an affair, didn't you?" Anne said, wonderment coloring her voice. "You knew it because you *planned* it. It was all a plot."

Patsy leaned an elbow on the wing of the chair she'd been sitting in. "Call it whatever you want, Anne. Whatever lets you sleep at night. A plot. An affair. A seduction." Her mouth hardened. "An investment in your future."

"This had nothing to do with my future." Anne had trouble getting the words out. Her throat closed with helpless anger. They'd been so much more devious than she'd ever imagined. How would she ever dispute this? It had been too well planned. Too coordinated. Too overwhelming.

She felt herself shrinking before the woman's hatred.

"You're right," Patsy said. "It had to do with Connor's future. You were never important. You were just an annoyance." She put one hand on her hip. "You couldn't even have been that important to him, did you ever think of that? Think about it now, Anne. Consider the fact that I never had to show him that check until yesterday."

Anne stood still, her breathing shallow.

She was right. Anne had often had that very thought herself, that if Connor had really loved her surely he would have contacted her at some point in the years after he'd left that last summer.

But he never had. Even after she'd sent him the note when his father had died, she'd heard nothing.

And the only reason she was seeing him again now was that he was selling the place and getting away from her forever.

Defeat washed over her. She looked down at the check in her hands.

Patsy had won again.

Anne's shock gave way to a cold calm. Something inside her couldn't accept it. People couldn't do this, they couldn't manipulate others' lives for their own ends. This wasn't a soap opera—this was her *life*. And Patsy Emory was not going to shape it for her. Not again.

Anne looked back up at her. "But you did have to show it to him," she said. "Even after eleven years, you still needed to use this check—this half-truth—to get him away from me." She shook her head, a slight smile on her lips. "*You* think, Patsy. You think about *that*."

Patsy walked to the door, opened it, and stood imperially next to it. "I want you to leave this room immediately, Anne Sayer. You've had your say, more than you deserved. Now get out of here before I have the police take you away."

"The police," Anne repeated with a laugh. She

crumpled the check in her hand and let it drop to the floor. It didn't matter what happened to it now. Connor had seen it.

"I don't like to resort to threats, Anne, but you seem to require them no matter what the situation. I want you to leave this house and not come back. You are *fired*. Do you understand me? And if you choose to speak of this to anyone, I will personally make sure your name is dragged through the mud of this town until everyone knows what a harlot you truly are. No one will trust you within a mile of their husbands. Do you think any of the society women on this island will hire you to plan so much as an afternoon snack once they hear what I've got to say? These women are my *friends*, Anne. They will listen to me. And I'll tell them everything."

Anne shook her head and spoke quietly. "I don't need your friends, Patsy."

"And they don't need you. But that's not all, Miss High-and-Mighty. I'll invent the most heinous, disgraceful reasons for why I let you go now, and I'll make sure they're heard from one end of Candlewick Island to the other. It won't matter whether or not they're true," she said lightly. "It will only matter that everyone hears them. And that everyone will include Delores Sayer."

For a second, Anne pictured her frail grandmother in her nightcap, her spindly legs covered in the nursing home's thick, industrial sheets. And she thought about how her grandmother was the one who'd enabled Patsy to bring this whole thing on now. If it hadn't been for Delores Sayer's manipulation this would all just be behind them. Nothing but ugly stories with no proof.

"As I recall," Patsy continued, "Delores was always deathly afraid of a scandal, was she not?"

Anne looked at her as if she were seeing the face of the devil for the first time.

Deathly afraid, Anne thought. Truer words had never been spoken. Despite her grandmother's complicity in all this, if it were to be aired in public, in her grandmother's declining state it could kill her. And this woman—this hateful, powerful woman—was just the one to do it.

Anne's blood boiled. The woman was trying to corner her again. To blackmail her with the emotions of another to keep her from doing what was right and fair and true. Well, it wasn't going to happen again. Not this time. Anne was going to salvage what she could from this fire, and if nothing else it was going to be her own sense of destiny.

A steely calm descended upon her. "You can't fire me, Mrs. Emory," she said. "Connor is in charge of this house now, and Marcello will be after him. So I do not accept your invitation to leave my position early."

"What? There was no *invitation*," Patsy sputtered.

"As for your ruining me on this island, you're welcome to try. I believe I have more sway with these people than you do, at least with the ones whose opinions I care about, and the rest, well . . ." She shrugged. "I can take or leave them. You can even threaten me with telling the story you told Connor, going out on a limb and slandering your husband just months after his death. But how bad would that make *you* look, Patsy? I'm sure you've thought about that, though."

"I could tell—"

"And you can say what you will," Anne spoke imperviously over Patsy's voice. "But my grandmother is an old woman who has lived through far worse things than having her granddaughter lied about by a woman who hasn't visited the island in a decade, and who by all accounts is a few marbles shy of a set in her own right."

Anne was so angry at her grandmother for cashing that check she half hoped Patsy *would* spread the scandal.

"So tell your cronies what I've supposedly done," she continued. "Make up more things, if you want, there's nothing and no one to stop you. But I, for one, will not be ruled by your deceitful blackmail anymore. You can no longer intimidate me."

Anne stopped, took a deep breath, and ran her damp palms down the sides of her skirt. "Now if you'll excuse me, I have a party to plan."

Patsy's face was nearly purple. *"You,"* she

breathed with perfect Hollywood villain venom, "will live to regret this day. I will see you humiliated beyond—"

"Good day, Mrs. Emory." Anne inclined her head courteously and swept past her out the door.

"Gramma," Anne said, modulating her voice to keep the hard edge off of it as she opened the curtains in her grandmother's room. Late afternoon sunlight blazed through the windows. "I need to ask you something."

Anne's anger and worry had worn her down to a state of near emotionless fatigue. She'd gone home immediately after talking to Mrs. Emory and had tried to calm down, but her thoughts had been a roiling, tumultuous mess.

In an attempt to find perspective, she'd reminded herself of all the reasons she'd broken up with Connor all those years ago. No matter what she told herself now, no matter how much she wanted to blame Patsy and Bradford for destroying her future, she knew it hadn't been entirely because of the debacle with Connor's father that she'd given Connor up.

The fact was, she had known Connor wasn't going to marry her, and the thought of spending years waiting for the two or three weeks each summer he might be able to visit, of wondering what he was doing in Atlanta all winter and agonizing about him meeting someone else, of finding everyone else inadequate because her heart was held by a man so incomparable no one could hold a candle to him, had scared her to death.

She'd seen her future becoming just like her mother's past. Her mother had essentially withered away pining for the man she naively called her fiancé, turning away all other suitors because there was only one man she'd wanted. But that man had left and never came back, dying in an accident just months after abandoning her pregnant mother.

Anne might have been a simple island girl, content with the small and ordered life of Candlewick, but she'd had no intention of letting history repeat itself. Her mother had become someone pathetic, someone living for a pipe dream. Anne would not follow suit and pin her hopes on a fantasy that had very little chance of coming true.

Of course, she hadn't planned to break things off with him. She had thought she would wait and see how the coming months went, see if her relationship with Connor would change with his going to work instead of school. If he'd continued to talk about a future, if he'd continued to keep in touch and even talk about her coming to Atlanta, she might have allowed herself to hope.

But then along had come Patsy Emory and her ugly scheme. The hand of Fate, Anne had thought at the time. Not only had Patsy threatened to expose her for something she wasn't but she'd also put into hard words all the fears Anne had had about any future she might have had in Connor's life, and about what might have been expected of her if the improbable had become reality. Patsy had intimidated her into seeing that she would never have fit into Connor's real world, and that eventually Connor would have grown to resent her for it.

That had been the biggest reason she'd broken up with Connor. And that was why she'd foolishly believed they might be able to start anew now that he was back.

She wasn't the same scared girl she'd been in 1992. She'd matured in ways she hadn't thought would be possible when she was nineteen years old. Making her living throwing parties and catering to the wealthy people who owned most of Candlewick Island's properties had taught her how to deal with the elite. It had also taught her that they weren't so very different from everyone else.

Over the years she had actually engaged in conversations with congressmen and "captains of industry," the very people with whom Patsy had tried to scare her. She had hobnobbed with foreign dignitaries and even joked with the Canadian ambassador at Sea Bluff functions.

She could handle Connor's life now.

She'd just never have the chance.

Still, Anne had to get to the bottom of what had happened. She'd needed to talk to her grandmother, but she couldn't just have gone barging into the nursing home and accusing the old woman of sabotaging her. No matter what her grandmother had done, she was too old to pay for it now.

So Anne had calmed down. And now, here she was, exhausted, but on a mission for the truth.

Delores Sayer sat in her bed, in a pink-and-blue flowered robe. Her body appeared tiny in the billowing robe, and her face was as lined and weathered as a beach piling. Still, she wore pink lipstick and had curlers in her hair.

"Well, go ahead and ask," her grandmother said, in a voice incongruously strong compared to her slight body. "I'm not going anywhere."

Anne faced her. "Where did you get the money to pay my college tuition?"

Her grandmother, pulling spongy pink curlers from her hair with gnarled fingers, paused. "I told you. I put by money over the years. And there was a little inheritance from your grandfather." She continued pulling out the curlers and dropping them in her lap.

"But Gramma." Anne turned back to her. "When I looked into college after high school you said there was no way we could afford it."

Her grandmother's thin shoulders rose and fell in a shrug. "Really? I don't remember."

"So how did you suddenly come up with the money not three years later? Surely you didn't have forty thousand dollars 'put by' that you'd forgotten about earlier," Anne said, thinking she must have been the most gullible person in the world not to have questioned it before.

Delores pulled the last of the curlers from her hair and began pushing at the iron gray curls with unsteady hands. "I told you, I don't remember."

"I think you do." Anne came to the bedside and moved the chair from against the wall so that it faced her grandmother. "I think the source of that money was probably a pretty memorable event for you."

"What are you getting at, girl? Don't pussyfoot around, just say it." The words were tough but Delores's fingers patted and pinched the curlers in her lap nervously.

"I found out about the money, Gramma." Anne's voice was hard. "I know about the fifty thousand dollars."

Her grandmother's jaw worked, as if rearranging her false teeth, and her rheumy eyes stayed defiantly on Anne's face.

"Aren't you going to say anything?" Anne asked.

"That man *owed* it to you. That Bradford Emory," she spat the name. "Oh, wasn't he a piece of work. Taking advantage of everyone on the island like he owned every single one of us. Well, he wasn't going to take advantage of the Sayers. We've been through enough hard times. *They* knew you weren't going to stand up for yourself, but I could."

Anne's breathing accelerated. "What do you mean? What did you do?"

"I went up there to that house and I talked to the son of a bitch."

Anne still winced when her grandmother swore. For years Delores had been a model of propriety, but during the last few she'd seemed to have given up holding back.

"Oh, he tried to weasel out of it," Delores continued. "He simpered and apologized and even tried to say that you asked for it, but I wasn't having any of that. I set him in his place but good. That man wasn't getting away with any of that bullcrap with me."

"Oh my God," Anne breathed. It was true. It was all true. It was all unbelievably, horribly true.

"We both knew what we were talking about," Delores continued, warming to her story. "He was a lecherous old bastard who tried to take advantage of you. You, a pretty, innocent little girl. Damn near scared you out of your wits, too, I recall. Don't think I didn't know we could have sued them, either, rotten rich bastards, and I told them I knew it. I was an old woman even then, but I've never been stupid." She made a fist, misshapen by arthritis, and brought it down decisively on the curlers. "They paid up but good once I told them, too. Sent you to college. Got you a good education."

Anne closed her eyes. "Oh, God, Gramma." The pride, the defiance, the raw *protectiveness* in her grandmother's words diffused much of Anne's anger.

"And I didn't use any of that money for myself. No, ma'am." She shook her head vehemently. "It all went to you and your education. There's even a little bit left over, but that's safe in a bank account. You'll get it when I go." She nodded to herself. "They paid up, just as they should have."

"But Gramma—"

"Don't you 'but Gramma' me. You should be thanking me, is what you should be doing. I went up there and got you your due from those people."

Anne remembered how desperately she'd wanted to hide from her grandmother that day. She'd left for home immediately, but her clothes had been torn and she couldn't stop crying, and the second she'd walked into the house her grandmother had spotted her.

It might have been a small thing, she thought now, if it had just been allowed to fade away. Instead it had mushroomed without her even knowing it into an ugly scandal waiting to explode.

"But Gramma, you gave them proof. You gave them something to tell—to *show*—Connor. Or anyone else, for that matter. It was probably worth every penny to them."

Her grandmother looked at her with sad eyes. "He wasn't ever going to be yours, Anne. You knew that. You'd have stood on your pride and let his parents walk all over you, and for what? So he'd think well of you when he went back to his rich world and married some socialite?"

"At least what he'd known about me would have been the truth," Anne said. "Now . . ." She shook her head.

"The truth. Huh. He should know the truth

anyway. You didn't do anything. It was his father. And me. I wasn't going to sit by and let them take advantage of you like that. They knew you were a nice, quiet girl, but they didn't count on me." She cackled proudly. "No siree, they didn't count on me."

"Actually, Gramma, maybe they did." The weight of the world seemed to be bound to Anne's heart, dragging it so low in her chest that she felt sick.

"What do you mean?" Delores's eyes narrowed.

Anne shook her head. "They saved that check, Gramma. The cancelled check. And Patsy showed it to Connor. He left this morning believing I had an affair with his father. That's what Patsy told him, and he believed it as soon as he saw that check. I don't think he's ever coming back."

Delores was silent a long time.

Anne sat looking at her hands in her lap. She'd never felt so defeated. She'd been paid off. It didn't matter that she hadn't known it until this minute. She had been compensated, as Patsy had put it, and compensated handsomely. For an incident that had lasted all of two minutes and cost her the love of her life.

"If Connor Emory believed that," Delores said finally, "if he decided to trust that wretched woman's story instead of trusting what he knows about you, then he doesn't deserve you."

Anne laughed sadly. "All he knows about me, Gramma, is that I'm the one who dumped him for no reason he could discern. Until now. Now he thinks I dumped him for his father."

"Then you tell him to come talk to me, if you're so dead set on having him." Delores's old voice rasped fiercely. "I'm the one saw your face. I'm the one saw you crying hysterically, scared and ashamed and fearing it was *you* who'd done something wrong when that man mistreated you. I'm the one who sewed up your shirt, too. How many women having an affair get their shirt ripped open? Yes, you tell Connor Emory to come and talk to *me* about what his father did. I got no qualms about telling that spoiled boy what his old man was really like. And I'll tell him what I did to make it right."

Anne sighed, a lump in her throat. Her grandmother had done it for her, she believed that wholeheartedly. Delores had honestly thought she was doing the right thing.

But it couldn't have been more wrong if it had been scripted.

"You can't tell him anything, Gramma. He's gone."

Chapter Nineteen

He came at me, stumbling a little, and just grabbed on. At first I thought I'd done something inadvertently, smiled the wrong way or looked at him too long, something that would make him think I'd invited him into my room with me. But then I realized he'd been drinking.

The words could have been Anne's, Connor thought, watching the Maine coastline run beneath him like the white lines on the highway. But they weren't. They were Diana Bell's, and she hadn't been asking for seven million dollars. She'd found an old check from his father for seventy thousand that she'd tried to cash and couldn't.

No, I wouldn't call it an attack. It was more like having a dinner guest you couldn't get rid of sitting on your couch. Only instead of the couch, he was hanging on me, telling me how beautiful I was, how kind, how gentle. It's really hard to throw someone off who says that kind of thing. And who seems so sad.

His father had sent the check to her parents' house years ago, with a note explaining why. He hadn't known, Diana explained, that she and her parents hadn't spoken for years. They hadn't even opened the envelope. They'd just stuck it in a box with a bunch of her other stuff.

The good news was, she and her parents had reconciled. The bad news was, she'd found the check and it was now too old to be cashed.

"We're about ten minutes out, Mr. Emory," the helicopter pilot said.

Connor nodded and gave him a thumbs-up.

The other interesting thing about Diana Bell's story was that she said his father was renowned for going after the pretty, young employees. Most of them treated it like a joke. He was never scary or brutal. Some of them didn't know how to handle it, though, and would quit. That's why there was so much turnover, Diana explained. Not because they were all having affairs with him.

Connor thought about the file folder full of checks made out to various women. Maybe they'd taken the money as settlement for being harassed. If that were the case, he certainly wouldn't blame them. His father's conduct had been inexcusable.

He thought again about Anne, about how insistent she'd been that nothing had happened. And about how she'd probably brought it on herself.

She had been, he saw clearly, doing what she'd

always done—taking the blame for something that was not her fault.

The Anne of old had always been feeling guilty about one thing or another that could not possibly have been her fault. Usually it had been something with regard to her grandmother, whom Connor had wanted to throttle on a regular basis for unfairly burdening Anne.

Maybe it was the fact that the new Anne seemed so confident. And capable. And sexy and desirable. Connor closed his eyes and clenched his teeth. He'd been jealous, and that was why he hadn't been able to believe she'd been innocent in the affair. Jealous of a situation in which an old man had come on to a young, pretty girl.

He rubbed a hand over his face. He owed her an apology. He just didn't know how to make it big enough.

He'd been gone nearly three weeks. He'd gotten home to a slew of mail about real estate inquiries he'd made, most of them in California, and he'd had to wait almost a week before being able to meet with Diana Bell.

During that time he'd also been in close contact with Marcello about the sale of the house. He'd had to procure various documents from the safe-deposit box in Atlanta and fax papers and signatures back and forth for the closing, which had taken place the previous Monday without Connor's presence.

Then he'd packed up his belongings, put them

in storage, and put his condo on the market. He wouldn't be going back to Atlanta.

The helicopter circled over Sea Bluff and descended. He'd arranged for Franklin, the gardener, to meet him with a car. He wasn't ready to go into the house just yet. Since the place was teeming with caterers, florists, musicians, guests, and an entire television crew, he didn't think he'd be noticed arriving and then driving right by the house.

Connor threw his bags in the trunk and shook Franklin's hand.

"Thanks for your discretion, Franklin," Connor said. Then, on a whim, he asked, "Found that treasure yet?"

Franklin looked startled, his milky blue eyes growing wide in his face. "Treasure, sir?"

Connor laughed as he dipped into the driver's seat. "Guess you're just going to have to keep looking, then."

Franklin ducked his head. "Yes, sir. Thank you, sir." Amazement tinged his gravelly voice.

Connor started the car, one of the mansion's Toyotas kept for the guests, and U-turned away from the helipad. He passed the house, circled the drive on the far side, and headed for town.

The day was crisp and clear, perfect for the party that was to be held that night. Marcello had told him all was in order when he'd called a final time the night before. Marcello also said he'd been successful at keeping Patsy at bay, allowing Anne time, space, and support to get the whole thing organized.

The television crew had been coming and going for the last two days, setting up shots, making sure the lighting was adequate, and ensuring that the decorations would not get in the way of the cameras and vice versa. Some corporate bigwigs had also arrived for the party, so helicopters had been in and out of Sea Bluff all day, which was just what Connor wanted. He didn't want Anne to know he was back. Not yet.

As he neared town, he slowed the car and headed past the grocery store. He turned the corner and drove slowly by Anne's little clapboard house, looking at the plants hanging on the front porch and wondering who she'd sat on that porch swing with in the last eleven years. He shoved aside regret that it had never been him. *Life takes you in many strange directions*, he thought, *but if you get back to the one you started out on, you're lucky.*

He drove up the hill on the other side of town to the long, low building that was the Candlewick nursing home. He parked the car and walked slowly into the lobby.

"Can I help you, sir?" A pert voice from behind a counter to his left drew his attention.

A girl in a pink-striped apron looked at him with interest.

"Yes, I called yesterday. My name is Emory, Connor Emory. I'm here to see Delores Sayer."

The girl's eyes widened. "Oh, yes, Mr. Emory,

sir. Of course." She giggled, then quickly stifled it. "I heard you were coming. I'm so sorry for not recognizing you."

"Have we met?"

She giggled again. "Oh, no, sir. It's just, we all know who you are. I mean, you know, your name. And your house. Because we all know Mrs. Sayer's granddaughter, Anne, who works there, you know."

He smiled. "Yes I know. Is Mrs. Sayer up?"

"Oh! Let me just check." She picked up a phone.

He looked around the lobby. It was clean and fairly welcoming. The floor was carpeted in a deep burgundy, and the front desk was made of some dark wood. Large ferny plants stood in the corners, and the lighting was overhead but not fluorescent.

From here he could see what must be the public room. An old woman sat on the couch with a younger man and woman. A toddler with a beaming smile hung onto her knobby knee without regard to its fragility.

Across the room an old man in a wheelchair sat nodding in the sunlight from a window, a book open on his lap.

"Right this way, Mr. Emory," the striped girl said. "I'll show you to her room. She's expecting you."

Connor had a lot he could say in response to that. He knew Delores Sayer would be expecting something, but he was pretty sure it wasn't what he had in mind.

He followed the girl down a silent hallway that smelled of rubbing alcohol and Lysol. Occasionally they'd pass a door through which the sound of a television blared, but for the most part the hall was library-quiet.

They stopped at room number 3, and the girl knocked briskly, opening the door well before the raspy voice inside bade them enter.

"Here we are!" the striped girl chirped. "This is Mr. Emory. Do you remember we told you he was coming?"

"I know who he is," Delores growled. "I've been expecting him for years."

Connor strode past the receptionist into the room and turned to the wizened little woman in the bed. "Hello, Mrs. Sayer."

She nodded once, her face a prune of discontent. "I guess you think I should be honored by a visit from an almighty Emory." She turned her head to the young girl. "Well? What else do *you* want?"

The girl blushed. "Oh! Nothing. I just wanted to be sure you remem—that is, that everything was all right. You don't need anything, do you?"

"I need a new bag of bones and some lipstick, but I don't expect any of that from you." Delores raised a haughty eyebrow at the girl.

"Okay." She sidled for the door, her perky smile wavering. "Good day, then." She glanced at Connor and renewed her smile, blushing deeper as she closed the door behind her.

"You might as well sit down." Delores indicated the chair against the wall with a gnarled hand.

Connor moved toward it.

"Anne usually sets it over here, so I can see her when we talk."

Connor lifted the chair and moved it next to the bed, where she'd indicated.

"So. You're late," she groused.

Connor smiled slightly as he sat. "You think?"

"You should have come to me ten years ago. I could have told you some things."

Connor gave her a steady look. "Maybe. But you wouldn't have."

To his surprise, she cackled at the remark. "You're right about that. So what do you want now, pretty boy?"

Connor leaned back in the seat and tilted his head, studying her. Anne had always been so afraid of this tiny, hostile woman. He wondered if she still was, or if Delores's power had worn off over the years.

"I want to know," he said slowly, "why you were always so dead-set against me."

She narrowed her eyes. "Oh, come on, now. You look like a bright boy, Connor Emory. You haven't figured that out in all these years?"

"I want to hear it from you."

She sighed, put-upon. "It's not any big mystery. You know how it is in small places like this. The local girls always fancy the handsome summer boys. They fall in love, make plans, dream dreams, and give away everything they've got to give. But do the boys fall in love with them? Do the boys dream those same dreams?" She shook her head, her mouth twisting sourly. "No, they don't. They use those girls and they leave them. And you were no different than the rest of 'em."

"That's not true. I was in love with Anne. I think you knew that. And I think that's what scared you." He kept his voice even, his eyes candid. To his own surprise, he didn't feel anger for this woman. He felt, more than anything, sorry for her. "I think," he continued, leaning forward in the chair, his elbows on his knees, "you were afraid I'd take Anne away, and then what would you have? No one to pick on. No one to boss around. No one," he paused significantly, "to take care of you."

Anne's grandmother scoffed and knotted her hands together in her lap. "That's a fine, self-serving theory. But don't kid yourself, because you're not kidding me. You weren't in love with her. And you've proved it, these last eleven years."

Connor shook his head. "The only thing that was proved over the last eleven years is that lies and manipulation can work for a time, but not forever. As far as I'm concerned you were just as guilty as my stepmother of keeping Anne alone and afraid. You undermined her confidence at every turn, and now you want to blame *me* for her disappointment? What about *my* disappointment? What you and my parents did to Anne and me was selfish and unforgivable."

Delores's mouth moved in a way that made Connor think for a moment she was preparing to spit at him. But she worked her teeth into place and crooked a finger at him. "If you had truly loved Anne, if you had known her at all, believed in her at all, you wouldn't have spent the last three weeks trying to prove her story. You'd have just believed it. You would have known she'd never have taken that money. Just as I knew it. That's why I had to go get that check and why I had to cash it."

Connor laughed wryly. She was right about one thing. He *had* spent the last three weeks trying to prove Anne's story. And he had. "It would have helped if you hadn't cashed that check."

Delores shrugged elaborately. "It would have helped if she'd been born rich."

"So you're telling me it was the fact that I was a 'summer boy' that you held against me?"

"Damn right it was. Still is. You come and you go, you take what you want and you leave. Anne's father was a summer boy, did you know that?"

Connor's face must have shown his surprise, because she chuckled in a self-satisfied way.

"That's right. Her mother, my daughter, got knocked up just like any other stupid young local girl, besotted with a rich kid just like yourself. She believed he was going to marry her. Well, he didn't marry her, though we told everyone he did. Told everyone he died in a car crash before Anne was born, too, and that was true enough. Before Anne's mother even had a chance to change her name, that's what we said. And it would have been true, if the boy had ever married her."

Connor's understanding of Delores's hostility and Anne's tenacious underconfidence was suddenly complete. "Does Anne know the true story?"

"Enough of it." Delores nodded.

He thought about the life this woman had led. Raising a daughter, then having to raise her daughter's daughter. She was hard, but she'd been dealt a tough hand.

He brought his gaze back to hers. "Well, Mrs. Sayer, I'm here to tell you I'm not just another summer boy. I'm here to ask you for your granddaughter's hand in marriage."

Delores's eyes lit shrewdly at his words.

"And it won't matter if you won't give it," Connor added, "I'm going to marry her anyway. But I thought I'd give you the chance."

"What about your father? What about the money? What about the fact that your stepmother can't stand her?"

Connor did not take his eyes from her face. "I'm going to ask Anne's forgiveness for the behavior of my entire family. Most especially my own."

"You gonna do that on one knee?" Delores asked, a devilish glint in her eyes.

He leaned back in the chair. "Is there any other way?"

Delores Sayer's face broke slowly into a smile. "Well, I'll be damned . . ."

"I'm sure you will be," Connor agreed with an answering smile.

The old woman leaned forward and reached for the drawer of her bedside table. One thin, misshapen hand closed around the handle, pulling weakly, but she was too far away, and the angle was awkward.

Connor reached over and opened it for her.

She grunted what might have been meant to be thanks, reached into the drawer, and pulled out a folded sheet of notepaper. She handed it to him.

"Read that."

He took the note and unfolded it. At the top of the yellowed sheet was his father's name, engraved in his trademark font. The sight of it sent a chill down his spine. This was one thing he hadn't expected.

His father's bold script filled the rest of the page.

Dear Anne,

This letter conveys my apologies and shame for what I've done. I have no excuse other than that I am a weak man, beset by a wife of strong opinions

and ideals. I want you to know that you will al-
ways have a job at Sea Bluff, if you want it. In ad-
dition, you will never have to suffer my unwanted
advances again. I'm afraid I cannot explain them,
I can only apologize for them. The check enclosed
is for a college education, which I understand
from my son that you desire. I beg of you to accept
it. I have known you since you were a child, Anne,
and I see great things in store for you.

> *With most sincere regrets,*
> *Bradford Emory*

Connor studied the note for a long time, recognizing his father's stilted speech, seeing clearly
his weakness and his conscience, and valuing his
admission that he was too often ruled by his
wife's strong opinions.

"Anne doesn't know about that note yet," Delores said.

Connor looked up.

"I got it out to show it to her, now she knows
about the check. But she doesn't have to know
about it," she added. "I'll leave that up to you, Mr.
Emory."

Connor folded the note and handed it back to
her. "I'm going to marry your granddaughter,
Mrs. Sayer. Maybe you ought to call me Connor."

She gave him a look that he thought might have
a trace of respect in it. "All right, then. Connor.
You might as well call me Delores."

He smiled, his heart lighter than it had been in years. "All right. So what are you doing tonight, Delores? Would you like to come to a party?"

"I put Mr. Baxter in the room where Dill knocked down the wall," Lois said, catching Anne in the sunroom, where she was instructing the florist. The long breakfast table and four bistro tables were all covered with flowers in various stages of arrangement.

"Great," Anne said. "I guess it's a good thing he took that wall down after all. Someone like Percy Baxter would never have been satisfied staying in the nanny's room."

Anne suffered a momentary pang, thinking about that day in the nursery when Connor had found her holding up the wall. How many times in the last few weeks had she thought she and Connor had been getting closer, remembering their similarities and forging a new appreciation of each other.

Only to have it all obliterated by one exaggerated lie.

It had been all Anne could do the last several weeks to keep from giving Patsy another piece of her mind. But Marcello had been a pretty constant companion, keeping Patsy at bay and simultaneously telling Anne he was sure Connor would come around, that he would talk to him, that all was not lost.

But Anne hadn't been convinced. If she'd been

Connor and had been faced with the evidence he'd been faced with, she wasn't so sure she would have "come around" either. She had to admit, a cashed check for fifty thousand dollars was pretty convincing evidence of wrongdoing. *Whose* wrongdoing was another subject.

Still, she was the one who had lied to him. She *had* told him she didn't love him anymore, even though that had been the furthest thing from the truth. And she *had* told him it was over. There was no reason in the world he should not have believed her.

"Anne, can I talk to you a minute?" Lois asked, stepping close to Anne. Lois's eyes shifted to the florist several yards away at the table. "Alone?"

Anne looked at her in concern. "Of course." She led her toward the door, and the two of them stepped onto the patio. But three men were there stringing lights, and one of the florist's helpers was setting up a large urn full of gladiolas.

The two women moved down the steps and onto the lawn, heading for the edge of the garden, beyond the potting shed. As they approached, Anne saw a mound of dirt under a large aspidistra. Getting closer, she saw a hole dug about three feet deep.

"What in the world? . . ." she muttered.

Lois leaned over and looked, too. "Think it's Franklin, looking for treasure?"

Despite her somber mood, Anne started to

laugh. "Oh, my God. I think it's Gabriella's ghost!"

"What?"

"You know, the ghost she saw a few weeks ago, out here in the garden. Digging."

"Ohhhh." Lois looked back toward the house. Gabriella's room was just to the right of the patio, upstairs. "She'd have a perfect view of this spot."

"And Franklin could easily have draped a sheet—" Anne stopped and glanced at Lois.

Lois's eyes narrowed shrewdly. "Which brings me to what I wanted to ask you about. I've gotten wind of some rumors . . . and what with all this stuff that Dill's been doing, I'm wondering if they're true."

Anne inhaled deeply. "They're true, Lois. I'm sorry, I wanted to tell you, but I was afraid you wouldn't approve of what we were doing."

"You mean . . ." She looked shocked. "The place really *is* being condemned?"

This time it was Anne's turn to look shocked. "Condemned?"

"That's what Nicola said. At least I think that's what she was saying. And I've got to say, the place has needed an awful lot of work lately."

Anne started to laugh in earnest now. "Oh, my God. Did she also say it was haunted?"

"Well, yes. But of course I didn't believe that part. She told me about Gabriella's ghost, and some of the stories Prin's been telling them. That one about the headless dog was a classic."

Anne's laughter increased. "Oh, Lois. I'm really so sorry. How long have you been hearing about this?"

"A couple weeks, now," she said, looking perplexed. "But I didn't hear the condemned part until yesterday. Is it really true?"

Anne sighed and composed herself. "No. It was a plot. A *failed* plot, on my stupid part. Connor told me when he arrived last month that he was selling the place to Marcello. So Dill, Prin, and I cooked up this plan to make the place look like it was falling apart so maybe Marcello wouldn't want it."

"And the ghosts? . . ."

Anne smiled. "A brilliant bit of ad-libbing on Dill's part. He found out Gabriella is deathly afraid of spirits." Her smile disappeared, and her heaviness of heart returned. "Unfortunately, none of it worked. The sale went through last Monday."

Lois's face was amazed. "I can't believe you didn't tell me."

"I know. I'm sorry." She laid a hand on Lois's forearm. "I just—we were being so underhanded. And you're always so honest. I'm sorry."

"God, Anne. I have to say, I'm really offended."

Anne briefly put a hand over her face. "Please don't be. It wasn't that I didn't trust you. It was only because I thought you were above this kind of thing."

"Above it, my ass!"

Anne dropped her hand.

"I can be a ghost as good as Franklin's, I'm sure," Lois continued. "And I wouldn't have used the opportunity to look for any buried treasure, either. I'd have scared the bejesus out of that girl, and been happy to do it, too."

Anne gaped at her.

"Is it too late? They settled already?"

Anne nodded.

"Well." Lois put her hands on her hips, her face the picture of practical consideration. "That doesn't mean we can't still scare the little brat, does it?"

Anne laughed and hugged her. "Oh, Lois. I will never keep anything from you again."

Lois smiled as the two parted. "I guess there's a bright side. Marcello's not a bad guy. I wouldn't mind working for him. As long as we can frighten Miss Scaredy-Cat back to Italy."

Anne shook her head. "He's already told me he's bringing in his own staff. People who've been loyal to him for years, he said."

Lois's face fell. "Oh." She thought. "So we're all going to be out of a job, is that it?"

Anne nodded. "They're giving us a generous severance, though. And they're going to help find jobs for all of us. And anyway, Lois, I was going to talk to you about joining my side business, if you're interested."

Lois brightened. "Heck yeah, I'm interested."

Anne smiled. "Great. Let's talk about it later. Right now I've got to make sure the string quartet isn't crowded out of the front foyer by the television crew intent on capturing the celebrities as they enter." She rolled her eyes and began to turn toward the house.

"Good luck with that. Hey, I hear Connor's coming back today."

Anne stopped and jerked back. "Really?"

"Yeah. Did you think he'd miss the party?"

She shrugged. "No. But then I hadn't heard anything about his return, so . . ."

"Really?" Lois's brow furrowed. "Marcello told me last week. Said he was flying in today sometime."

"Marcello did? I wonder why he didn't tell me?" She looked at Lois. "Why didn't *you* tell me?"

Lois smiled wryly. "A familiar refrain today, huh? Actually, I thought you would already have known. Plus, I haven't exactly seen a lot of you the past week."

"I know." Anne sighed. "If this party doesn't kill me, I'll be amazed."

"Well, just remember," Lois said as they started walking back toward the house, "what doesn't kill you makes you stronger."

Five hours later Anne was ready. In a white backless dress with gold jewelry and a light spray of perfume, she was cruising the rooms of the house making sure everything was in order.

The evening was perfectly gorgeous, with a

clear blue sky, gentle breeze, and temperatures that promised to stay in the low seventies even after the sun went down.

Anne, however, was battling sweating palms and heart palpitations, wondering with every corner she turned if she was going to run into Connor.

She'd passed by his room a dozen times during the day, waiting to see if a suitcase or any other evidence of someone having returned might be spotted. At five o'clock, just before Anne had to go home to change clothes, the door had been closed, sending her pulse and anxiety level into the stratosphere.

He was back.

What would she say to him? What would he say to her, if anything? Would he still be angry? Might he have thought about all she'd said and, perhaps, come to understand a little of what she might have done and felt during that awful time eleven years ago?

Or maybe, just maybe, had he come to the conclusion that he could forgive her regardless of what he thought she'd done?

She was just checking the front wraparound porch when she encountered Marcello. Though he was a nice-looking man, with his slightly portly build and white tie and tails he gave form to the expression "penguin suit."

"*Bellissima*," he said, extending his arms and regarding her as he might a painting by an old master. "You are as lovely as I have ever seen you.

How do you do it, *cara*, with all the work that you have had to do, eh?"

Anne smiled wanly. "You're too kind."

"*Sí*, I know. That is true." He gave her a wicked grin. "But not in this case. In this case I am honest."

"Mr. Tucci." Anne put a hand on his arm and smiled at the man. "I'm glad we have a minute to talk. I wanted to thank you, for all you've done to help me the last few weeks."

Marcello flipped his other hand out dismissively. "Bah, what have I done? Nothing. You have done it all, *bella*."

Anne shook her head. "That's not true. I could not have pulled this party together without you. At least," she gave him a sly smile, "not without having to include a bunch of horses in tutus or parachuting Elvises."

These were actual suggestions Patsy had made in an effort, she'd said, to make the party truly memorable. Nobody wants to watch a bunch of people walking around in tuxedos. They were, in case anyone'd forgotten, going to be *on television*, she'd said. As if anyone *could* forget with Patsy making that very declaration every time anyone mentioned the party.

Marcello's laugh boomed over the front lawn, causing Anne to laugh with him. The man was so wholeheartedly genial, so unabashedly open and happy, that it was impossible not to feel good around him.

"But I'm not just talking about the party," she

continued, growing serious. "You've helped me in many, many other ways. I think you know what I'm talking about."

Marcello sobered too, and he patted her hand on his arm. "And I hope to continue to, *cara*."

They shared a smile.

"Now," he said briskly, "come with me. We have some last-minute business to attend to."

"What? No, I've got to make sure the punch—"

Marcello waved a hand again. "Prin will take care of the punch. Come."

She followed him around the porch to the front door and into the foyer. At the same moment, Connor was descending the stairs.

Anne's heart jumped to her throat. She felt suddenly sick. She must have clenched her hand on Marcello's arm because he patted it again with his other hand, prying her fingers loose with a thumb.

"Ah Connor, *il mio ragazzo*," Marcello said, the smile on his face once again broad. "Just the person who I was hoping to encounter."

Anne glanced at Marcello. At least he was admitting it now. She shifted her gaze back to Connor.

He looked so good he took her breath away. Tall, broad, handsome, and perfectly at home in his classically tailored tuxedo. He smelled good, too, she noted as he neared.

His expression was grave as he descended the last of the stairs and shook Marcello's hand.

Anne's stomach rolled in somersaults. He looked like he hadn't forgotten a word of their last conversation. He looked like he might even repeat a few from it.

"You're looking very handsome, *figlio*," Marcello continued, looking inexplicably pleased as he looked between the two of them.

"You're looking pretty dapper yourself," Connor said with a slight smile.

Anne's heart danced in her chest.

Connor turned his gaze to her, his smile disappearing. "Anne, you look beautiful."

A blush flared up her neck to her hairline. "Thank you."

"Doesn't she!" Marcello turned, stepped away to stand next to Connor, and regarded her like a sculpture he'd just completed. "The very picture of splendor."

Anne's self-consciousness quadrupled. "I should check on the—"

"No, no. I will do it," Marcello pronounced.

"But I didn't—"

"It does not matter. I will check on *everything*." With that, he strode away from them.

In the foyer, a man hung from a platform on the ceiling, where he was adjusting some kind of television camera. Three musicians were setting up chairs in the corner, clattering music stands and shuffling sheet music while discussing the order of the songs they would play. Behind her, Anne could hear the clinking of glass and silver-

ware as the bartender in the front parlor set up.
And through it all, she could hear the ominous
ticking of the insane grandfather clock just behind Connor.

Still, with all the bustle, Anne felt as if every eye
in the room were on them, wondering if Connor
would speak, turn away, or berate her for her part
in the destruction of his father's memory.

"I—I guess Marcello wanted us to"—halfway
through the thought Anne wondered at the wis-
dom of saying it, but she had no choice other than
to finish—"be alone?"

To her surprise, his mouth curved again in a
smile. "At least he didn't lock us in a room somewhere again."

Anne smiled tentatively back. "I didn't mind
that so much." The words were soft.

Connor took a step closer. "Anne—" He
reached out and took one of her hands. Anne
looked down at it in astonishment.

"Hey! Would you guys mind moving closer to
the front door?" the guy on the camera platform
called down to them. "I just want to check the
light, if you don't mind."

Anne jumped and Connor exhaled, not turning
to the man, who was in the upper corner of the
vaulted ceiling, behind his back.

"Sure," Anne called.

"No they won't either," Prin's voice announced
as she emerged from the front parlor. "I'll do it.
You two go right on ahead talking." She shooed

Anne and Connor back into their conversation with one hand.

Anne laughed nervously. Connor smiled, his eyes dead serious.

"Where can we go?" he asked. "Is there a spot in this house without someone in it?"

Anne looked frantically around. "I honestly don't think so."

"Fine, then," he said. "I'll do it here."

Anne looked at him in fear. Fear of what, she wasn't sure. She just knew she had to be prepared for anything, from anger to comeuppance to—she hoped and prayed—forgiveness.

"Anne," he said, "I owe you an apology."

Chapter Twenty

"A—an apology?" she repeated.

"Yes. For being an ignorant jerk. For blaming you for a situation that couldn't possibly have been your fault. And most of all, for not believing in you."

Anne couldn't get her mind around what he was saying, it was so unexpected. "You mean, about . . . about your . . . about the check?"

Connor's hand squeezed hers. "Let's forget about the check. You deserved that and more. I'm apologizing for not understanding. For being too hurt and self-centered and stubborn to see what you must have gone through. I can't even imagine the pressure you must have been under to do what you did eleven years ago. My parents . . ." He scowled. "Well, they were always unforgivable when it came to you. And I always thought I was above that." He shook his head. "Apparently I wasn't, and I want to ask— no, *beg*—your forgiveness, though I certainly don't deserve it."

Anne's eyes dropped to his mouth. "You're asking *my* forgiveness?"

He expelled a breath. "God, yes. Though you'll be a bigger person than I am if you can give it."

She shook her head, still disbelieving. "Connor, there's nothing to forgive. You were the victim here. You were lied to, by me, by your parents, by everyone."

"*I* was the victim?" Connor smiled and shook his head. "Anne, you are amazing. You've got a lot to learn about self-righteous anger, I can tell you that. Though, frankly, at this moment I'm glad of it. We don't have time for you to give me the lambasting I deserve."

"Here they come! Ron, move nearer the door. You can get 'em as they come in," the voice from the rafters called to his buddy, who had just entered the foyer with a shoulder camera.

A moment later the musicians started up with the first strains of Vivaldi's *Four Seasons*.

The sound of car doors shutting outside reached them, and Connor and Anne looked at each other.

Anne wanted the moment to go on forever, but they only had seconds left before the first guests appeared.

He *understood!* her mind sang. Anne's heart rose with the violin music, carried up to the ceiling on wings of joy.

Connor leaned in to speak directly into her ear. "Meet me back here at midnight."

Anne's breath caught. She nodded, and, with a squeeze of her hand, he was gone.

The party was an unqualified success, Anne thought as she wandered amongst the glittering guests over the next few hours. Of course, she would have deemed it a success if no one at all had showed up.

Several hours into it, Anne came across Gabriella on the front porch arguing vociferously in Italian with a young, dark-haired man dressed in a black suit and tie. She was gesturing wildly, and he was poking at a fistful of newspaper clippings. Anne wondered how they understood one another, speaking at the same time as they were. She also wondered who on earth the young man was. She hadn't seen him before this moment, and she didn't think even Gabriella could get into such an argument with someone she'd just met— particularly not in Italian.

A second later, she noticed Marcello standing next to her.

"Mr. Tucci, what are they saying?"

To her surprise, Marcello was smiling. "They are arguing," he said, leaning close to her, his eyes on his daughter, "about a series of gossip columns in which Gabriella's name appears, or rather, is implied."

Anne looked closer at the clippings the young man held.

"Are those? . . ." She looked up at Marcello. "Are those from the *Candlewick Island Herald Press*?"

"They are, indeed," he said with a beatific smile.

"The ones about her and Connor?" she insisted.

"The very ones."

Anne stared at him. "How did he get those?"

Marcello brought his hands out in a helpless gesture. "Who can say? News travels far in this day and age."

Slowly, the truth began to dawn on her. "Is he Gabriella's boyfriend?"

Marcello put a finger to his lips, then gestured toward his daughter.

Anne looked back at the two. The young man was on his knee, and Gabriella was crying. Then she was exclaiming, *"Sí, sí,"* and kneeling on the floor herself, taking the boy's face in her hands and kissing it all over.

"Maybe later I should tell them about the villa on the Riviera I have bought for them, *sí?*" He glanced at Anne with a smug smile. "They look busy now, don't you think?"

Anne turned slowly to Marcello. "So *that's* why Sean was writing all that stuff. You were using it to make that poor boy jealous. Why you sly old . . ."

"Careful, *bella.*" He grinned at her. "I'm very sensitive about my age." With a burst of laughter he wandered away from her.

Anne made her way back to the kitchen. Prin was there surrounded by white-coated servers and lab-jacketed caterers whipping up dips and sauces, puffs and pastries, roasts and side dishes.

She made her way over to her little desk, looking at the mass of papers, receipts, and lists and orders for the party that would all be over in a few short hours. She felt like pinching herself to see if she was awake. Connor had apologized to her. *Apologized!* She'd been hoping for forgiveness, and what she'd gotten had been total vindication.

She breathed easier than she had in many years.

All night long she'd had him in her sights. He was magnificent, she thought. Handsome and composed, genial and relaxed, the perfect host for the perfect party. It almost broke her heart to think it was the last time he'd be a host at Sea Bluff. Certainly it was the end of an era.

Her mind strayed to Connor's last comment. *Meet me here at midnight.* Why? she wondered. What more could he have to say? She didn't dare think. Midnight in the foyer where TV cameras and partygoers and caterers and musicians loitered was hardly the setting for anything terribly romantic. Still, it was a mystery.

She looked at her watch. Eleven-fifteen. Midnight was never going to come, she thought. She was going to wake up at eleven-fifty-five and discover it was all a dream, that Connor was still in Atlanta and nothing had changed.

Prin spotted her and, as if reading her thoughts, approached and asked, "So what's going on at midnight?"

Anne's heart skipped a beat. "What?"

"Mr. Tucci was just down here telling all of us to

be in the front hall at midnight." She wiped her hands off in her apron. "What do you think that's all about?"

"Oh," Anne said, deflated. She leaned toward Prin so as not to be overheard. "He must be planning to announce the sale of the house."

Prin nodded, consideringly. "Yep. That must be it."

Anne sighed.

"You look good tonight, honey," Prin said with one of her rare, warm smiles. She preferred being a curmudgeon, but Anne knew that hid a heart of gold. "Any man worth his salt should be throwing himself at your feet."

Anne smiled wanly. "Thanks, Prin." She looked down at her shoes. "But as you can see, there's no one there."

Prin patted her cheek with a callused hand. "There will be. If that boy's got any sense at all, there will be."

But Anne knew it wasn't true. She'd fantasized briefly after the *Meet me here at midnight* comment. But it was obvious now what that was about.

Forty-five minutes later it seemed the whole party had congregated in the once-spacious foyer. In the middle of the crowd were Marcello and Connor. Just off to one side stood Patsy, resplendent in lavender sequins and a real diamond tiara.

"*Attenzione, attenzione,*" Marcello called, his hands in the air.

Anne looked up and could see the cameraman on the platform near the ceiling adjusting his aim toward Marcello.

The crowd quieted.

"My favorite nephew and I have a very important announcement to make," he continued.

Anne looked around the crowded room. Toward the back, near the kitchen hallway, she spotted Prin, Dill, and Mr. Franklin. Trudy stood at the top of the stairs with Lois.

"As most of you know," Connor said, stepping forward, "Sea Bluff has been a commercial property the last ten years or so." His glance flicked around the room, found Anne, and rested on her. His lips curved into a smile. "So when Marcello Tucci approached me about possibly buying the place I was amenable to the idea."

The crowd murmured. Anne saw Sean Crawford near the front door with a cat-that-caught-the-canary grin on his face. He must have been involved in the sale somehow, she thought.

"Last Monday, that sale became official. You are all looking at the new owner of Sea Bluff. Mr. Marcello Tucci." Connor fanned a hand out toward Marcello and stepped back. Someone in the crowd started to clap, and the others followed suit.

Wait'll they hear what he has in mind to do with it, Anne thought. But he was such a likeable man they would probably be won over by him just as she was. After all, she was losing her job because of this sale, and even she liked the man.

Patsy stepped forward, and the crowd quieted again. She twisted around until she spotted the television camera with the light on, at which point she turned and stepped back, nearly treading on Marcello's toes, to beam at the camera.

"I would like to say," she said with a broad grin, once she was situated next to Marcello, "how happy I am that this sale has taken place."

Sure, you're happy, Anne thought. *You've just made two and a half million dollars.*

"Marcello Tucci has been a friend to our family for many, many years," Patsy continued. "And I have every confidence that he will be a faithful steward of the place, maintaining its historical integrity as well as its benefit to the Candlewick Island community. I further suggest . . ."

Patsy continued in this vein for some time, espousing Sea Bluff's importance to the island and Marcello's qualifications for maintaining it, until the crowd's feet began to shuffle and murmurs of boredom began to surface. Connor then pointedly cleared his throat.

"So in conclusion," Patsy said loudly over the discontent, smiling so forcefully into the camera that Anne thought her face must surely hurt, "I personally hope to be able to maintain the Emory ties to Sea Bluff and the island by visiting often, representing both the past and the future, the family and the history, of this richly significant property."

A brief smattering of applause greeted this conclusion.

Anne glanced across the room at the crowd near the door. It seemed to be parting slightly, and a second later, a nurse pushed a wheelchair to the front. In that wheelchair, to Anne's complete surprise, was her grandmother.

She was too far to reach, and Marcello was about to speak again. Anne couldn't go to her to ask what was going on, but she couldn't take her eyes from the old woman. She had even dressed up, Anne noted, in her favorite pale peach dress.

"*Signora Emory,*" Marcello said, issuing a short bow in Patsy's direction. "That is a lovely sentiment. And I hope that you will indeed *be* able to visit, but that will not be up to me."

Anne's eyes returned to Marcello. *Be able to visit?*

"You see, I have decided," Marcello said as he cast a devilish eye over the now dead-silent crowd, "that instead of keeping the property, as I had once planned, I will bequeath it to a steward far more dedicated and trustworthy than I."

Oh my God, Anne thought. *He's going to give it to the state. The Historical Society has finally gotten their way.*

Her eyes sought Connor's. He was watching her with an expression she found impossible to read. Did he know about this? Was he happy about it? She had no idea. She was so engrossed in his look that she didn't notice Marcello approaching her until he took her hand in his.

She started. He pulled her into the center of the room. In disbelief, Anne watched him reach into his jacket and pull out a folded sheaf of papers, tied with a red ribbon.

"I am giving Sea Bluff to you, my dear," Marcello said and bowed deeply over her hand.

Anne's mouth dropped open, and she thought she might faint. Her eyes sought Connor's. *Was this really happening?*

Connor was grinning at her.

The crowd broke into wild applause. Patsy looked as if she'd just been shot in the chest.

Anne glanced up at the camera and thought she saw it diving in for a close-up of Patsy's livid face.

She started to laugh, put her hand over her mouth, and looked again at Connor.

"Marcello," she said, gripping his hand and pulling him toward her. "This is crazy. I *cannot* take this." She pushed the papers back at him.

Marcello laughed and pulled away. "No, no, *signorina*. The damage is done. The papers are in order. The place is yours."

Anne's eyes scanned the crowd, barely focusing on the faces it contained until she came to Prin's. The cook was laughing and crying, rubbing tears from her cheeks with her apron. Dill had his fists over his head in a triumphant "Rocky" posture, which made Anne laugh.

She turned and looked at her grandmother, who wore the broadest smile Anne had ever seen on her face.

"But there is one more thing," Marcello said.

Anne turned back to him, shaking from her

head to her toes. "Marcello, no, you can't—"

"It is not from me," he said with a wink. He inclined his head toward Connor.

Connor stepped toward her and took both of her hands in his, their fingers combining over the sheaf of papers Marcello had handed her.

"Anne," he said, so low the crowd immediately stopped talking. "This has been far too long in coming. But I found over the last eleven years, in looking for someone to share my life, for a woman with whom I could fall in love, that nobody else ever came close to you. You are the one, Anne, and you always were."

Anne watched, dazed, as he reached into his pocket and pulled something out. She glanced at his hand. Gleaming in his fingers was an emerald-cut diamond in a white-gold setting. Two carats, she would bet, remembering his words in the wine cellar, sized to that blade of grass he'd tied around her finger so long ago.

"Anne Sayer," he said, bending down on one knee.

Tears and laughter simultaneously bubbled up in her chest. She put her right hand to her mouth.

"Will you marry me?"

She couldn't breathe. "Is that? . . ." she whispered. "Is that the same ring?"

He nodded, grinning. "You were the only one it would fit."

She laughed.

"Is that a yes?" he asked.

"Yes!" she said, laughing and looking at him in amazement. "A thousand times yes!"

He slid the ring onto her finger. The crowd burst into applause. From the back hallway came a chorus of whistles as Connor stood up and took her in his arms. His mouth came down on hers in a bruising kiss, and her arms twined around his neck.

Just then the grandfather clock chimed, and an audible gasp went up in the room, followed by laughter. At the third ring people started counting along with it. At the eleventh ring Connor and Anne looked at each other in disbelief. The crazy thing was going to ring the correct time.

For the first time in anyone's memory, the twelfth chime sounded as the clock, albeit a few minutes slow, read twelve o'clock.

"To Connor and Anne!" Marcello boomed, holding aloft a glass of champagne.

The crowd, too, held up glasses that had mysteriously materialized in their hands.

"Connor and Anne!" the crowd roared.

Connor leaned down and kissed her again.

Whereupon the clock struck one last time.